WORLD OF IF

By
ROG PHILLIPS

I0616787

ARMCHAIR FICTION
PO Box 4369, Medford, Oregon   97501-0168

*The original text of this novel was first
published by Century Publications*

Armchair Edition, Copyright 2012, by Gregory J.   Luce
All Rights Reserved

*For more information about Armchair Books and products, visit our
website at…*

www.armchairfiction.com

Or email us at…

armchairfiction@yahoo.com

IN THE COMPLEXITIES OF THE DREAM WORLD THERE ARE ALWAYS VARIANTS...

In our reality, the past is fixed, what happened to you yesterday can never be altered. But, what IF you could be placed under hypnosis for an eight-hour period, each second in the real world equaling a year in the dream world, and dream a whole different lifetime. And suppose that in that lifetime, some things were completely different, and some the same? Would you marry the same person? Witness the rise of Communism? Have the same trusted people by your side? But most importantly, what could there be to learn in your dream world that could be brought back—back to the world of reality? Are all of our fates linked by the same differences and similarities in both the real world, and in the Worlds of If..?

Find out the answers in this long-forgotten gem from master science fiction author, Rog Phillips.

FOR A COMPLETE SECOND NOVEL, TURN TO PAGE 127

CAST OF CHARACTERS

JOHN DOW
A big cheese in the business world, his life was about to become surprisingly different—in more ways than he could imagine.

DR. SIMON FRENCH
Having a subject to participate in his experiment was all he wanted and needed.

JOE PACE
He had plenty of secrets to keep—and more than his share of blunders to fix.

STEFFEN TOMBS
This big-shot communist leader doled out severe punishment with an evil glint in his eyes.

CLOE
Dow's personal secretary…she was very, very efficient, and wanted to be very, very personal…

GLORIA DOW
She had to put her foot down when it came to her husband coming home with lipstick on his lips.

CHAPTER ONE

JOHN Dow lifted the phone from its cradle on his large walnut surfaced desk. "Yes?" he said absently, knowing that he was talking only to the switchboard girl, who would tell him who was on the phone and give him a chance to be "out."

He was in keeping with his large elaborate office. Neatly combed gray hair, a face marked with the indelible stamp of authority, a well-tailored brown suit designed to conceal an average paunch.

Beside the phone was a thick tablet, the top page of which said Thursday, November 5, 1981.

"There's a Dr. Simon French to see you, Mr. Dow," the pleasant voice of the switchboard girl said. "He says he wrote you."

"Oh, yes," Dow said into the phone, picking a letter out of the pile on one corner of his desk.

"And your wife's on the phone," the girl added.

"Put her on," he said, "and tell Dr. French to come in."

His eyes were scanning the letter he had received the week before. Dated October 27, 1984, the letterhead was that of a well known research group that put out an annual booklet on business trends for the coming year, among other things. He had never heard of Dr. Simon French though, until he received the letter.

"Hi, Gloria," he said into the phone.

Dear Mr. Dow, the letter began. *On Thursday, November 5, 1984, at two P.M. I will call at your office on a matter of extreme importance to our research organization.*

"What!" Dow shouted gleefully. "Frank's wife is going to have a baby?"

The door opened. John glanced up at the man who was entering.

Cupping his hand over the mouthpiece of the phone he nodded toward a chair and said, "Sit down, doctor. I'll be with you in a moment." Then, uncupping the phone, "Oh, not until February," he said, disappointed. "Does Frank say in his letter whether he got that promotion? Oh, not yet, huh."

Our circulation department informs me that you have been a subscriber to our business-forecast service for the past ten years, the letter went on, *so you are acquainted with one of the research departments of our organization. The matter I wish to discuss with you, however, has nothing to do with business forecasts, but lies in another field of research. I most sincerely hope in view of our past service to you that you will grant me the time to explain to you in person.*

"Yes, I'll be home on time tonight, Gloria. If something comes up so I'm delayed I'll call you... Bye now."

He hung up, his eyes surveying the man seated across the desk from him. A young man, in his late twenties, unusually high forehead, steady blue eyes, well formed features.

John smiled and half lifted the letter, letting it drop back on the desk surface. "From your letter you sound rather anxious to talk with me about something, Dr. French."

"Yes sir," the young man said. "Have you much time to spare?" As John Dow looked at the clock he added, "it will take a little time. Maybe half an hour or more."

"That's not too long, Dr. French," John said, leaning back.

"I'll make it as short as possible," Dr. Simon French said. "I doubt you know anything about our organization other than that it publishes the business forecast. We don't explain our methods in print, leaving the readers to draw their own conclusions as to where we get our data that enables us to make such remarkably accurate predictions.

"We use a combination of several methods and co-ordinate the results of all of them. Where they agree, the predictions are generally accurate. Where they disagree we have found over the past ten years that one particular method we have been developing is usually the most accurate. That method is rather involved. It employs, among other things, a form of hypnosis."

"This sounds like it might be rather interesting, Dr. French," Dow said.

"Hypnosis," Dr. French continued, "has several different types. There's the kind where the hypnotist lulls the subject into a passive sleep by suggestion. No machine of any kind is used unless the hypnotist uses a bright object to aid in inducing sleep."

"I've read about that, of course," John Dow said. "Even saw it done on a stage several years ago. Was it at the Great Northern Theater? Well, it doesn't matter."

"We began with that type of hypnosis," Dr. French continued. "At first we were studying the possible effects hypnosis might have on the brain waves picked up by the electro-encephalograph. To see, among other things, if the alteration in mental activity brought about by hypnosis was different than the alteration brought about by just naturally falling asleep."

"And did you find a difference?" John Dow asked, interested.

"Quite decidedly yes," Dr. French said, smiling. "We continued our researches along that line, finding the electro-encephalograph a valuable tool in perfecting hypnosis techniques.

"I don't know whether you have read much on the subject or not, but have you ever ran across the idea of pushing the mind back into childhood under hypnosis?"

"I think I read something on that," John Dow said. "If I remember correctly, the theory was that when the adult subject was taken back to when he was eight years old he made the same mistakes in spelling."

"That's right," Dr. French said. "Our research explored that line quite thoroughly, along with the other phases of the subject.

"Then, one day, we tried something different. We jumped a subject around until he was completely lost in time, and told him it was a certain date six months in the future."

"And what happened?" John asked.

"He lived out a few hours of that day just like it were as vivid a memory as any of the past!" Dr. French said.

"What!" John said. "You mean he had a memory of the future?"

"Not quite," Dr. French said, smiling. "You see, when we had the same subject live out that same future date a week later it came out differently."

"Oh," John said, settling back. "I get it. His imagination rationalized things by inventing what happened in the future."

"You could call it that," Dr. French agreed. "Except that when we tried the same thing on several different subjects on the same day they agreed in general about the overall events of that particular date."

"Something like, if X had lunch with Y on that future date," John Dow said, "then Y said he had lunch with X?"

"Substantially that," Dr. French admitted.

"Oh!" John exclaimed knowingly. "So that's how you gather your business predictions for the coming year!"

"That's one of the systems we use," Dr. French said smiling, "but don't tell anyone. It's our big secret."

"Uh—then you had in mind asking me to be a subject for finding out what will happen next year?" John asked doubtfully.

"Let me go on," Dr. French said smoothly. "If you remember, I said that events for any particular date changed from day to day. To use your illustration, if X and Y said they had lunch together on July 8, 1985, when they were under hypnosis on May 6, 1984; then when they were under hypnosis on June 6, 1984 maybe they didn't have lunch together on July 8, 1985."

He grinned at the bewildered expression on John's face.

"Then how do you account for their agreement on having lunch together and then not having lunch together?" John asked.

"We finally evolved a theory," Dr. French said with slow emphasis. "I want you to understand that theory, because it plays a very vital part in what I want to tell you about a little later."

"Picture yourself," he went on, "suddenly kidnapped from here and placed in solitary confinement in a plain cell somewhere for an indefinite period. Today is November 5, 1984. If you were in that cell until this time next year, then on November 5, 1985, you would do certain things and think certain things during that day. But if you weren't kidnapped and placed in that cell until tomorrow, then on November 5, 1985 you would behave slightly differently, and think of something different. The events of the next twenty-four hours will then have altered that day a year in the future, everything else being the same."

"That's open to question," John Dow said. "There would be no way of comparing. But I can see vaguely what you mean."

"Good," Dr. French said. "But get this: not all events changed. Maybe X and Y had lunch together on July 8th next year from the hypnotic point, May 6th of this year, but not from the hypnotic point, July 8th of this year, so that that particular event was a variable. But at both hypnotic points they may have agreed that it was raining all day that day in the future. And also there may have been several things they disagreed on."

"Hmm," John said. "I can see the possibilities. If the future doesn't exist until we come to it, then two different people shouldn't agree on what will happen on that day, of such an insignificant character that nothing in the present could cause their imagination to arrive at a common conclusion."

"That's right," Dr. French agreed. "The very fact that they do agree indicates something more than imagination enters into it. And the fact we have found to be borne out that the elements that don't change—we call them hypnotic invariants—generally come true when that future date, arrives, shows that there is something, we don't know what yet, that ties the future with the present in men's minds. That's how we make our business forecasts almost exclusively now. It isn't infallible. Working with the thing as I have for the past ten years, I've gained a sort of feel for the whole setup.

"The way I visualize it, the mind of any individual is somewhat in tune with those of others around him, millions of others. The hypnotic dream of what goes on at some future date is drawn from that mass mental complex. Anything external to that mental mass is a variable. And everything being impressed on the mass is constantly altering future possibilities."

"Then the population of Chicago could be likened to me being kidnapped and placed in solitary confinement," John said.

"That's what I mean," Dr. French agreed. "So long as you aren't in a controlled and isolated environment, your environment is altering your probable behavior in the near future."

Dr. Simon French paused, lighting a cigarette, his eyes studying John Dow thoughtfully.

"We perfected that phase of our research," he said abruptly, "and systematized it as a going enterprise to give us an income for further study."

"I think I see why it won't work for more than a year in the future," John said. "A couple of years from now so many new factors have influenced the population that detailed events are completely unpredictable."

"Exactly," Dr. French said.

"This mass mind business interests me," John said slowly. "I see what made you bring that in. The fact that two persons could agree on something six months away without comparing notes ahead of time. It would have to be a sort of mass telepathy or mass consciousness that the individual draws on."

"Under this deep hypnosis we have perfected," Dr. French added. "Under normal consciousness and normal sleep the individual is never aware of it as an influence on his thoughts."

"This is the most amazing thing I've ever heard of," John Dow said. "I gather you're after me to become a subject of this—ah—research?"

"Let me go on," Dr. French said. "To answer your question, no. We have something far more important to us in mind. It has to do with another branch of our research."

"Another branch of research?" John echoed. "What you've outlined seems more than enough for one research organization to concentrate on. What else could you be doing?"

"The past is fixed," Dr. French said. "What happened to you yesterday can never be altered. What happened to you twenty years ago on September 4th can't be changed. We could place you under hypnosis with our perfected techniques and you would live out every minute of that twenty-four hours in detail. We could do it again a year from now and the details you would relive would be exactly the same."

"Of course," John said.

"But," Dr. French said slowly, "suppose we convinced you under hypnosis that on some particular date ten years ago something happened that actually didn't? It would be an outside factor."

"Just like the outside factors impressing on the mental mass of humanity, altering the course of the future?" John said.

"Just like that," Dr. French said.

"You mean that it would make me remember under hypnosis a whole future stemming from that date, that wouldn't agree with what actually happened?"

"Eventually, yes," Dr. French said. "It would be the unfoldment of your life *as IF that event had actually happened.* We could start you off with that change, and allow you to live right up to the present and find out what the world of today would be like IF that event had happened."

"A sort of *World of If?*" John Dow suggested, smiling dryly. "What good would it be?"

"That's what we asked ourselves when we started that line of research," Dr. French said, matching his smile. "But very quickly we ran into things similar to what we ran into in our research into the future. We ran into independent people agreeing remarkably on events. Specific events that didn't happen, deriving from the introduction of this one foreign or superimposed factor."

"An event of general importance like some prominent man dying before he actually did," Dr. French said, "brings out a consistent and sometimes very remarkable 'history' dating from that event."

"Yes?" John Dow said. "Interesting. I mean from the standpoint of your research. It would have no practical value, such as that derived from your study of the coming year in order to map business curves. I can truthfully say that I save several thousand dollars a year by following those predictions in my business."

"You've been in the publishing business for many years," French said. "As far back as 1953?"

"I thought you said you knew nothing about me except that I'm a subscriber to your annual booklet," John Dow said, smiling.

"Actually that's all I do know about you directly," Dr. French said, seeming to choose his words cautiously. "But I gather the answer is yes?"

"That's right. The Moore Publishing Company. I was editor of their Western magazines. But why do you pick that particular year? I was there until 1957. Started in 1951—no, it was the fall of 1950. Left them in 1957 to start the Dow Publishing Company. Started with a Western and a Fact Detective and the business has grown into nine national magazines and fourteen Daily newspapers, all published in the largest cities in the country." John Dow frowned thoughtfully at Dr. French. "I catch some sort of implication in what you said—'all you know about me directly.' I'm beginning to put two and two together."

"How do you mean?" Dr. French asked, a smile tugging at his lips.

"This business of agreement existing among independent subjects under hypnosis," John said. "You've been leading up to something. In some way my name appeared in your research into the *Worlds of If* as you call them. I gather you located me, then looked in your subscription list to see if I was there. That would give you an opening cue in contacting me, but was an afterthought, rather than the reason. Wasn't it?"

Dr. French concentrated very deeply on the task of taking out a cigarette and lighting it. Finally he looked up.

"You're right, Mr. Dow," he said.

CHAPTER TWO

JOHN GRINNED COMFORTABLY at the doctor. "Go on," he said. "I can see that your research into the if-world is deadly serious to you, as it should be. What part do I play in it? It must be a very important part, from your manner."

Simon French hesitated, seeming undecided what to say. Suddenly he relaxed.

"Your grasping the essentials has been swifter than I expected," he said. "For a moment you had me off balance." He pursed his lips, hesitating. "I'll tell you this. You do enter into those if-worlds. I'll also be quite frank with you. My intention was to get you interested without telling you in what way you played a part in their history. I still want to play it that way for more than one reason. The main reason is that I want to maintain the same independence from pre-influence in your case as in the others."

"You want me to be hypnotized and live out part of an *if-life* of the past, then," John Dow said.

"Yes," Dr. French said. "Will you?"

"How much of my time will it take?"

"It can all be done in one day, preferably a Saturday when you could be completely free to relax," Dr. French said.

"I'll think about it," John Dow said. "Tell me more about these if-worlds. They could be a fascinating study. You could for example go back to before Roosevelt died and have him live another ten years, and get an entirely different story of the cold war than that under Truman. You could go back before that even and not have the atom bomb created, and see how the war would have ended without the bomb."

"That's correct," Dr. French agreed. "And we have done all that."

"Hmmm," John Dow said, looking sharply at Dr. French's expressionless features. "Tell me this, then. Suppose I go into this, some Saturday. Will I remember it when I wake up?"

"That's up to our discretion," Dr. French said. "We can have you remember it or know nothing about it. We generally do the latter. Our subjects for these experiments are usually office workers or laborers who like the idea of getting fifty dollars for just sleeping all day. So far as their conscious mind is concerned they come in at eight o'clock in the morning, lie down under a machine, and at five o'clock they wake up, get their pay, and leave."

"What part do I play in these experiments with Worlds of If?" John asked abruptly.

"A very peculiar part," Dr. French said slowly. "I won't tell you anything specific. You remember what I said about invariant elements of these dream worlds? The invariants are the things that remain the same over many successive or different changes of basic conditions of departure." He took a quick deep breath. "I'll go farther than I had intended to go with you beforehand, and tell you this. In every if-world we have explored, you play one definite final part. And it's not the part you play today in real life.

"And now that I've gone that far I'll go a little bit farther and say that we have become convinced that if you submit to this experiment we will almost certainly find something—how should I say it? It's a certain event connected with you in some way. Something that either did or did not happen, we don't know which."

John Dow frowned at the clock on his desk. "I take it that everything you learn about me under hypnosis is considered in the light of a sacred confidence?"

"Of course," Dr. French said hastily. "In fact, in the past so many of our subjects have refused us permission to make public vital information about them that we've discarded the idea of ever publishing anything about our study of this phase of our research. Anything detailed, that is."

"I suppose you would like me to show up this Saturday, day after tomorrow," John said.

"If you want to," Dr. French said. As John Dow nodded, the doctor let out a long breath of relief.

John Dow stared at the door long after Dr. Simon French had closed it, oh so carefully, on his way out, as though fearing that to let it shut loudly might upset everything he didn't want upset.

His thoughts were whirling around in his head with all the possibilities and implications opened up by his conversation with the research scientist. And strangely, that long sigh of relief, the release of terrific inner tension, that Dr. French had emitted when he had agreed to submit to the experiment, disturbed him.

He waited until he felt sure Dr. French must have gone from the outer office, then he reached for the phone. His hand drew back. Dr. French might be waiting outside on some pretext, waiting to see if he made a phone call.

He got up and went to the door, opened it and strode into the outer office casually. Dr. French was standing near the switchboard talking to the girl.

When she saw her boss her smile died. She glanced meaningfully at the doctor.

Dr. French stood up from his position of leaning against the switchboard and turned casually.

"I'll see you Saturday at ten, Mr. Dow," he said smiling, then with a smile at the switchboard girl he left.

John went past the girl and pushed open a door to a large office. Twenty desks were evenly spaced over the floor. At most of the desks were young ladies busily typing. John's eyes went over the room, coming to stop on a man at a desk in the far corner. He caught the man's eye and jerked his head imperceptibly, then returned to his own office. Shortly the man came in.

"Frank and Mattie are going to have a baby in February, Joe," John said.

"Well I'll be darned," Joe Pace said happily. "That'll be their third one. You'll be the proud grandpa again. Don't forget the cigar."

"How much capital reserve do we have available?" John asked, suddenly serious.

"I don't know offhand," Joe said, studying John's face. "Somewhere under twelve million and over nine. Not very much."

"It's almost four o'clock," John said, looking at the desk clock. "I want you to go back to your desk, and from there find some way of getting rid of the switchboard girl for the rest of the day. Then I want you to find out all you can about the Rexler Research Corporation by five o'clock. Who owns the stock? Get a photostat of the articles of incorporation, whether stock is listed, who owns their buildings. Everything."

"By five o'clock?" Joe Pace said, surprised. "Say! That's the business research group that puts out the business forecasts for the coming year!"

John handed Joe the letter on his desk. Joe read it, his frown deepening. "What's it all about?"

"I'm not sure," John said. "I just spent an hour and a half with Dr. Simon French. I learned some very startling things. I'm just beginning to sense some of the implications of what he said."

"What things?" Joe asked.

"No time to go into it now," John said. "Get going on this. I want to know whether I can buy that research outfit. I don't think I'm going to feel safe until I own it. Not only that—get busy, Joe."

When Joe left, there was a dreamy, pleased look on John's face. He tapped his fingers absently on the desk top, nodded to himself.

At five minutes to five Joe came into the office without knocking. In his hand was a slip of paper.

"What did you find out?" John asked.

"Rexler Research owns its own building," Joe said. "It used to be a bank and office building. The corporation was formed twelve years ago, in the State of Illinois. Its capital stock amounts to two thousand shares at a thousand dollars par value. Two hundred shares are offered on the exchange at twenty-three hundred—"

"Get me the stock exchange," John said briskly into the phone as he scooped it up. A moment later, "George Bennett...Hello George. This is John Dow. I want that two hundred-share block of Rexler Research... Yes, today. I don't care if it is only two minutes to closing time. Get it or else." He slammed the receiver and looked up at Joe. "Go on," he said.

"One thousand and one shares are owned by the estate of Samuel Rexler, the founder," Joe said quietly. "The other seven hundred and ninety-nine shares are owned by several individuals and one holding company. Five of the shares are owned by your Dr. Simon French."

"I'm going home," John Dow said. "By morning I want all the dope on the estate, who administers it, who the heirs are and all about them and the administrators. Get Will Jones on it with his entire staff of detectives. Direct things yourself. Work all night on it if you have to. By morning I want to know everything necessary to acquiring ownership of Rexler. By noon I want to own it. But I want it done so that no one knows I own it—especially Dr. Simon French. Understand?"

After phoning the garage John put on his hat and left. On his way from the elevator to the building entrance he kept his head straight, but let his eyes turn to see into the coffee shop. Dr. French and the switchboard girl were sitting at the counter where the doctor could watch who left the building through the backwall mirror.

At the curb John climbed into his car. The garage man slid out on the driver's side.

"Just a minute," John said. "I want you to do something."

"Yes sir," the man said respectfully.

"In the restaurant are two people," John said. "They're sitting at the counter. One of them is my switchboard girl. Know her?"

"No Sir."

"All the better," John said. "I want you to keep those two there for at least ten minutes. Here's fifty dollars for doing it, and you can keep your job as long as you want it. Understand what I mean? I own the garage."

"Yes sir. I know that," the man said.

"The girl is pretty, twenty-three, blonde. The man is in his late twenties, high forehead, black hair. Don't let the girl leave. If you have to, pretend she's your wife who has left your bed and board and you want her back. Don't worry about police. Just keep her there until the police come."

John slowly pulled away. In the rear view mirror he saw the garage man enter the building.

Less than five minutes later he turned into the entrance of the police garage and went up in the elevator to the Chief's office. He went in without knocking.

"Do you know who I am?" he asked.

"Of course, Mr. Dow," the police chief said, rising from his desk with a puzzled frown.

"I want you to do something without delay," John said. "It's absolutely vital. I want my switchboard girl arrested on suspicion of some old murder in Kansas City or Miami or someplace and held until at least Monday. Right now she's in the street floor restaurant of my building."

The police chief studied John's face, hastily reviewing all he knew of the setup of the city. Suddenly he reached for the phone. "Get me connected to radio," he said. Then to John Dow, "Description?"

Ten minutes later he picked up the phone and listened for a moment. He looked up at John. "They're bringing her down now."

"Make it look good," John said. "If possible, make it a genuine suspicion. Picture vaguely resembling her, actual case. Murder, so she can't get out on bail. Keep her here until Monday. Don't let a man in his late twenties with a high forehead and black hair see her or talk to her."

"Right," the chief said.

John went down in the elevator and drove his car out. There was a quiet smile on his lips as he turned on the car radio and, listened to the news.

Fifteen minutes later he drove up the winding driveway to the side entrance of the Colonial styled lake shore mansion that was his home.

"Put it away, Jerry," he said to the man who took his place behind the wheel. "I'm expecting company tonight, so be ready for their cars."

Inside he walked over thick oriental carpets worth a fortune until he reached a walnut paneled door. He paused there, his features relaxing into a warm smile before he reached out and twisted the knob.

"Hi, Dear," he said to the white haired woman inside.

She turned and darted him a welcoming smile, then laid down her brush and stood back from the canvas on which she had been painting.

"Not bad," John said, putting his arm around her and studying the lines of paint. "But what is it?"

His wife kissed him then pushed him away.

"It's a mood," she said. "The only trouble is my mood won't stand still long enough for me to paint it."

"Should it?" John asked naively. They both laughed.

CHAPTER THREE

"HELLO, JOHN," the new arrival said expansively, allowing the servant to remove his black topcoat.

"Good evening, Senator," John Dow said, smiling. "Make yourself at home. How was the trip?"

"Never better, John," Senator Larimon said. "Tail wind all the way from Washington." Then, lowering his voice and mumbling his words so they wouldn't carry to the departing servant, "Lantrop will take orders from you when he's elected, so we're giving the go-ahead to the machine."

John Dow nodded expressionlessly and turned to the next arrival…

From time to time he searched out Gloria Dow, his wife, over the heads of the growing group in the huge drawing room. A look of quiet pride crept over his face as he watched her white head and gracious bearing, as she moved among the guests making them welcome. Once she sensed his eyes on her and turned, smiling at him.

When the last of the guests had arrived he joined her, standing beside her with possessive pride.

"You're wonderful, dear," he whispered in her ear once. She blushed with pleasure.

Servants moved through the little clusters of standing and sitting people, serving drinks. Three teenage girls dressed in Dutch maid costumes served food at the long buffet table on one side of the room.

After a while servants began setting up card tables at one end of the room. The women drifted over to them, sitting down together.

John squeezed Gloria's hand and made his way to a side door. Steps on the other side led down.

With his departure there was a slow movement of the men toward that door, until there was no one left in the room except the women. Dow playing Canasta, and the servants.

A servant who had moved about during the earlier part of the evening giving orders to the others now took his place at this door, closing it and remaining there.

This had not been the first time this group had gathered here. The wives of the men played cards unconcerned over the departure of their husbands, knowing that they were now "in conference."

Directly underneath them, in a room they had never seen, their husbands were seating themselves in a room notable for its sound-proofing, among other things.

The two tables were round, and covered with green felt. John Dow himself was standing behind a counter and handing out stacks of red, white, and blue poker chips in exchange for crisp new currency.

Shortly the men were playing poker with an intensity that would have made an outsider think that was their only concern in being here.

But now and then one of the players would rise and walk over to the counter where John Dow remained, and stand talking to him for several minutes, the conversation inaudible two feet away of the general murmur of conversation.

At one thirty, as at a signal, the players began taking their chips up to the counter. John Dow pressed a small button under the counter. The servant outside the door up above came down. He expertly counted each player's chips and paid out the crisp bills that had been taken in earlier.

The men drifted upstairs in two and threes, engaged in small talk.

When they appeared it was a signal for the breakup of the Canasta games. By two o'clock the last guest had left. The servants were busy cleaning up after them.

Gloria Dow linked her arm in her husband's and led him up the winding stairs to the ornate balcony, and into their bedroom. When the door closed her air of leisure vanished.

"What did they say?" she asked, almost fiercely.

He smiled at her quietly for a moment before answering.

"It's going to go over," he said. "Only Australia is holding back on the signing, but that doesn't matter, now that the rest are going through with it."

John Dow walked through the door from the hall to the front office at half a minute after nine, which was within three seconds of his customary time. His cheery smile toward the switchboard was habit. There was a different girl there. He remembered last night suddenly.

"Tell Mr. Pace I want to see him in my office," he said as he swept by the switchboard.

In his office he sat down at his desk and began going through his morning mail. Several times he frowned at the phone as though annoyed that it didn't ring. Finally he picked it up and called the unlisted number in the Mayor's private office.

"Hello, Fred. This is Mr. Dow," he said. Then suddenly, "What! Let me get this straight. You say she really IS wanted by the Los Angeles police for questioning, that there's no question about the identity? Hey, wait-a-minute. I hadn't bargained on this. It's unfair... Yes, I know. I still want her held until Monday, but the Los Angeles police aren't to be notified... They have? Then tell him to wire them it's all a mistake, that they've checked and she can't possibly be the same girl... No, nothing like that. She made good her escape from California; she's doing a good job here. It was a dirty trick having her picked up but I had to keep her where she couldn't talk too much until after Saturday. I had no idea this would happen. Tell that police captain that after this when I tell him to do something not to exceed his instructions. In a way he didn't. I told him to try to make it authentic, but where's his sense of sportsmanship?"

He glanced up as Joe came in and nodded a greeting to him, noticing the tired grayness to his complexion.

"O.K., Fred," he concluded his telephone conversation. "Tell him to use his brains and get her completely in the clear. I don't want this to go on. It could get out of hand. You know what I mean. A little thing like this could make real trouble. Big trouble." He dropped the phone. "Our switchboard girl was in the coffee shop with Dr. French. I had the police pick her up for the weekend on suspicion of some out-of-town thing. They made it too good. She's actually wanted by California. Now I may have trouble getting her out by Monday."

Joe grinned mockingly. "Don't you know better?" he said. "Three out of five people, if they were picked up by the police, would either confess to something or be pinned with something inside of twenty-four hours."

John Dow nodded glumly. "It was stupid, but there was nothing else to do without letting Dr. French suspect I didn't want him talking to her. What'd you find out?"

"There are seven heirs," Joe said. "They all want to sell."

"Good," John said. "Buy."

"But they can't sell," Joe added. "It's in trust, and the executor has sole discretion. He has refused to sell before, and the heirs can't force him to."

John looked at Joe, trying to read what was in his mind. "Give me the worst," he said. "I know you've got bad news."

"The executor is Stephen G. Burk, president of the Bank of Commerce," Joe Pace said. "Age, fifty-four, no past. We could buy a controlling interest in the bank for fifty million dollars, approximately, and have the power to fire him. But he's independently wealthy. Mostly Government bonds and gilt edge stocks." Joe smiled dryly. "Your law firm also handles his legal matters, so in any legal conflict between you, you would each have to get a new law firm to handle it."

"A good man," John said admiringly. "The will? Can it be broken? Or could the heirs by a concerted pressure make him willing to sell for them?"

"They've tried both things," Joe said. "They aren't satisfied with the amount of money they make off the stock. Too much of it is plowed back into research. I've been up all night on this. The law firm says you have only one angle you can work with any chance of success."

"What's that?" John asked.

"The heirs are the legal owners of the controlling interest," Joe said. "Burk has assumed the authority to vote for them ever since Samuel Rexler died. In court it might be possible for the heirs to take that authority away from him and control the company themselves, even though they can't sell the stock or force him to sell it. It's a fine point, but a good law firm might be able to win such a case.

"I think they would play along with enthusiasm if they could be sure their income from Rexler would be doubled."

"That would take time," John said. "And also it would show our hand whether we won or not. Or, maybe not. What happens when Stephen G. Burk dies?"

"Not a chance," Joe said dryly. "He's sound as a dollar. Will Jones has an idea to use if nothing else will work. I suspect he's used it before, he had it down so pat."

"Hmmm," John said, studying Joe carefully. "Tell Will to go ahead with his idea and not to bother me with the details. I have a hunch."

The phone rang. John picked it up. "Yes?" he said.

"Washington is calling," the girl at the board said.

"Put them on," John said curtly.

"Hello, John," a voice he recognized said heartily. "I thought you'd like to get the news right away. Australia is signing."

"Good," John Dow said, his face brightening. "I thought they would, but didn't want to raise all your hopes too much. Now the world front against communism will be solid. There can be no secession for any country from this union of democracies, and international policing of elections will keep would-be dictators out of the picture."

"It won't be smooth," the voice said. "I'll make a prediction that within two years we'll have the first country trying to withdraw from the union."

"And a brief war of occupation," John said. "Much better than a world war."

"Anything you want to say to me while I'm on the phone?" the voice asked carefully.

"Nothing," John said. "I may be in Washington soon. We can have a long talk then. You're doing all right."

"O.K., John," the voice said.

Almost immediately the phone rang again.

"Dr. Simon French is on the phone," the girl said.

"Put him on," John said, licking his lips nervously. "Yes...I heard about it this morning, doctor. You were having coffee with her when it happened? Yes, they talked to me this morning. Someone, a garage mechanic or somebody, recognized her as a suspect in something that happened in California. I didn't get the details. Of course it's a mistake. I'd stake my life she's innocent. She'll be out of jail by Monday or I'll see if my friendship with the Mayor doesn't rate a few heads in the police department... No, not too busy... You're downstairs? Well come up. I'll be able to see you for a few minutes."

He jiggled the phone button until he got the switchboard girl. "Connect me with Mr. Pace... Joe? I'll be downstairs in the coffee shop... No, I don't want the details of what's happening to Burk... Arrested for hit-run driving? Don't tell me any more. He's out of course... Half an hour after he was taken in? *We* have a good law firm, he and I." He chuckled, then hung up.

Simon French's high forehead was glistening with a light film of perspiration as he came into the office. He shook hands with him gravely, then slid into the chair opposite him.

"You're sure she'll be out by Monday?" Dr. French asked without preliminaries.

"Of course," John said. "I like the girl. I know she couldn't be guilty of anything more serious than taking a day off for illness to take in some shopping."

"I hope so," Simon French said. "In a way I feel responsible."

"Why?" John asked sharply.

"Oh, I just have an uncomfortable feeling that if I hadn't been talking to her she wouldn't have been picked up," the doctor said.

"Yes?" John said.

"You see," the doctor said, "she was on her way out of the building. I was still in the lobby. I invited her to have coffee with me. If I hadn't done that this mechanic wouldn't have spotted her and called the police. She'd still be free.

"Oh," John said, relieved. Then, abruptly changing the subject, "tell me more about what we'll do tomorrow at your laboratory. What day of my life am I going to live over?"

"Not just a day," the doctor said. "Several years in one day. The whole thing will be completed tomorrow."

"Several years?" John said.

"Yes. You see, under hypnosis, with the mind divorced from the flywheel of the body for its conception of passing time, we can impress on it that each heartbeat is twenty-four hours."

"I see," John said. "That means I could live out a theoretical lifetime in the course of a day then."

"Just about," Dr. French said.

"But how do you know what's going on then?" John asked.

"We ask you from time to time," Dr. French said. "Not too often. And at the end of the period we half wake you, with all your fictitious memories still fresh, and we ask you all about yourself. You talk to us about all that's happened. Just like right now you could tell us the story of your life as you remember it."

"Will I remember it when I'm fully awake?" John asked.

"It's better not to," Dr. French said.

"Well, I want to," John Dow said. "In fact, unless I can I refuse to go through with this."

"You may regret it," Dr. French said, smiling. "Sometimes parts of it are pretty ugly. It would be better if you didn't know what we know about you."

John shook his head. "You do what? Keep notes? Make recordings?"

"Keep notes," Dr. French said. "We have a huge vault that used to belong to a bank. We keep them in there."

"Good enough," John said, thinking of Stephen G. Burk. "I'll be in your office promptly at ten o'clock tomorrow morning."

CHAPTER FOUR

THE PHONE STARTED RINGING the moment he closed the door. He took his time sitting down, then answered it.

"Mr. Pace is on the phone, sir," the girl said.

"Put him on," John said. "Joe? …O.K., come to my office."

He drummed his fingers on the desk until Joe appeared. "What's the excitement?" he asked.

"Will Jones had me investigate ownership of the stock in Burk's bank," Joe said. "A couple of million dollars worth is owned by three friends of yours."

"Well, what of it?" John asked.

"Will wanted to know if you would have these friends offer to sell considerably below market at the last minute today."

A gleam appeared in John Dow's eyes. He lifted the phone and asked for a certain number.

"Hello, Harry," he said, winking at Joe. "You own some shares in the Bank of Commerce don't you? Well, listen carefully. At ten minutes to five I want you to put them on the market at three dollars below list. At three minutes to five I want you to drop your asking price another five dollars. There won't be much time for buyers to come in…I don't care if you do stand a chance to lose your shirt. Do it or you'll lose more than that… That's right the market is going to drop anyway. I'll tell you when to start buying back… Sure, sure. It's my doing, but I thought I'd do you a favor and let you in on the play. You won't be the only one." He winked at Joe again and hung up.

Five minutes later he had the word of two more people they would dump.

Then he called another number. "George Bennett…Hello George. What's the list price on Bank of Commerce? …O.K., listen carefully. Put up an ask eight dollars below list… That's right. And don't buy more than two hundred shares before closing time for me. Under procedure K. Monday morning put my ask down another three dollars."

"Procedure K," he explained to Joe as he hung up, "is a kind of running play. Five dummy buyers take all that's offered for a while at the asking price, then one of them suddenly tries to sell. The other four drop their ask a notch. He drops to meet them. Meanwhile they're picking up a lot of bargain buys from panic sellers. Get it?"

"That'll do what Will wants," Joe said. He sat down and crossed his legs, taking out a pack of cigarettes. "Would you mind telling me why you're so hot about this Rexler Research Corporation all of a sudden?"

"I found out how they get their dope on business trends," John said. "I want it. In fact, I have to have it."

"Why?" Joe persisted.

"Do you believe in prophecy?" John asked. Joe shrugged indifferently. "Well, their system is the nearest thing to genuine prophecy there can be. This Dr. Simon French is a Simon-pure simpleton outside of his research. He doesn't fully realize what he has. In a way he does, but Rexler Research isn't handing out anything except business trends. They get more. Much more. For example, they know right now whether the President will be alive a year from now or not. They know whether it will be raining six months from now."

"Go on," Joe said quietly.

"It's hypnotism," John said. "No, wait a minute. Don't look at me like I was going batty."

He explained what he had learned from Dr. French. Joe smoked his cigarette, apparently interested only in the swirling smoke from it.

"So," Joe said when he had finished, "Dr. French says you play an important role in these histories the way they went when certain events that didn't happen are made to 'happen' in the dream. He called the role you play all invariant. I read a story something like that once. The guy wanted to live his life over and not make certain mistakes. He didn't make those, but he made others that caused him to be hanged in the end anyway, so the result was the same. His being hanged was an invariant.

"How do you know Dr. French won't find out all the ramifications of your real life from this? Maybe in these if existences you have the same setup."

"He said no," John said.

"But he doesn't know what you are right now," Joe said quietly. "He doesn't know the people who call you for instructions, the Senator who—"

"Shut up, Joe," John said.

"All right," Joe said good-naturedly. He looked at the rug for a long minute, frowning in thought. Finally he said, "I'm trying to figure what his motive could be for contacting you at all. He apparently knows all about you as you would have been if something that didn't take place a long time ago had taken place, or vice versa. Why does he need to check with you?"

"I'm not sure," John said. "I have a distinct impression that he told me, but I've forgotten what he gave as the reason."

"You sure he didn't hypnotize you?" Joe asked sharply. "What better way to rule than to rule the ruler? That's the way you—"

"He didn't hypnotize me," John said.

"Maybe not," Joe said. "I think I'll be there when they put you to sleep tomorrow."

John hesitated. "Good idea," he said, giving in. "We've been together a long time, Joe. More than once I would have blundered without you. This may be one of those times."

"Yes," Joe said dreamily. "We've had good times together. We make a good team. I'm a kibitzer, you're a doer. There are the times you would have cracked up on the rocks if I hadn't seen the rocks and steered you clear. But you were the one forging ahead. I was just along for the ride."

"You see what I want though, don't yon?" John said. "As owner of the Rexler Company I'd have access to those secret files. It'd be like playing poker with a marked deck. You know the old saying, you can't lose at if-poker.

"By the way, Australia is signing. Washington called, told me this morning. My dream of a civilized union of democracies with policing of elections by international armed force to guarantee democratic processes is going to come true. Eventually, as the

Communist World State loses its grip on the satellites, democracy will spread."

Joe grinned crookedly. "But in any of those countries another John Dow could rise, to dictate behind the scenes, seeing that only his boys got elected—in both parties."

"Within the Constitutional guarantees," John corrected. "And you know my greatest hold on my boys. It's their conviction that I have no desire for personal power, and that my plans are for the good of the world. Once I went off the beam they'd soon desert me, and threats wouldn't hold them."

"They get to know you," Joe said, rising. "Like I do. Come by in the morning in time to stop in and have a cup of Martha's coffee. It'll make her feel good."

Gloria Dow stood for several minutes looking across the large room, vacant now, which had been full of activity the night before.

Dwarfed to insignificance in a chair on the side opposite her, her husband sat, apparently asleep. At his elbow was a radio console. From it music was flowing with a force suggestive of Niagara.

She crossed the room, her steps soundless on the thick rug.

John's eyes opened. He turned his head, watching her approach. The scowl on his face was replaced by a smile, but the brooding look in his eyes remained. His hand reached out and turned the volume down as she sat on the arm of the chair.

"Something's troubling you, John?" she asked. "It generally is when you play Liszt's Hungarian Rhapsody No. 2 over and over."

"Maybe," he said with an effort at cheerfulness. "But it's nothing for you to bother your still beautiful little head over. Did you ever listen to Liszt over and over?"

"How could I help it?" she chided.

"I mean *really* listen," he answered seriously. "It's the history of humanity. You can feel it, sense it. He didn't intend it that way, but he didn't know what he wrote. Its opening bars are the Genesis of the Bible. The Creation, God's resting on the seventh day, Eden, the fall, the descent of Adam and Eve out of Eden, the murder of Abel, history down to today and on into the future to the final whatever is coming." He was staring into space again, the scowl on his face. "You can even hear the coming of the twentieth century, and feel the too joyful hysteria of the world with the atom bomb hanging over its head, its sudden calm once more when the perfect defense from it was found."

"That's just your imagination," Gloria said. "What I get when I listen to it is the—those ten days in the hospital when Sisty was born. Its closing bars are when I was getting ready to come home. The second time it plays carries her into her first day in school. Remember that teacher? Miss Fleury?"

"Yeah," John said absently. "Seventh grade history. All the time she had been slanting history. They didn't know it until the loyalty checks on city employees and found she belonged to the communist party. Then I began to realize why Sisty had some of the crazy ideas she talked about."

"Probably the Communist bloc will never know that that was the cause of your going the way you did," Gloria said, "after you started making real money."

"If I hadn't," John said, "someone else would have, or some group would have."

CHAPTER FIVE

THE SIGN ON THE BRONZE DOORS of what had obviously been built to be a bank said "REXLER RESEARCH CORP." Jose Pace held the door open for John to enter.

A slender young man with dark eyes and light hair escorted them along the graveyard of long deserted tellers' cages to an elevator in the back that lifted them to the second floor.

When they stepped off the elevator he remained on, closing the doors on them without explanation. They stood in a large deserted office. Half a dozen desks were distributed without plan, their surfaces covered with untidy piles of papers.

Dr. Simon French appeared after a short wait, the smile on his lips changing to a questioning pout as he noticed Joe.

"This is a very close friend of mine, doctor," John said casually. "Dr. Simon French, Mr.—ah—Craig Downing."

"Glad to know you, Mr. Downing," Dr. French said, shaking hands cordially. "But I'm sure you'll find the whole thing very boring. Mr. Dow will be sleeping practically the whole of the ten hours he will be here."

"Nevertheless," John said, "I've asked him to be present during the experiment." He smiled significantly. "I don't want to leave myself *wholly* at your mercies, doctor."

"Quite right," Dr. French said, laughing briefly. "Well, come this way, gentlemen. I'll take you back to one of the laboratory rooms. The one where I'll put you to sleep."

"What if I'm one of those people who can't be hypnotized?" John asked.

"We haven't found any like that," Dr. French said without turning to look at them. "You'll see why in a minute. We use a foolproof system. Even if you intended to fake being hypnotized, you wouldn't stay awake long enough to do it."

He pushed open the door of a small room. Its walls were padded with soundproofing. The windows were double, a dead air space between them. A window air-conditioning unit was humming softly.

Against one wall was a bed. At the end of the bed was a heavy table with several electronic cabinets on it. Beside the table was a small hand truck on which two tanks of gas perched. To their left as they stood in the doorway was a glass case containing what seemed to be surgical tools of some kind.

"If you'll pardon me a moment," Dr. French said politely, "I'll get a comfortable chair for Mr. Downing to sit in." He left the room.

"I think you're being foolish to go through with this, John," Joe said. "You always go getting yourself involved in something that complicates matters. What can you gain from doing this?"

"A first hand working knowledge of Dr. French's experiments," John said. "If we can't do what we're trying to do, we might have to duplicate his work."

"Aha!" Joe said knowingly. "I'll keep that in mind."

The doctor returned with an upholstered chair.

"This should do, Mr. Downing. After Mr. Dow is asleep we'll have coffee brought up. Now, Mr. Dow, if you'll lay down with your head on the pillow. It would be a good idea to take off your shoes so you'll be as comfortable as possible.

"First I'll give you a few whiffs of gas. It's a very common gas, used by dentists to relax their patients and also kill pain without putting them completely to sleep. It's ideal for this work, because going into a drugged sleep partially defeats our purpose. You must go into a hypnotic sleep so that we can follow you, so to speak."

John had been taking off his shoes. Now he laid down, stretching out luxuriously. Dr. French turned a knob on one of the gas tanks and unwound a quarter inch red rubber tube, bringing its end just under John Dow's lips.

"Don't breathe deeply," he instructed. "Just let its coolness touch your nose while you breathe."

He pressed a button on the wall by the door. Two young men came in so soon after that they must have been standing outside waiting. Without waiting for instructions they went to the table and began placing small copper plates on John's wrists, smearing a jelly on the skin beforehand. Other plates went on the ankles.

"Now we'll raise your head so this support can go under the pillow," Dr. French said calmly.

A hood whose interior surface was a forest of small metal heads held out by fine springs was lifted off the table and clamped to the head of the bed so that it fit over his cranium.

The two silent men in white uniforms connected wires from the machines on the table to the hood and to each of the small circular plates fastened to the wrists and ankles by tight fitting straps.

Dials on the panels of the instruments lit up. Needles moved up from their zero marks. For a good ten minutes the two men adjusted the hood to various positions until they seemed satisfied with what the meters said.

They stepped back. One of them nodded to Dr. French. He returned the nod. They left the room.

"Now we're all ready," Dr. French said. "How do you feel, Mr. Dow?"

"Relaxed," John said calmly.

Joe was watching the panels. The instrument connecting to the hood was a large one, with several dozen small meters arranged in rows. Those on the right side of the panel were fluctuating more wildly than those on the left.

Dr. French took a small device out of his pocket. It was the size of a pocket watch, with a long thick handle like that of a flashlight. The silver dial on it began to whirl slowly. Very slowly. There were small black dots evenly spaced on it.

"Now I want you to watch the dots on this little revolving mirror, Mr. Dow," he said. "Try to pick out one and keep your eyes on it, following it around and around and around. It should be very easy, since it goes so slowly.

"You're getting along in years. Aren't you? Your two children are grown and have their own families now. Sometimes you miss the days when they were little and still at home."

"Sometimes," John said with a smile.

"Maybe you didn't have the comforts you have now," Dr. French said, sitting carefully on the edge of the bed and bringing the whirling little mirror closer to John's eyes, "but there were other things you had then, more precious. You worked for the Moore Publishing Company then, didn't you. Little responsibility compared to what you have today.

"A certain insecurity, perhaps, but the thrill of buying your first home, the one where your children and your young wife were waiting for you when you came home at night, of worrying about the pennies, budgeting your salary so you could make the monthly payment on your house.

"*Nineteen fifty-three!* The last week in April. The new President was in office. His name was—"

Dr. French leaned over and whispered in John's ear. Joe couldn't make out what he said.

"No!" John said, shaking his head with drugged motion. The panel instruments fluctuated wildly.

"Yes!" Dr. French said. "You know it's true. Of course it is! Isn't it?" His hand stretched toward a panel. A finger jabbed swiftly at a red button. John shuddered, then relaxed.

"Y—yes, it's true," John whispered. "Funny...for a minute there...I...thought..." The last word was formed only by his lips. His eyes, unblinking, were following the small black dots around in the small mirror. But the mirror was growing larger and larger, and the dots were going faster and faster...they were blurring...

"Now, Mr. Dow," the scientist's voice seemed to come from a great distance, "tell me what happened at this time that almost changed the entire history of mankind."

CHAPTER SIX

THE BUS PULLED TO THE CURB with its brakes squealing. John lifted his eyes from the book he was reading, blinking them tiredly. It was hard to read the small print when it bobbed around in front of his eyes that way.

He hastily closed the book and joined the line leaving the bus. On the sidewalk he shouldered his way past people into the grocery store. In the rear was the meat counter...

"Good evening, Mr. Dow. I think you're next." Mr. Schmidt, the butcher, laid four fat, white fingers over the top of the meat counter and smiled fleshily. "What'll you have tonight?"

"My wife called up and told me you had a chicken ready," John Dow said, glancing up from his newspaper.

"Oh yes." Mr. Schmidt turned away and sorted a small pile of packages, returning with one with the name "Dow" scrawled in pencil over a fourth of its perimeter. Underneath was scrawled the price, two eighty-four.

John adjusted his sack of groceries and brought out his billfold, extracting three ones and laying them on the counter with a crab-like distortion of his body so as not to dislodge the grocery sack on his hip and the roughly folded newspaper barely secured under his arm.

While Mr. Schmidt went to the cash register he tried to perch the wrapped chicken on top the already filled grocery sack, thought better of it, and managed to squeeze it under his arm in such a way that it rested partly on the groceries.

"Eighty-five, ninety, three," Mr. Schmidt said, smiling. With a final friendly nod he turned his attention to the next customer, an impatient woman.

John Dow scraped the change off the top of the enameled counter and dropped it in his pocket, then turned away, making his way through the crowd to the front of the store while trying to read the paper again.

"Hi, John." John looked up to see who had spoken to him.

"Oh, hello, Fred," he said.

"Some excitement—about those communists," Fred said.

"What's that?" John asked disinterestedly.

"Just noticed the headlines on the extra at the corner when I came in," Fred elaborated. "Some longhair madmen tried to turn loose some poison gas on an army installation in New Mexico, I think it said. As if the atom bomb stockpiles were that easy to take. Fort Knox would be easier—I'll bet."

With a farewell grin Fred pushed through the turnstile into the self service grocery section and was quickly lost in the crowd.

John folded his paper and tucked it down into the grocery sack. Out on the sidewalk he fished a handful of change from a pocket and tried to isolate a dime from the rest in his palm with his fingers.

The newsboy was shouting, "Extra! Extra! Communists seize atom stockpile!"

"Here!" John said sharply.

A paper was thrust in his hand and the dime extracted skillfully. A second later three cents were slid into his fingers. He tried to get them in his pocket while holding the paper, but finally had to transfer the paper to his already overtaxed left arm.

With the change safely put away he unfolded the Extra and read the headlines. His feet automatically turned at the corner and led him down the side street toward home.

COMMUNISTS LOOSE POISON GAS AT ATOM STOCK-PILE, the headlines in red ink screamed.

John's feet slowed as his attention sharpened. There were several short news items under the brief, almost tersely worded account of the explosion of several poison gas bombs in New Mexico. One told of reports of fishermen, sighting large, unidentified planes at sea, coming from the direction of Russia. Another told of a highway patrol car stopping a truck loaded with cylinders of gas just outside Chicago. A third was a report of a farmer in Idaho seeing parachutes dropping just over the hills from his farm.

After reading each of these, John whistled. He suddenly thought of the radio and reluctantly kicked himself for not waiting to get the latest on the six o'clock news.

The thought of the radio quickened his pace. He folded the paper and thrust it under his arm with the other, and looked ahead for the first glimpse of his house, crowded in between two others in the densely packed residential block.

When he saw it he glanced at his wristwatch and saw it was four minutes of six—just time to get in the house and get the radio warmed up before the news.

He opened the front door. The radio was already on. Pleasant food odors from the kitchen greeted his nostrils as he dropped the two newspapers on the davenport in the living room and crossed the rug to the kitchen door, which was open.

"Hi, Gloria," he greeted his wife casually. She straightened up from the oven, wiping her hair back from her forehead with the wrist of a hand that held a meat fork.

"Hello, darling," she said throatily. Obediently she crossed the kitchen and planted a kiss on John's lips, her eyes surveying the grocery sack and meat paper wrapped chicken.

"Hi, daddy!" two voices exploded at his back, in the living room. An eleven-year-old blonde haired boy, and nine-year-old black haired girl, rushed into the kitchen and swarmed onto their father.

Gloria rescued the groceries from the attack and retreated to the stove to finish taking the roast beef from the oven and slam the oven door on the not yet done baked potatoes.

"Quiet down now," George ordered his youngsters, dropping them off as he fought across the kitchen to the radio. "I want to listen to the news. Some communists tried some funny business today and I want to learn what it was."

"Quiet, Franky," the nine-year old girl said, aping her father's authoritative tone.

"Quiet yourself, Sisty," Franky shot back, pouting his lips at her.

"Both of you be quiet," their mother said with finality. To emphasize her order she let the roast plunk more forcibly than necessary onto the large oval dish on the kitchen table.

"Shshsh," Franky and Sisty said to each other, their eyes mischievously bright.

"—ELGRUG IS GURGLE SPELLED BACKwards," the radio said, dropping off to a whisper. The pointer moved to five ninety and another voice said, "—and the news."

John Dow straightened and turned away from the radio, for the first time looking about him with interest.

"It seems we have a revolution of sorts on our hands," the news commentator began. "Perhaps it will turn out to be a good thing, because it will now give the government reason to deport or execute or imprison every known communist in the country."

During a pause John examined the roast beef hungrily.

"At three o'clock this afternoon several cylinders of an as yet unidentified poison gas were dumped from a speeding dump truck just outside the army reservation in New Mexico where it is rumored extensive underground storage rooms house a goodly portion of our atom bomb stockpile.

"Censorship was immediately clamped down on the extent of the damage, but observers report a heavy cloud of gas covering the entire area, and a civilian pilot who flew over the area less than an hour ago reports that several cars could be seen through the fog, in ditches, with what seemed to be people lying on the pavement near them.

"Undoubtedly the Army Chief of Staff is aware of the gravity of the situation. Of course, it is always possible that this insane act was perpetrated by home grown communists in the hope of capturing our atom stockpile, and with the belief that if they could in some way render it ineffective, then the enemy would be in a position to declare war on us. But the odds are against this being any such far-fetched scheme. To me—and please, I don't want to alarm you, because there is no hope of this succeeding—it seems certain that the gas attack at what seems likely to be one of our atom stockpiles must have been carefully planned, and must be part of a larger scheme which they hope will succeed. This larger scheme could hinge about the capture of an atom stockpile in two different ways. It could first have no other design than to take the stockpile out of action as a threat to invading forces, which might already be on their way here. But the more probable scheme is to—not take the atom bombs out of the running—but to gather American communists in the areas surrounding that stockpile, and for invading enemy bombers to land there and load up with our own bombs to use against us.

"I sincerely hope that the army strategists have guarded against this possibility so that the saboteurs and red traitors and enemy invaders, if they materialize, will find themselves effectively checked in any attempt to use our bombs!

"A humorous report has just come in over the teletype. It might be titled 'Communist Rebels Capture American Town.' Two young men with red armbands on their sleeves with black scythe-and-hammer emblems on the bands drove into Little Mesa, Colorado, parked in front of the sheriff's office, calmly walked into that office and informed the dozing sheriff that they were taking over. They locked that dignitary in one of his cells and themselves proceeded to doze. They were sound asleep when, some hours later, the sheriff's wife marched in to see why her lord and master hadn't come home for lunch. Unimpressed by the armbands, she took over, locking the young men in another cell, then releasing her husband. So, for a few hours today, Little Mesa, Colorado, belonged to Soviet Russia instead of the United States, but its two hundred and thirty stalwart citizens were completely unaware of the change!

"There are the various rumors and reports of the sighting of huge airships in the north Pacific, headed toward our shores. As soon as any of these are confirmed we will report them over this station. Right now there seems to be an air of tension building up. Washington has nothing whatever to say. The same is true of the enemy capital.

The radio became silent for a pregnant moment.

"Flash!" it came to life again. "Our Senator Donald Webster of—has just taken off in an army plane, presumably for Washington. Most of the Senate are already in Washington. It may be that before morning we will be at war. But, knowing how the Communists work—and don't we all—it will probably be called an internal revolution by the Communists."

"Dinner's ready," Mrs. Dow said loudly above the voice on the radio. "Have you children washed your hands?"

"I haven't," John Dow said, heading for the bathroom.

"Daddy is a chi-uld," Sisty chanted at his retreating back.

"Oooooh," John Dow groaned, opening his eyes and blinking them slowly. "Uh!" he said, sitting up. His feet searched for and found their bedroom slippers while he rubbed his eyes with his knuckles.

As he stood up his eyes sought the clock. It said seven minutes after seven. He blinked at it in annoyance. For three days running now it had said that—exactly that. It gave him the feeling it was stopped, but the fine red second hand churned slowly around the dial.

The clock said fifteen after when he returned from the bathroom. He remembered the news when he had one arm in a clean shirt, and turned the bedroom radio on before sticking the other arm in.

It was nineteen minutes after seven when he remembered the radio again and frowned. It should have been giving with the news by now.

Holding up his trousers with one hand, he turned dials, but, though the pilot light and the tubes were glowing, not a sound came out of the little white plastic radio.

"Damn," John muttered, shutting it off. The "Damn" was at the prospect of having to bypass three or four scarce dollars into getting the radio fixed, rather than at missing the news.

He strode to the bedroom door while slipping his tie under his collar.

"Gloria!" he called. At her "Yeyus?" from the kitchen he called, "turn on the radio. The bedroom one is on the fritz."

He left the door open and turned back into the room, standing before the dresser mirror to tie his tie. He had forgotten about the radio again.

With a final glance at himself in the mirror he left the bedroom, catching his suit coat off the hanger in the closet and slipping into it as he crossed the hall to the kitchen.

Suddenly he remembered the radio again, and glanced at the kitchen wall clock. It said twenty-two minutes after seven.

"Why didn't you turn the radio on?" he complained. "The seven fifteen news will be over before we can get it now."

"It's on," Gloria said matter-of-factly without looking up from the eggs in the skillet.

John twisted the dials on it. Other than a faint A.C. hum there was no sound.

"What the heck's the matter with our radios?" John said in a complaining-to-God tone of voice. He sat down in the breakfast nook opposite Franky and Sisty, rattling his silverware as a mild outlet for his mild annoyance at the radios. They prudently kept quiet. Breakfast time, they had learned, was no time to assert their personalities.

"Oh well," John said to no one in particular, after he had emptied his glass of orange juice. "I can buy a paper on the way to work." The thought made him feel better. He gave his two children a fatherly smile as they squeezed out of the breakfast nook to go to school.

When they were gone Gloria poured herself a cup of coffee and sat down opposite John. She always did that, waiting until she had the house to herself before eating her own breakfast.

"Better call the radio repair shop this morning," John mumbled through a bite of toast. "We can't have BOTH radios on the blink."

"Funny they should both get out of order at the same time," Gloria said thoughtfully. "Do you suppose it could be the radio stations?"

"Huh?" John grunted. "Nonsense!" He glanced at his wrist. "My watch!" he exclaimed. "The radio made me forget it."

He slipped out of the breakfast nook and went to the bedroom, returning at once, strapping on his wristwatch.

"Well—" He kissed Gloria impersonally on the lips, stood back and looked thoughtful—like someone who has sampled something cooking, then took her in his arms and gave her a long kiss. "Bye, Cookie," he said with satisfaction.

"Bye," she whispered as he disappeared through the door to the living room. She stood there until the sound of the front door closing told her he had gone. Then she turned to the stove and dropped an egg in the skillet for her own breakfast, humming softly.

CHAPTER SEVEN

JOHN REACHED THE CORNER just as the bus pulled into the curb. Expertly he picked four cents out of the change he held in his hand, and exchanged it for the morning paper. Picking out another dime for bus fare, he dropped the change back in his pocket and joined the line of those boarding the bus.

As he sat down in the rear seat he saw a news truck come to a stop just behind the bus. A man jumped out with an armful of papers, went to the man on the corner, exchanged the papers for the old ones, and scurried back into the truck again, which pulled around the bus with a clash of gears and speeded away.

"Darn," John muttered. "I'm always buying a paper a minute before the next edition comes out." He eyed the possibility of opening the window and demanding the later edition. The bus started forward.

With a sigh of resignation he spread out the paper to read the front page.

COMMUNISTS ATTEMPT REVOLUTION, the headlines said. In the right hand double column the items elaborated on the headline. Communist paratroopers had landed in New Mexico and various other places. There was street fighting in Kansas City. Los Angeles had been taken over by the Communists, and the Governor had called out troops to go in and restore order and drive out the Communists.

A Communist newspaper had appeared in the enemy capital two hours before the first sign of trouble in the United States with the news that there was a revolution in America—proving that the revolution was enemy inspired. There had been a hot exchange of notes between the two capitals during the night in which Washington had accused them of starting an undeclared war. The enemy had at first insisted that it was revolution and nothing more—and finally sent a note at four in the morning which said that they could no longer recognize the Washington Government as the American Government, since it no longer was in a position to act.

John read all this silently, then turned to the comic sheet. There was a worried frown on his face as he read the comics, however, and he wished that he had been able to get the later paper.

He finished the comic sheet and searched through the paper for the cartoons, pausing here and there to read some item with an interesting headline. Finally, a few blocks before where he was to get off, he finished the paper and dropped it under the seat.

When he saw the next stop was his, he stood up and went down the aisle to the door. Traffic held up the bus. He extracted a cigarette from his shirt pocket and got out his lighter ready to light the cigarette before emerging from the bus onto the street.

Finally the bus pulled in and the door opened. Hastily lighting the cigarette, John Dow stepped out of the bus. Only then did he notice the crowd and the scattered newspapers. His eyes uncomprehendingly read the huge headlines.

COMMUNIST PATRIOTS LIBERATE AMERICA FROM CAPITALIST SLAVERY, the headlines read.

The crowd was more interesting. John squeezed his way unobtrusively through it to the focus of interest. His shocked eyes recognized the face on the sidewalk as that of the old man who had always sold papers on this corner.

It was a blood streaked face now, and John saw that it belonged to a dead man.

"What happened?" John asked the man next to him. "Get hit by a car?"

The man turned dazed eyes at him.

"He refused to sell those papers and they blackjacked him," he muttered nervously.

"Oh," John said vaguely. "Oh!" he added with dawning comprehension. He hastily extracted himself from the crowd and scurried down the street to his office building. As he slipped into the revolving doors he heard sounds like gunshots a block away.

"Morning, Mark," he muttered to the elevator man as he squeezed into the already crowded elevator.

"Morning, Mr. Dow," Mark answered, reaching out to close the doors.

He brought the elevator to a stop just above the top of the first floor doors.

"The building is full of commies," he said in a tight voice. "The best thing for all of you to do is go to your offices and stay there and NOT ARGUE. That way you won't get shot—and we all know that this revolution won't succeed, so it's better to not run any risks of getting killed. Before the day's over the army will reach the city and run out the commies."

There were gasps as Mark started the elevator again.

"Ooohh," a feminine voice said. A shapely blonde closed her dark eyelids and started to slump.

"Cut it, Gertrude," a practical female voice said clearly. "This thing is serious."

"Oh!" the blonde said half-afraid, half-exasperated, as she caught herself and opened her eyes.

There were nervous titters as the elevator came to its first stop at the fourteenth floor and three people stepped warily into the hall.

There followed a succession of surges, stops, and door slammings, until the elevator stopped at the nineteenth floor. John stepped out nervously.

There was no one in the hall. John, and the three others that had emerged from the elevator with him, made their way down the deserted hall to the frosted glass doors of their office.

MOORE PUBLISHING CO., the lettering on the door announced. John unconsciously read this every morning before opening the door and stepping onto the thick, sound-deadening carpet floor of the luxurious outer office. He did the same this morning, then opened the door.

There was a man slumped down in one of the oversize lounge chairs. John recognized him. He was one of the union officers— Harvey Brage—assistant business agent or something.

Harvey Brage pulled himself forward from the depths of the chair and stood up. It was then John Dow noticed the armband on Brage's right arm. It was dull red, three inches wide.

"Good morning, John," the assistant business agent said familiarly. His eyes took in the two stenographers behind John and nodded to each, speaking their names.

"Good morning, Harvey," John said, his voice almost questioning.

"Everything's all right," Harvey Brage soothed them. "Take your desks, but don't do any work until you get your orders. I think there's going to be a general meeting of all employees first—in about a half an hour."

The outside door opened again to admit more of the office personnel. John nervously scooted across the reception room and escaped into the inner hallway to the various offices.

Mr. Moore's door was wide open as he went by. A stranger was sitting at the large desk. The stranger looked at John with a fishlike glaze to his eyes as John paused involuntarily.

John went on to his own office, wondering who the stranger was.

He had worn a red armband too.

"Hello, John," Cloe Stevens, his secretary, said, as he pushed open the door.

"Hello, Cloe," John said with an attempt at his usual frame of mind. "Take the day off."

"I already did before I came down to the office," Cloe shot back in the same spirit. "Only—" Her voice became worried. "I think it'll be safer right here at the office today."

"You and me both," John agreed. He started to take off his suitcoat, thought better of it, and slumped behind his desk with a sigh. There was a full five minutes of silence, marred only once by the faint sound of more shots coming through the open window from the street below.

"Do you think they really—that it's going to—?" Cloe asked faintly.

"I don't know what to think," John said gravely. "I've always thought—well—it's just one of those impossible things. I can't adjust myself to realize it all, I guess."

"Me too," Cloe said in a faint voice.

"I'd better call Gloria," John said suddenly. He lifted the receiver and dialed nine, then waited for the hum.

"No outside calls for the present," a male voice said presently. John slowly placed the phone back in its cradle.

"What's the matter?" Cloe asked.

"No outside calls," John said. "Well—I don't suppose they'll murder her. She'll be all right." He said it as if he wanted to believe it.

Another five minutes of silence followed. John idly tapped the eraser end of a pencil against the desktop. Cloe chewed at a finger-nail, occasionally pausing to inspect the damage she had done to it.

The door popped open and an office boy said they were to go to the conference office, then disappeared again.

"Well, this is it," John said grimly.

"Gee, I'm scared," Cloe said unsteadily.

John gave her an encouraging grin and held the door open for her. In the hall they met Harvey Brage again. Harvey was standing in front of the door to the conference office, stopping each person and whispering something to them.

It came John's and Cloe's turn. Harvey Brage took each of them by the arm with a friendly pressure and whispered in a voice that was inaudible to others.

"The man who's going to speak is your new boss," he whispered. "I'll be in there, and when I lift my hand I want you to clap your hands loudly. I'm on your side, but we want to steer clear of trouble—especially with the man in there. He's a bigshot communist and can cause not only you, but our union, a whole lot of trouble."

Without waiting for their reaction he let them go and took the next two arms in a friendly vise.

John and Cloe lifted their eyebrows at each other and entered the large room. The man who had been in Mr. Mear's office was seated at the head table. His armband, now conspicuous, had the enemy insignia in black on its red.

He was a young man, in his late twenties, unusually high fore-head, steady blue eyes, well-formed features. His eyes under heavy dark brows were intent on a sheet of paper lying on the table before him.

John jerked his eyes away from the man and looked around him. The thirty-seven employees of the Moore Publishing

Company were now all in, and Harvey Brage entered, closing the door behind him.

He strode around the wall until he was in back of the stranger, bent over and whispered to him, then stepped back against the wall.

The stranger waited a moment longer, then suddenly raised his head.

"I am Steffen Tombs," he introduced himself in a deep, not unpleasant voice. He smiled crookedly. "I will—for a while at least—be in charge here—a worker just like the rest of you."

He paused expectantly. Harvey Brage lifted his hand behind Steffen Tombs' back and waved his fingers violently. The sound of one person clapping loudly broke over the still room. Steffen Tombs coughed and frowned. Other sounds of clapping came, half-heartedly.

John turned his head and looked at Cloe. Together they began clapping. Everyone was clapping now. Harvey Brage lifted both arms and brought them down in a signal that it was enough. Steffen Tombs smiled frigidly.

"Thank you," he said. "I shall not forget the warm reception I've received, I assure you."

John was sure he detected a malicious smile in the depths of Tombs' pale blue eyes.

"As you are all no doubt aware," Steffen Tombs went on. "The people have thrown off the yoke of the Capitalist Masters, and a People's Government is this very moment in the process of being formed.

"It was inevitable," he added, an inner fire lighting his eyes for an instant. "You, here, are in a special position in relation to the new state of affairs. Today, in every publishing house in the country, must begin the gigantic task of going through all material to be published, and—as you call it—slanting it for the purpose of aiding the population in their necessary adjustment to the new ideas."

Again that inner fire lit his eyes briefly.

"It is not your jobs now that hang in the balance," he said. "It is your freedom and your lives. You are now living in a people's state."

He paused. Harvey Brage lifted a hand again. Everyone clapped quietly. The business agent smiled his approval.

Steffen Tombs cleared his throat. "What does living in a people's state mean? It means that you are all employees of the government, basically, and inefficiency or failure at your duties can be considered treason. Remember that."

Again Harvey Brage lifted his hand.

It struck John Dow as being a funny place to clap. He felt like laughing instead. As a compromise he put all the force he could into his clapping. The others seemed to have the same type of reaction. The applause was deafening.

Harvey Brage frowned and frantically signaled them to stop. When they did, Steffen Tombs remained silent a moment, frowning thoughtfully. Then he went on.

"Much of the material on hand here," he said, "is perhaps going to be scrapped. Form letters will be here from the printers this afternoon or tomorrow which you will send out to all authors, instructing them about the type of story they must submit from now on. Your duty until desirable stories come in is to carefully study what you have on hand with the idea in mind of altering it here and there to bring in the idea of a people's government and life under a people's government.

"When you have changed a manuscript so that you think it will be acceptable you will send it to my office. Under me will be one whom you all know—Mr. Alex Been. Step up here, Alex."

All eyes turned on Alex Been as he stood up. His face was slightly red with embarrassment. Harvey Brage lifted his hand for applause but no one noticed it. He opened his mouth, then closed it and dropped his hand. Alex Been walked to the front of the room and stood beside Steffen Tombs who placed a heavy hand in seeming affection on his slim shoulder.

"Say a few words, Alex," Steffen Tombs said smoothly. "You are now assistant manager in charge of the publishing details of the Moore Publishing Company."

"I—I suppose you're all very much surprised to learn that I'm a communist," Alex Been said haltingly. "I only want to say that I've known for some time that this was coming, and that when you get used to it, it won't seem so bad at all. For one thing, you won't have to worry about losing your jobs any more. There isn't going to be any unemployment. Everybody's going to have a job—the job they want, if they can handle it. I—I've spent years studying and know just what Mr. Tombs wants in the way of changes in manuscripts; and I'll help you catch on in every way I can.

"I—I just want to say one more thing. There'll be some trouble here and there in the city as a few foolish people try to object to the changes going on, but if you all pitch in here, and don't let the few talk you into being foolish, you'll find that everything will be fine."

With an apologetic smile Alex Been sidled in the direction of his chair. There was a heavy silence—suddenly broken by the explosive sound of a female voice.

"Well I'll be damned," it said. "To think that all this time I've been secretary to a stinking communist!"

John turned to look. It was Mary Phillips, Alex's secretary, now standing up her eyes aflame with anger and recklessness.

"But Mary—" Alex Been said pleadingly, advancing toward her.

Violently she spit on him. Then with a defiant toss of her head she turned toward the door to leave.

Steffen Tombs nodded his head, smiling twistedly. John jerked his head in the direction of Tombs' gaze and saw two men standing on either side of the door. Strangers.

Mary didn't seem to see them. She marched to the door and reached for the knob. One of the men reached out and took a generous amount of her hair in a fist and lifted. The other slapped her face sharply with the back of his hand.

He repeated the slap. Mary screamed and tried to pull free of the hand holding her by the hair.

The sound of the hand against Mary's face was monotonous and without feeling. John, his senses paralyzed, could not pull his eyes away. He half rose, instinctively preparing to rescue Mary.

"Keep your seats!" the peremptory voice of Steffen Tombs said from the front of the room.

A vision of Gloria rose in John's eyes. Slowly he forced himself back. He closed his eyes to blot out the horrible nightmare. Mary's head was bruised and limp. Blood streamed from her nose.

The sounds ceased. John opened his eyes again to see Mary's unconscious, pathetically crumpled body on the floor.

"You will return to your desks," Steffen Tombs' voice ordered.

Dull eyes turned to look at him. He stood there, a statue of inflexibility. Voiceless, the men and women trailed from the room.

CHAPTER EIGHT

"GET YOUR PAPER. Get your paper. Abso-lutely free!" It was a young man with a red armband. The body of the old man was gone. The strewn papers of the morning were cleaned up.

John took the extended paper and smiled at the man.

"If they're free, how do you pay for them?" he asked.

"They gimme ten bucks for distributing them," came the explanation. "Get your paper. Absolutely free..."

John climbed into the waiting bus and made his way to the back. Everybody had a newspaper.

"Ha ha!" a man in overalls laughed. "No wonder they're free. Listen to this. 'Workers overjoyed as new city government takes over industry for the masses.' Ha ha ha! What a laugh."

"Better keep quiet," the man sitting beside him said. "Some redband will blackjack you."

"What are you, a—communist?" the man in overall said belligerently, turning to glare at his seat companion. His eyes widened as he saw the fresh bandage covering the man's scalp under his hat. "Oh," he added lamely. "I see what you mean."

John sat down in the back seat and opened his paper to see for himself. It was true! The front page was full of similar "news" items.

According to the paper everyone was going around with tears of happiness at being rescued from the slavery of the capitalists.

His eyes settled on a double column spread. It said that in the early morning hours Russia had answered the plea of the American people for aid in their battle for freedom, and had sent thousands of planes and paratroopers over to land at strategic points. Communist patriots in the armed forces, in the government, and in every key post, had suddenly risen and in less than twenty-four hours everything had changed.

The atom bomb stockpiles were now under the protective custody of Soviet paratroopers and would be shortly moved to safety behind the iron curtain. Washington had been taken during the forenoon, and the ringleaders of the war-mongering capitalist clique had been arrested and were being held for trial before a hastily set up war crimes court.

Maxim Vopinski, formerly a high officer in the Soviet Army had been suddenly discovered to be an American Citizen, and had been hastily elected President of the United States by the telegraphed votes of the Electoral College.

"For the first time since the days of Lincoln," the paper said, "America has once more a truly constitutional government."

"My God, look!" the man sitting next to John said, grabbing his arm.

John looked where the man pointed, out the window. The sidewalk for a distance of twenty feet was thickly strewn with corpses, their clothing riddled by dozens of bullets.

Men with red armbands, and with army rifles on their shoulders, paced slowly along as the bus passed the scene. Then— it was time to get off the bus, and John Dow awoke to the fact that he had been sitting in a daze, the newspaper on his lap, his mind frozen by the sight of such callous death.

The thought that he would shortly be home revived him. In his mind as he got off the bus he was telling himself to let none of the day's horrors intrude at home. He would go home with his usual casual manner as if nothing had happened.

He stopped in at the grocers and found that Gloria hadn't phoned in her order—that phone service had been "out" all day. At the meat counter he discovered that panicky housewives were buying enormous quantities of meat in anticipation of rationing, the devaluation of their money, their money becoming no good, or whatever might happen. Seeing it would take too long to get waited on, he turned away and hurried out of the store.

"Get your paper. Get your paper. Free papers," the man on the corner was droning nasally, as John Dow hurried past.

As his house came into sight, nestled in its place among the others, it seemed that he hadn't been home for months. It surprised him that everything was as it should be. Two neighbor teenage boys were in the street playing catch with an indoor baseball. Just beyond the point where his own sidewalk met the street were four little girls playing a game of hop skip. Mrs. Johnson, farther down, was calling for her Georgey at the top of her voice—and Georgey, ignoring her, was one of the two boys playing catch.

John cut across his lawn to the front porch and opened the door. Voices came from the kitchen.

"Maybe so," Gloria's voice sounded politely.

"Of course it's so," a woman's voice said emphatically.

"I'm home, Dear," John called.

"Oh, Johnny," Gloria called. She appeared in the doorway, paused while her eyes surveyed him anxiously, then rushed across the room and put her arms around him with a choked sob of relief that he was all right. She huddled in his arms for a moment, then lifted her head and rumpled his hair with one hand.

"I tried to call you this morning when the radio came on and told me what had happened," she said. "While I was trying, the radio said phone service would be out indefinitely." Her lips trembled. "I've worried."

"I tried to call you, too," John soothed. "Don't worry. Everything's going to be all right."

"That's what I've been telling her," a voice sounded from the kitchen doorway.

John looked up. It was Mrs. Patty, who lived in the next block. No one ever associated with her, because she was a communist. Now she stood there, proudly serene. He frowned at this callous invasion of the privacy of his greeting to his wife. He opened his lips to order her out of the house, then with great effort forced them closed. His smile as he nodded at her was, he explained later to Gloria, his supreme moment as an actor.

"I must be getting home," Mrs. Patty said. "Rog should be getting home soon, though it wouldn't surprise me if he didn't, his new duties will be taking all of his time. What I really came over for in the first place was to ask you to come over for the party tomorrow night. We're holding a victory dinner, and I'm sure that you folks will be wanting to get into the new swing of things, now that the party has taken over."

She crossed the room to the front door and turned, smiling at John and Gloria. "You're lucky. If you run into any trouble with anyone just mention my husband's name. No friend of the Patty need fear anything now. G'ba-ee."

John, his arm still about Gloria's waist, watched the front door close without moving.

"I didn't know what to do," Gloria said hastily. "I wanted to tell her to leave, but every time I tried I thought of you and the children, and couldn't. Oh, Johnny, what'll we do?"

"We'll just eat our dinner," he said. "Where's the kids?"

"Here we are, daddy," Sisty said gravely from the hallway door. She and Franky came into the room and went into the kitchen.

"What's the matter with them?" John mumbled to Gloria.

"I'll let them tell you," Gloria said, following them into the kitchen. "Come on and eat. It's ready."

"All right, kids," John said grimly when they had all been seated in the breakfast nook.

Franky and Sisty looked at each other. Franky seemed to decide he was to be the spokesman.

"Well," he began. "Miss Fleury, the seventh grade history teacher, made herself principal today. She wore a red band on her sleeve and made the other teachers call a convocation and she spoke to all of us, including the teachers and Mr. Raft, the principal—I mean the old principal."

"And she said we were to—" Sisty broke in.

"I'm telling it," Franky interrupted her. "She said we wouldn't have to learn any more of the capitalist lies any more and we were to write a theme tomorrow on what our parents thought about what was going on, and we were to write down what our parents said at home tonight and hand it in first thing in the morning, and we weren't to tell our parents anything about it."

"Oh?" John said quietly.

"And she said if we didn't," Franky rushed on, "we wouldn't get a grade for tomorrow's schoolwork, and then we wouldn't pass into the next grade and would fail."

"And we all held class in the auditorium all day," Sisty broke in, successfully this time. "Even the teachers had to be students, and Miss Fleury was teaching us the new alphabet, and it's funny. They have letters like we do, but some of them are turned around and some of them are different. They have a lot more letters, too."

"I see," John said, his lips grim. "Anything else?"

"This afternoon a man came and talked in front of us," Franky took up the tale. "He said we weren't our parents' children any more, and that we must always remember our first duty is to humanity and to the state. He said we were all brothers and sisters now and that we were the first real American citizens, and our parents had been slaves of capitalism and were now freed slaves."

"And he said there wouldn't be any more war," Sisty said eagerly. "He said there wouldn't be anybody to fight now because with everybody under the same party they would be able to make the world over into one family."

"I see," John said gravely. "Well, let's eat our dinner now, and then after we eat we can talk about all this."

"O.K., daddy," Sisty said.

John turned on the radio. When it had warmed up he searched until he had found a faint station.

"That's that Canadian station I found a couple of weeks ago," he said to Gloria.

"Oh," she said, understanding.

"—crisis," the voice on the radio said faintly. "The enemy representative vetoed the move to oust the newly appointed United States members, and warned that the party and the United States now hold absolute power in the world and in the United Nations, and would tolerate no interference from Capitalist slave nations. After some violence the meeting came to order and the new United States members were seated.

"Europe is quiet today. There seems to be an air of waiting and it is generally conceded that if the coup in the United States succeeds the rest of the world, including Canada, will go communist. Hourly it looks more and more as though it would succeed. In New York, Chicago, Seattle, San Francisco, Los Angeles, and Kansas City, the communists have gained control. In the capital there is street fighting. The President has been captured by the paratroopers of the self appointed Maxim Vopinski; but the Vice President and about half the Senators and Congressmen are barricaded in the Capitol Building, protected by American troops, under siege.

"The atom stockpiles are now in the hands of enemy troops, and are being flown out of the country as fast as enemy planes can take them. A small area of southwest Alaska is in control of the enemy, and they are defending it against the isolated American outposts further north; but it seems that incredible amounts of aviation petrol were stored in that area—perhaps by saboteurs within the American armed services, in preparation for this moment. At any rate, the enemy planes are stopping there to refuel, both coming and going.

"At this moment the big question is, where are the elaborate American defense plans? Where are the American troops and state militias? Where are the American high command? And where are the American mothball fleets of planes that were to be ready in two hours if anything happened? The answer, fantastic though it may seem, is that the communist coup was planned so well that it took care of every detail, and in one fell swoop napping America has fallen—and the rest of the World with it. That is the inescapable FACT we Canadians must face tonight. Whatever comes, whatever the future holds in store for us, at this moment we must realize that henceforth we must recognize Communism as THE great power that is to mold the future of the World, and whatever she dictates is to be the law we must follow—or perish.

"It will be interesting to follow the events of the next few days in America, for what happens there will in all likelihood happen to us very soon—just as soon as the communists have made secure their grasp on the United States and can turn their attention safely elsewhere. It is certain that we will be next."

CHAPTER NINE

JOHN SHUT OFF THE RADIO. He ate in thoughtful silence, and his wife and two children did the same, instinctively waiting for him to voice his decisions and assume his leadership.

In John's mind, as he chewed his food absently, rose the memory of those bodies he had seen on the way home. They had been very close together, some laying partly on top of others. A crowd—a group of angry people ordered to disperse, and then mowed down by machine guns. Mrs. Patty standing at the front door, a triumphant light in her eyes, determined but friendly—for a price, that price being that they show up tomorrow night at the "victory" dinner at her house. The Berlin blockade and the Soviet technique of telling lies that everyone knew were lies, and repeating them again and again and again until the cry of liar faded into tired silence.

Footsteps on the back porch interrupted his thoughts. He went to answer the door, grateful for the interruption that had broken in on his defeatist mood. He opened the door.

"Hi, Joe," he said, his eyes lighting up in welcome. "It's Joe Pace and Martha, Gloria," he announced over his shoulder to his wife. "Come on in, Joe. How ya be?"

Joe, grinning, stepped inside, followed by his wife, Martha, who was carrying what seemed to be a homemade pie covered by wax paper.

"We thought we'd have our dessert with you folks," Martha said. "So I brought the pie with me." She laughed gaily.

John's eyes came to rest on the red armband on Joe's sleeve.

"What's this, Joe?" he asked incredulously.

"Just playing it smart, John," Joe said. "Tell you about it later. Let's have some dessert first, huh?"

"O.K.," John said, his mind getting bewildered again. "How— how's the coffee, Gloria? Enough?"

"I think so," Gloria said gaily, not seeing the red armband. "Martha, you're a dear. I'll bet you baked that pie just to bring over."

"What kind is it?" Sisty asked boldly.

"Now you be quiet, Sisty," Gloria admonished mildly. "You aren't supposed to ask questions like that."

Sisty subsided, pouting.

"It's an apple pie," Martha said.

"Apple," John said. "Ice cream would go nice with that. Franky, run down to the store and get a quart of vanilla. Hurry back."

"I'll go too," Sisty spoke up brightly.

John gave Franky a dollar bill. A moment later the front door slammed.

"All right, Joe," John said grimly. "Out with it before they get back." He made a wry face. "It seems the teacher at school assigned homework for the kids—reporting what their parents say and think."

"It's simple enough," Joe said, his eyes wary. "We all know what communism has done in other countries. This afternoon it became obvious the revolution was going to succeed, so I decided the best thing was to play along and join the party. We all have to live, and party members will get the best of it. You should do the same—for the sake of Gloria and Franky and Sisty. You'll be left alone then, and you'll still have—this." He looked around the kitchen meaningfully.

John opened and shut his mouth several times, clenching and unclenching his fists. Suddenly he turned away, his back to Joe, Martha, and Gloria, his fingers twisting at the salt shaker on the breakfast nook table.

"I don't know what to think," he said, his voice muffled. "Maybe you're right. You've always been a pretty sensible person, Joe and a good friend and neighbor. Maybe you're right. But I can't seem to get used to things. I keep wanting—" He turned and faced them, his eyes blazing. "I keep wanting to—do something desperate—to—to bring back what we had yesterday and the day before."

"So do I, John," Joe said quietly. His eyes met John's and held. Under Joe's steady gaze John slowly relaxed.

"It shouldn't be too much different under the communists," Joe said suddenly. "No matter who runs the country they have to pretty much let the common man make a decent living and be at peace with himself. There'll probably be some injustices, and a lot of cheap crooks will grab local offices and throw their weight around. But that won't be half as hard to take as—Siberia. And being separated from Gloria and the kids and losing your house. A lot of down and outers are joining the bandwagon and tomorrow or next day they'll be crying for a nice house in the best part of town and getting it. And whom do you think will have to move down into the tenements they move out of? It won't be party members in good standing. You have to think of those things, John."

"I—" John sighed deeply. "I guess you're right, Joe. Where do I go?"

"That's the spirit," Joe said. "I'll take you down after we have our pie." He slapped John affectionately on the shoulder.

Gloria and Martha put their arms around each other and started to cry. The sight of them, so miserable, struck John and Joe as being extremely funny. They laughed—a bit too loud.

Stamping of feet on the front porch announced the return of Franky and Sisty eager to get a taste of the pie and ice cream.

"We'll be back in an hour," Joe told the women confidently. "And don't worry about us."

"No, don't worry about us," John echoed, glad he hadn't told Gloria about the dead people on the sidewalk.

The two men got into Joe's car and were quickly driving across town to the place Joe knew of for joining the communist party. Joe was talking swiftly as he drove.

"One thing you gotta be prepared to do, John," he said. "And that's to lie like hell—right and left. You gotta swear on your honor things that nobody with honor would swear to, and sound like you mean it. For example, you'll have to swear allegiance to the Party. Just think of all the dirty rats that swore allegiance to the United States of America in order to be here where they could destroy it, and swear as earnestly as the local sinner getting saved for the fifth time.

"They'll tell you when you're a member the height of nobility in the party is to make friends with people and get them to say nasty things about the communists so you can squeal on them and get them in trouble. You'll have to say that that agrees with your idea of being noble, and that you have a few friends you'd like to see squirm, too. That'll go over big.

"Give them the same line I did—that at heart you've always been a fellow traveler, and now we are communist you could hardly wait to get down and join up."

"I have to swear to all these things?" John asked.

"Sure," Joe said, his eyes on the traffic. "All of it."

"Then it's out," John said flatly. "Turn around and go back. I'll take my chances and hang onto my decency."

"Look, John," Joe said pleadingly. "This won't be a Holy pact you're entering into, but a pact with hell—a hell on Earth, of lying, cheating, cheap little bastards who would rather spread misery than justice and brotherhood of man; and the only way to take care of yourself and your family is to play along with them and forget about honor with them. Believe me, any honor you would put into the deal would be strictly one sided!"

"I'll take my chances," John said grimly. "Turn around. We'll go back and forget about this."

"You're thinking of yourself too much," Joe said, a shade of coldness in his voice. "You'll go down with flying colors and a noble light in your eyes—but what will Gloria and your kids do then? Does your honor mean more than they do?"

John sighed deeply in resignation.

"Yesterday I would have never believed I could do a thing like this," he said with a bitter laugh.

"Here we are," Joe said, pulling into the curb. "Remember now, swear to everything they tell you, and agree that everything they say is true."

John looked out across the sidewalk at the building.

"What's this!" he exclaimed. "The union hall!"

"Sure," Joe said casually. "Absolutely free of communists, it says here. Just some more of what I was telling you. The members never knew it, and even some of the officers never suspected it until yesterday, but a lot of those leaders and union officials that swore solemn anticommunist oaths were all the time holding their tongue in their check and kneeling toward the East every morning when they said their prayers. The only communist union leaders who refused to take the anticommunist oath were those who refused so they could cause trouble."

Joe saw the expression on John's face and laughed dryly. "You'll have to get used to it, John," he said. "From now on the lie must be a part of your equipment, ready to be used just as fast as the Truth. Communism is the only true democracy. Democracy is freedom, and only communism teaches you to be free to tell a

Lie. Under Capitalism you are a slave to Truth and Honor—decadent concepts inherited from the dark ages."

"Only," John said softly. "The communist party will expect you to tell them the truth and tell others the lies."

"Oh, yeah?" Joe snorted. "Listen, John. In there, they will all know you're lying when you swear away your honor. They won't be so stupid as to believe a word you say."

"But—But—" John said, bewildered.

"They don't care," Joe said patiently. "They know what they want. In exchange for keeping your home and family and job, all they want is your signature on papers swearing you are now a communist. When you have been a liar for several days you'll find yourself believing everybody's a liar, and slowly you'll learn how to get along with the Truth and Lies being handed to you all the time in the same kind of a wrapper. It's an art. Let's go in and get it over with—and *act natural.*"

CHAPTER TEN

"GET YOUR PAPER. Get your paper. Free papers."

John absently took the paper the newsman held out to him. His eyes were on the bright new Cadillac waiting for the light to change so it could go ahead. In the back were two men in uniform. He recognized the uniform and insignia of the American as that of a Major. The other man wore a communist uniform. From the way the two smiled at each other and laughed occasionally it was obvious they were on the best of terms.

The lights changed. The Cadillac started up and was out of sight when the bus pulled in to the curb. John boarded the bus and made his way to the back seat.

The news, as he skimmed over the front pages, seemed more factual this time. One item said that the airfield was lined with cheering citizens as enemy airborne troops arrived. The communist troops had come at the request of the American Government to help restore order. American troops, after a few Capitalist traitors had been shot, now were joining in with the communist troops in the task of maintaining order in the cities.

The paper was much thinner. John discovered that the want ads were missing. On page two he found a small item that said banks were being placed on limited service, and that only authorized withdrawals and payroll checks were being handled for the time being.

Back on page one again it said that for the first time in the history of the United Nations General Assembly there had been complete unanimity, with every resolution Soviet Russia introduced being passed without a dissenting vote.

John laid the paper aside and glanced over the bus passengers. They were all very quiet tonight, and he noticed that there were four other red arm bands besides his own.

He recognized the four as regular riders, and felt a little better at knowing he wasn't the only one on the bus that was playing it smart.

A truckload of Party soldiers passed the bus with roaring siren just before it reached his stop. The wail of the siren was dying in the distance as he alighted in front of the market.

He started into the market, then remembered they were to eat at the Patty's tonight.

"Well," he thought with a smile on his lips. "Rog Patty will be glad to see me with a red armband on my coat sleeve."

Whistling absentmindedly, he started into his own street. There was a moving van in front of the Forbes place. He lifted his eyebrows in surprise, wondering how anyone dared move right now and take the risk of losing out altogether on a decent place to live.

Mrs. Green, across the street, was watching the moving van through her front window curtain. As John drew nearer he spied Mrs. Forbes on the front porch, crying. She saw John and started off the porch toward him, then drew up short. As he went by she continued to stare at him with a wooden stare, one finger resting between her teeth as if she had forgotten it was there. When he smiled and nodded his head she didn't seem to see it.

Suddenly it occurred to him that maybe his red armband had something to do with it, and maybe the Forbes were being moved so some party member could take over their house.

"Of course!" he muttered. "The Forbes finished paying for their place last year and held a party in celebration of getting the deed to their place!"

He had been at that party. He remembered how happy and radiant she had been.

"Now," she had said. "No matter what happens we have a home for the rest of our lives!"

And now—except for following Joe's advice and example it might have been his own home the moving van was in front of! He hastened his step as a reaction to the thought.

Sisty came bounding down the steps to greet him. She wore a red armband like his own. He caught her in his arms.

"How was school today, baby?" he asked, hugging her close.

"I got an armband like yours in school, daddy," she said proudly.

"And how did you get that?" he asked.

"Miss Fleury said that since you were a communist party member now, I must join the junior communist league," Sisty said. "Franky joined, too. Only Franky has a black eye now from Harry Brown beating up on him for wearing a red armband, but Miss Fleury locked Harry in a closet and this afternoon some men came and took him away from school in a station wagon."

"So Franky has a black eye," John mused.

"Only a little black," Sisty said, kissing her father on the cheek for the dozenth time and then squirming to be let down. She ran ahead and opened the front door. "Franky made Harry's nose bleed, too."

"Oh," John laughed, wondering grimly what had been done to the Brown boy and where he had been taken.

"That you, John?" Gloria called from the bedroom as he stepped through the door. "Better change your clothes right away. We have to be over to the Patty's in half an hour."

"Right away," John echoed. He tossed the newspaper half way across the living room onto the davenport and went into the bedroom.

Gloria was sitting at the dresser putting finishing touches to her hair, already dressed. John crossed over and bent down, kissing her on the neck. He stayed bent over, waiting for her to turn her head.

"Well?" he coaxed. Gloria hesitated, then turned her lips to his.

"That wasn't a very warm kiss, Cookie," John said. "What's the matter?"

"I—I—nothing's the matter, John," Gloria hesitated. "I'll be all right. It's just that—well—I've been trying all day to get used to things."

Suddenly she was up and in his arms.

"Oh, John. I know you did it for me and the children," she said, her voice muffled against his chest. "But—but—"

"I know," John said stiffly. "It's hard for ME to get used to the idea of my being a liar and a cheat, too."

"No! No!" Gloria objected. "I didn't mean that, because you aren't. You're still the same John I married, honest, upright, sincere. You always will be. I know that."

"All right, Gloria, let's forget it," John said gruffly. "I understand. Only remember it's just as hard for me—the children in school—Miss Fleury—"

He turned away and started to undress.

"I'm sorry, John," Gloria said in a small voice, returning to the dresser mirror and her hairdo. He was unlacing his shoes and didn't look up. Gloria watched him in the mirror, expectantly. His hunched shoulders and bent head were expressionless. "I apologized, John," she finally said.

"For what?" John said, looking up. "For knowing that I lied right and left last night to keep my family from being moved out like the Forbes are being moved out right this minute?"

"Don't shout, John," Gloria said, her voice very gentle. "We don't want the children to hear."

"Of course not," John said bitterly. "They would have to write it all out and hand it in to Miss Fleury, so she can turn it over to the party."

"Don't shout," Gloria demanded. "I'm your wife. I'm still married to you. I'm not some of office worker that you can shout at."

"I don't shout at my office girl," John said.

"So you don't shout at Cloe, but you come home and shout at me," Gloria accused.

"I wasn't shouting," John said stubbornly. "Now let me get dressed or we'll be late."

Gloria angrily pulled her comb through her hair.

"Oh, darn," she said, exasperated.

"What's the matter now?" John asked in a patient voice.

"I broke my comb," Gloria said. "And I don't have another."

"Well use mine then," John grunted.

"I can't, because it doesn't have a rat tail on it," Gloria complained.

"Would a pencil do the trick?" John suggested.

"Ye-es," Gloria said doubtfully. "But you'll have to help me then."

John sighed in defeat. "O.K.," he mumbled.

"I look like a communist," John said as they left the house, rubbing his unshaven chin. He sighed again. Gloria, her hair done perfectly, dropped into step beside him. Franky and Sisty, hand in hand, skipped on ahead down the sidewalk.

John and Gloria walked in a strained silence. A voice calling to them brought them to a halt. It was Joe Pace.

"Wait a second and we'll go with you," Joe called from his front door. A moment later Martha and Joe came hurrying down their walk to the sidewalk.

"How'd everything go today?" Joe asked, conversationally.

"O.K.," John said. "Two of the others in the office signed up too, so it wasn't so bad."

"Good thing they did," Joe grunted. "They're closing their files tonight so nobody else can join up. Guess if they didn't they'd have everybody in the party, and then who could they kick out of the nice houses to make room for the party members?"

"Yes," John said, thinking of Mrs. Forbes as she stood on her porch looking at him. There was a light on in the Forbes house now. He looked in the lighted window. A short fat man and a heavy woman with a coarse face and frowsy hair were standing inside facing each other, talking. John decided if they were the new neighbors he didn't like them, but said nothing.

There were several cars in front of the Patty house. The windows were all lighted up, even on the second floor.

"Looks like there'll be more than neighbors," Joe said. "Wonder what kind of a job Patty got on the strength of his record as an old time communist."

"He'll tell us, don't worry," John said.

"He's quite a talker, all right," Joe agreed. "I suppose we'll have to play up to him from now on, though. He's a commy from way back, and probably has a top job now where he can throw his weight around."

They turned off the sidewalk and went up to the porch. Gloria rang the bell. Inside they could see people moving about. The door opened and someone they didn't know invited them in. It was a woman. She looked as if she had been crying.

As they stepped inside they heard Mrs. Patty's sharp voice, speaking loudly. Their shocked ears listened to a string of profanity, spoken clearly and bitterly.

"You haven't heard?" the strange woman asked in whisper. "Mr. Patty was killed today."

"No!" Joe whispered, the word a hoarse breath. "Who did it?"

The woman ignored the question and pointed to the clothes closet. In stunned silence they took off their coats and put them away. John helped Sisty. Then they all walked hesitantly into the living room—considerably larger than John's, but furnished without taste.

John was shocked at the change in Mrs. Patty. The day before she had been almost beautiful, in a mediocre sort of way. Now her face was drawn and with sharp lines in it. Her slightly graying hair was a mat of shapeless curls and bobby pins. Her eyes were red and raw from hours of crying.

From her disjointed sentences interspersed with invectives he pieced together what had happened. Rog Patty—"My poor little Rog," Mrs. Patty called him—had had his sweet little heart set on being mayor after R-Day; but a communist from New York had been given the job. When Rog had objected violently the Party officer in charge of things had calmly pulled a gun and shot him. At this point in the tale Joe caught John's eye and they went into the kitchen.

"We'd better get out of here," Joe said earnestly. "I have a hunch being around the wife of a communist who's been liquidated is extremely unhealthy!"

"You're right," John agreed in a low voice. "And some of the things she's saying about the communists are sacrilegious!"

"Ain't they, though!" Joe said in mock piety.

The two went back into the living room and motioned toward the front door after they caught their wives' eyes. Two minutes later they all had slipped quietly out the front door, without having been missed.

Before they reached the corner an army jeep-sedan turned into the street, siren wailing softly, and stopped at the curb in front of the Patty residence.

"Let's watch this," Joe said softly. They waited several minutes. Just as they were about to give up and continue on home, several figures erupted from the front door.

Two soldiers were half dragging a violently protesting Mrs. Patty. As they shoved her into the jeep a large station wagon appeared around the corner.

John and Joe said almost in unison, "Let's get out of here," as soldiers herded the other people into the station wagon. The Jeep and the station wagon hurtled past them a moment later, sirens wailing deafeningly. There was a photographic impression of pasty white faces peering helplessly through windows, and the two cars disappeared around the corner.

"Lucky us," Martha said. "A couple of minutes later and we would have been goners!"

"Will they kill all of them like they did Mr. Patty?" Sisty asked innocently.

"Hush, Sisty," Gloria said.

CHAPTER ELEVEN

ALEX BEEN MINCED into the office. There was a soft smile on his somewhat effeminate lips that was not reflected in his eyes. In the three weeks since R-Day his personality had expanded in unsuspected directions.

"I don't quite like the way you've handled the changes in this western story, John," he said. "The way you made the ranchers desire collectivization, while the villain fights to impose Capitalism on them is all right, but the villain reflects the Simon Legree personality too much, without enough Wall Street in him. You'll have to build him up as a big money man from New York who has gone into western ranching for the sole purpose of spreading the doctrine of Capitalism. The native ranchers are peaceful citizens on their collective ranches, against branding of cattle, against private ownership. Just good communists at heart. THAT part's all right. But you can't seem to put it over that the PEOPLE are the heroes. It's the PEOPLE who fight the Capitalist. It's the PEOPLE who finally take back the cattle the Capitalist gave them corrupted dollars for. It's the PEOPLE who drive the Capitalist off the land they sold him and got dollars for—dollars that were good only for buying liquor and gambling at the town saloon so the Capitalist could get his money away from them again."

John took the manuscript and stared at it doubtfully.

"I thought I handled it all right," he said. "I did just the things you say I didn't."

"You thought," Alex Been said, sneering. "It doesn't satisfy me, and I'm the one you have to satisfy around here now. Not Moore."

"How do you like his house?" John asked. "I hear you're living in it now."

"That's right," Alex said. "Nice house. A bit drafty, but I guess all those big, imposing houses in my neighborhood are the same way. Now get busy on this and straighten it out. It has to meet the deadline."

John stared at the closing door thoughtfully after Alex had gone.

"Pretty hard—working for a former half wit," Cloe said softly behind him.

"Huh?" John said, startled. "Oh. Yes, it is. This story is according to the best Marxist tradition, and paints communism as being the very heart and soul of the old West. It can't be improved. There's nothing I can do to it that will make it any better—for its purpose."

65

"Why not be subtle?" Cloe asked.

"Subtle? What do you mean?" John asked, puzzled.

"You know what's the matter with Alex," Cloe said. "He's afraid you'll get his job. The story is perfect, and he doesn't want it perfect. He wants you to botch it so he can get rid of you."

"I know that," John said hopelessly. "But what can I do about it?"

"Well," Cloe said dryly. "It's going to be him or you. Why don't you put him in a nice, gilt edged frame?"

"Huh uh," John said. "I'll—"

"You were going to say you'd quit first?" Cloe asked. "Silly boy. Siberia gets cold in the winter—even for the loads of American tourists that are finding it so popular now, it says in the papers."

"Everything's going to be all right," John said. "He'll get used to being a boss after a while and stop the petty stuff."

Cloe snorted and turned back to her work.

John Dow started through the manuscript of the western story. Aside from the rattle of the typewriter there was a deep silence.

"Cloe?" John said some time later.

"Yes, John?" she asked, pausing in her typing.

"Did you have anything definite in mind?" he asked.

"Well," Cloe hesitated. "The details would have to be ironed out, but the setup is a natural the way I see it. Nothing goes to the typesetters until it gets sonny boy's O.K., so if he was to O.K. a little pro-Wall-Street stuff—"

"My forwarding address would be Squeedunk, Siberia," John said. "I thought you mentioned the word, subtle."

"It was a passing thought," Cloe answered. "But give me time. I'll work on it."

"How hard?" John asked.

Cloe got up and walked over to John's desk. John swiveled his chair to face her, the grin still on his face. She sat on the edge of his desk, her dark eyes smoldering with a light John had never noticed in them before. His smile slowly faded as he became aware of other things about her he hadn't noticed before.

Suddenly she bent forward. Her lips pressed feverishly against his. She straightened again before he could move, and looked down at him, her lips slightly parted.

"Awfully hard, John," she whispered. Abruptly she turned and left the office.

"Get your paper. Get your paper. Right here. Get your paper," the newsman droned. John automatically held out his hand for one. "Two bits, mister," the newsman said, not releasing it.

"A quarter?" John exclaimed. "How come?"

"New policy," the man answered, grinning mirthlessly. "You're a party member? You'll find something that'll interest you on an inside page—about refunds. Better buy it."

"O.K.," John said, fishing out a quarter. There were only six sheets to the paper. All ads and comics had disappeared two weeks before. Now only news richly padded with propaganda.

John had heard a rumor a few days before that the other printing presses were being crated for shipment to Russia—but there were hundreds of similar rumors floating around.

The bus was waiting. He stepped aboard and got out a dime to drop in the coin box.

"Twenty-five cents, mister," the driver said. "New price schedule for city buses."

John dropped the dime back in his pocket and fished out another quarter.

"Here's your receipt, mister," the driver said, extending a narrow red slip of cardboard. It had printing on it.

John took it and went down the aisle to the back seat, reading it. It said, "Good for twenty-five cents upon presentation at your neighborhood bank together with your party membership card."

"What about people who aren't members of the party?" John thought. The thought was followed by, "Well, it means that I ride free now. That's a saving of twenty cents a day!"

There were two headlines. One said, EX-PRESIDENT FOUND GUILTY. Under it was the words, DIVORCE RACKET ENDED. The left-hand column was about divorces. John read, "Divorces under the Capitalist system were draining off millions of dollars from the wages of the masses to enrich the denizens of Wall Streets in every city. President Vopinski pushed through the Congress today a law that makes it possible to get a divorce simply and at a cost of only fifty cents by applying at the license bureau where you also get marriage licenses.

"If both parties agree to the divorce and appear together the permit will be granted immediately on payment of the fee of fifty cents. Where one party objects to the divorce, or alimony is requested, the party desiring the divorce must apply, and then return the next day for the decision of the clerk in regards to alimony, etc."

John skipped the rest of that and turned his eyes to the right hand column.

"The Ex-President," it read, "was found guilty today by the war crimes court of fomenting a third world war and of engaging in an undeclared cold war against the Soviet Union during his tenure in office and was sentenced to be hanged next Sunday morning at four A.M. When asked by this reporter if he would appeal the sentence he replied, "It is a just sentence. I will not appeal the decision of these more than fair judges. I confess that the charges are true, and though I deeply regret my former ambitions against the Communist Party, I realize that my crime is too grievous for any mercy to be shown me. My only defense is that I was an unwilling tool of the Capitalist Masters of Wall Street. I wish to say at this time that for the benefit of those people who are still deluded by the propaganda of Wall Street, Communism is the only hope of the world for peace and prosperity."

Suddenly John remembered what the newsman had said. He turned to the inside pages and quickly found a small square in the upper right hand corner of page five that was similar to the receipt for the bus fare. It said that twenty-five cents would be paid upon presentation of the cut out square with party membership card. He felt again a surge of gratefulness toward Joe for having talked him into joining that night. The party was taking members now under very restricted conditions.

On page two it said that the border between the United States and Canada was closed, and President Vopinski was viewing with grave concern the attitude of the Canadian Government about the return of five Senators and several prominent Wall Street figures who had escaped to Canada.

John tucked the paper under his arm as he got off the bus in front of the market. He hurried through the grocery department, getting the things on the list Gloria had given him that morning.

There were several women at the meat counter. John took out his paper and started to read again.

"What'll it be, Mr. Dow," Mr. Schmidt asked.

"Huh?" John grunted, looking up. "Oh, I'm not next. These women were ahead of me."

"You're next," Mr. Schmidt said grimly. "I don't have much left, and orders are that when I get low I have to save it for party members. They're waiting until just before closing time. Then I can sell to them."

"Oh," John said faintly. He looked around at the women. They stared at him with wide, dry eyes in which there was neither envy nor hatred, but only voiceless suffering.

"We have some nice T-bones today, Mr. Dow," Mr. Schmidt suggested. John looked at the display of steaks. "Better buy a lot if you can," the butcher added. "Rationing is coming next week."

"I—" John looked at the women again. He recognized most of them. They had been here the night after R-Day, buying all they could carry. "I'll take them all," he said on impulse. "No! Wait! I—I'll take just four of them."

"All of them," Mr. Schmidt said, as if he hadn't heard the last. He dumped them onto a paper and wrapped them up. He weighed them while the women watched silent. "That will be sixteen dollars and seventy-five cents, Mr. Dow."

The women drifted away, their shoulders drooping. John paid the money and walked quickly out onto the street.

"They wouldn't have lasted anyway," John muttered. "It's nearly an hour yet before closing time." He scuffed his shoes in anger at his feelings as he strode down his street.

There were lots of new neighbors now. He and Joe Pace were the only ones of the old bunch left. Other streets in the neighborhood weren't changing over so rapidly, but that was understandable. The nicest houses were here, next to his own. Joe had been so right about everything!

CHAPTER TWELVE

JOHN FORGOT ABOUT THE WOMEN at the market as he jumped lightly onto the porch and opened the door. A pleasant odor greeted him from the kitchen. Gloria was singing something. She broke off as he shut the door.

"That you, Johnny?" she called happily.

"You bet it is," he sang out. Tossing the paper on the davenport with a mental reminder to clip the coupon later, he went into the kitchen. "Mmm mh!" he said, pausing at the door and sniffing appreciatively. "Smells good."

Gloria looked at him, closely. "What's this?" she exclaimed, pulling up short. She reached up a finger and rubbed it against his lip and took it away slowly. John looked at it. It was stained with red!

"Well!" A doubtful smile flickered on and off Gloria's face.

"Oh! That!" John said, completely off balance. "Oh! I was going to tell you about it in a minute."

"Cloe?" Gloria asked.

"Please, honey," John pleaded. "It wasn't anything. I mean, I didn't even kiss her. She kissed me—before I could stop her!"

Gloria's shoulders continued to shake. Muffled noises came, tearing at John's heart mercilessly.

"Please, Gloria," John pleaded impotently.

"I'm not crying," Gloria said, suddenly straightening out. "I'm laughing—at me! You know the first thing I thought of when I saw that lipstick?"

"No. What?" John asked, taking a timid step toward her.

"They just changed the divorce laws so you can get a divorce as easy as you can get married—easier!" Gloria said. "I thought 'John got a divorce on the way home from work and is going to marry Cloe!'"

"Of course it is," John agreed quickly. "Anyway, I hadn't even heard of the change in the divorce law then. I only read about it in the paper on the bus." He bit his lip. What he had said sounded like he was putting his foot in it again.

"Oh," Gloria said vaguely.

"There's nothing to worry about, Dear," he said, taking another timid step forward, and cursing himself inside because it sounded to him precariously like he was lying.

"Are you sure?" Gloria asked in a tone that tore at his heart.

"Of course I'm sure darling," he said, taking the rest of the distance separating them with bold steps and wrapping his arms about her.

Heavy footsteps sounded on the back steps. John released Gloria, guiltily.

It was Joe, John discovered on opening the door.

"Hi, Joe," John said. "Come on in."

"I heard a rumor today," Joe said after he had come in and looked around inquisitively. "You remember Forbes? I guess he was one of them. It seems there was a secret organization forming to fight the communists—an underground. They found it out and shipped the whole kit and caboodle to the Uranium mines."

"Poor Mrs. Forbes," Gloria said, looking up from the stove where she was trying to salvage part of the dinner. "What will she do now?"

"She was in on it," Joe said grimly. "It was a close friend of her brother's that told me all about it. She's gone too. Why couldn't the damn fools have realized that an underground was futile? NOTHING will do any good any more. We didn't have sense enough to realize what the communists were before R-Day, and after that it was too late!"

Joe went over to the sink and got a drink of water. After he drained the glass and set it down he turned around and glared across the room.

"I wish I had been in charge of things before all this happened," he said. "I'd have executed every Communist spy in the country. I'd have tortured American communists to death. They're the scum of the Earth. Even communists don't have any respect for them—is liquidating them as fast as she can because she doesn't dare trust them. They were traitors once, and can be again—to Russia, now that they have learned that all isn't the bed of roses they thought it would be. Look at what happened to Patty. That was on deliberate orders of the Communist general—not a quarrel between him and a New York communist. The New York guy got it a few days later.

"What could a small band of underground patriots do, assuming their 'friends' didn't turn them in to get a chance at being a party member so they could ride the buses free and get free newspapers, and have a decent place to live? Nothing! Now that the United States has fallen—and half of South America, and France and Italy—and England might as well give up, and Canada goes over in next week's elections, there just isn't any use in fighting against it. It's done now. All over."

John and Gloria were looking at him. It was a different Joe than they had ever seen before. His eyes were flashing fire. His face was lit up with an inner spirit utterly different than that of the easygoing Joe who figured the angles to avoid any trouble, and looked out for them besides.

"It makes me sick when I think of it," Joe said bitterly. "All that talk right up to R-Day. Trying to fight a 'cold war,' as they so childishly called it, with Russia—and all the time they were unable to realize that you can't wage a fist fight according to rules with a thug that has a couple of knives, brass knucks, and guns, and is going to win by making his own rules. The only way we could have won would have been to do the same things—like taking an atom bomb into Moscow in a diplomatic trunk and making sure everybody was close enough to get what was coming to him before exploding it. That's the kind of stinking, dastardly game Russia would have played with us if she had had the atom bomb.

"Instead of doing that we passed laws making the communists solemnly swear they weren't communists. Now we know how many of the top commies swore that anticommunist oath, too—when it's too late. And a lot of them know how scared they are of proven traitors, too. If their rotten souls in hell know anything at all."

"What's got into you, Joe?" Gloria asked. "I've never seen you like this before."

"Aw," Joe growled, his temper subsiding. "Forbes was a friend of mine. I tried to talk him into doing what we did, John. He wouldn't have any of it. He tried to talk me into joining in with him on this underground idea he had. He had it even then. I'm sore because maybe he thinks I'm the one that turned him in. He must think that. Only day before yesterday he told me about it again and told me where they would be meeting last night—and last night was when they were rounded up."

"For the rest of his life he'll believe it was you," Gloria whispered.

"Yeah," Joe said. "Well. I gotta be getting home. I—I had to get it off my chest to somebody besides Martha," he added apologetically.

"Come on over after dinner," Gloria said impulsively. "You and Martha. You'd better not be alone tonight."

"Yes. Come on over, Joe." John spoke up. "We can play cards."

"O.K.," Joe agreed. "I'll see what Martha says."

CHAPTER THIRTEEN

JOHN DOW PUSHED THROUGH the revolving doors and crossed the marble floor to the waiting elevator.

"Morning, Mark," he growled.

"Morning, Mr. Dow," the elevator man said respectfully, closing the doors and starting up.

John rubbed his tired eyes with his fingers. Joe and Martha hadn't gone home until one o'clock in the morning. He groaned at the thought of having to work on the western manuscript again today.

"If it was the old days I'd turn around and go home," he thought.

"Twenty-one," Mark said, looking at him.

"Oh," John said, waking from his reverie. "Sorry."

He stepped out and walked down the hall to the door leading into the Moore Publishing Company. He read the legend and silently wondered where Mr. Moore was. He thought of him as a nice old duck, though he had been hard to please when he sat behind the desk in the throne room.

He went through the door and crossed the reception room to the one leading to the inner hallway and his office. If anything, the reception room was more ornate than it had been under Mr. Moore and Capitalism. That was Steffen Tombs' doings.

Steffen Tombs had proved to be a man of moods—and one known hobby, the reception room's appearance. Except for that one interest he ignored the publishing business, leaving the active management of it to Alex Been. For the most part he arrived at noon, went directly to his office without speaking to anyone, and stayed there without doing anything so far as anyone could discover, until five, when he left, still without speaking to anyone at all. On his rare appearances in the other offices he presented an almost boyish, subdued personality, seemed almost apologetic, and never stayed long. He would have been considered completely innocuous except for one thing—the sudden and unpredictable rising into his eyes of a strange, coldly analytical, keenly intelligent light, flashing for a brief instant and departing almost as soon as it had come, leaving the one on whom it had been turned in a cold sweat. That—and the memory of him standing there, his face coldly impersonal, while the two thugs had slapped Mary Phillip. Alex's former secretary, into unconsciousness. No one had forgotten that.

Steffen Tombs' office door was open and his chair empty as John passed it on the way to his own office. John pushed open his own door and tossed his hat on the shelf in the closet. Cloe was already there. She came toward him with an excited gleam.

"I've got it. John!" she said, coming to a pause in front of him.

"Hey!" John said, trying to prevent her arms from circling his neck. "Gloria found that lipstick last night. Just tell me what's this idea you have." He succeeded in pushing her away.

"Oh, good morning, Alex," Cloe purred, her eyes going beyond John.

John turned, alarmed at the thought that somebody was spying on them. Alex Been was standing in the doorway.

"May I come in?" The thought flashed through John's mind that is unusual for Alex who had been strutting his new authority to ask for permission. But it was a different Alex who stood diffidently beside the half-opened door.

"Sure, sure." John was guardedly polite.

It was a pale and worried Alex who closed the door carefully. John noted how drawn his eyes were, his face had an unhealthy pallor, his clothes seemed to hang listlessly on his frame.

Looking around as if expecting to find somebody following, Alex said softly, "Are we alone. Can I speak to both of you?"

Cloe assured him that they were alone.

"Look folks, I know you think I am an awful heel. The way I have taken up with these people and have been pushing you and everybody else around. Especially Mary Phillip." Alex slumped into a chair and put his head into his hands, groaning, "Mary, Mary."

John and Cloe exchanged startled looks.

Breathing deeply, Alex looked up, "I haven't been able to sleep a wink ever since they beat poor Mary. That's all I seem to think about. I can't eat and I can't sleep. When I try to sleep I can't get the picture of her poor body lying beaten and bloody on the floor out of my mind. I wish it were myself lying there. I feel every blow, night after night. I can't sleep, I can't sleep."

John moved uncomfortably. It isn't pleasant to see a man bare his soul. "Now, Alex," he tried to sound soothing, "there's nothing you can do about it now."

Alex without noticing John's attempt continued, "Nobody will talk to me. It's as if I were a leper, a leper I tell you." His voice began to rise shrilly. "Nobody talks to me. The minute I walk into a room everybody stops talking. Nobody talks to me; nobody will look at me. Oh, why did I do it?" Now he was shrieking, insanely.

Cloe walked over to his chair saying, "Now, Alex calm yourself." She put her hand on his shoulder but he shrugged it off.

His body was shaking as if in the hands of a giant, tears were rolling down his face. Finally the sobbing lessened and he seemed to get control of himself. He looked up smiling ashamedly. "Well, I got all of that off my chest." He got up from the chair with effort, pushing on the arms for strength, and staggered over to the large window that faced on the building courtyard. He stood a moment looking out and then suddenly wrenched up the heavy steel sash. The breeze swept in rattling the papers on John's desk.

Both John and Cloe were so startled by the change in Alex that they stood rooted in their tracks.

Alex turned to them, "Well folks I don't think I'm worth any worrying about." A half smile crossed his face and before either John or Cloe could move, leaped upon the windowsill and threw himself out. A shriek as of the wind came through the window. Cloe turned to John and buried her head in his shoulder, weeping, "Oh, John."

John pushed Cloe aside and rushed to the open window and leaning out guardedly saw the mangled body of what was Alex Been laying upon the roof of a lower part of the building.

Later John tried to trace all the events leading to Alex' suicide. He remembered how he came into the office, how he started talking. But from there on it all seemed to merge into a nightmare. Alex jumping on the windowsill, turning to look back for a moment and then gone. The others in the office had poured into his room and stood milling around. Nobody seemed to know what to do. Finally Harvey Brage spoke up.

"We'll have to call the police," he said reaching for the telephone. John recalled how everybody in the room seemed startled by the sound of Harvey's voice. The police came and took poor Alex' body away. Everybody tried to settle down but it was useless and Harvey got Tombs to issue an order closing the office for the rest of the day. Only the switchboard girl had to remain.

CHAPTER FOURTEEN

THE INTEROFFICE COMMUNICATOR buzzed. The light above the toggle connecting to Steffen Tombs' office glittered. John flicked the toggle switch.

"Yes?" he prompted politely, trying to keep the trip hammer blows at his heart from sounding too loud. "John Dow speaking."

"Come to my office, Mr. Dow," Tombs' voice sounded in the room. "Yes sir," he said, lifting the toggle to the off position again. He looked over at Cloe and grinned nervously. "This is it," he formed the words soundlessly. He held up his right hand and crossed two fingers meaningfully. White faced and tense, she crossed two fingers and nodded encouragement.

Steffen Tombs was sitting behind his desk as John entered. He didn't rise.

"Sit down, Mr. Dow," he invited, pointing with a wave of his hand at a chair across his desk. "Cigarette?" He bent forward and lifted the lid of a carved, ornate box.

"Thank you, sir," John said, taking one and pretending to concentrate on lighting it while he tried to quiet his mind and nerves.

"I think you're going to be all right," Steffen Tombs said, his face wreathing into a benign smile. "Yes sir. I think you're going to be all right." He chuckled throatily. "I couldn't have performed that little business with more finesse myself." He chuckled again.

"What do you mean?" John asked, trying to sound casual.

Steffen Tombs ignored the question and leaned forward, his enormous chest against the top of his desk.

"The party needs men like you at the top," he said earnestly. "It takes capable men, ruthless men, men who can look ahead and count the cost—and then act. Yes. You're going to be all right."

"I only did what anyone would have done, sir," John said. Steffen Tombs waved his own cigar in a gesture of dismissing what John had said.

"I've been just hanging around." Tombs said. "Just hanging around." Waiting. Men—the kind of men we want—aren't made in a day. They have to develop. Situations, circumstances, bring them out. After today this is your office, Mr. Dow. What do you think of that?" He chuckled again with good-natured jovialness. "Yes Sir, this is your office now. You're to run Moore Publishing Company. I'm washing my hands of it and good riddance. I never liked the publishing end myself, anyway. My forte is men. Yes sir, men. You're one of my men now. I'm not washing my hands of you. No sir. But I'll leave you alone for awhile until you get used to being on top."

He reached out a thick finger and pressed a buzzer. The side door opened and a stenographer came in.

"Take an inter-office memo, young lady," Steffen Tombs said expansively. "To all departments. Effective today Mr. John Dow is in complete charge of Moore Publishing Company. He will be responsible only to the Party—capital P, young lady. I notice in your spelling you don't have the proper respect toward the Party. Correct that in the future. Now run that on the mimeograph and see that it gets distributed immediately."

"Yes sir," she answered meekly, retreating to the door.

Mr. Tombs watched her until she was gone. Then he turned back to John.

"You will find a private phone in the typewriter compartment of this desk. Here is the key." He slid the key across the walnut surface. "The phone is connected directly to Party headquarters—the inner headquarters. You are to call every day at ten thirty sharp. Other than that I have no instructions at this time. Good luck, Mr. Dow, and get out. I want to pack."

He smiled again in high good humor, his shoulders shaking with silent mirth. They were still shaking with mirth when the outer door shut off John's view of him. The image of Steffen Tombs' cold face, wreathed in smiles, followed ahead of him as he went back to his office.

Cloe stood up and took a step toward him as he entered, one hand over her mouth, her eyes anxious.

"You're looking at your new boss," John said giddily. "Tombs is leaving for good. And I'm to be in full charge with no bosses over me—except the Party, of course."

"Wonderful!" Cloe said forcing herself into his arms. "Oh, you darling! Isn't it wonderful? And he doesn't blame you."

"I wouldn't be too sure of that," John said with a worried frown.

"Something gave me the impression that he suspects. But he doesn't suspect you were connected with it, so don't worry. You know—he acted like he knew all about it and approved of it. I wonder? Get to work now, employee. I've got to call home and tell Gloria the news.

"Oh, poo to you, boss," Cloe said, wrinkling her nose at him and kissing him before he stepped away.

Dropping into his swivel chair John planted his feet on his desk and dialed home. He hummed happily while the phone at the other end rang. It rang several times, and John was beginning to wonder if Gloria were home when there was a click and her voice sounded.

"Hello?" she said, her voice soft and impersonal.

"Hello, darling," John said. "Guess what! I'm the new manager of the Moore Publishing Company—in complete charge. Mr. Tombs is leaving, and I'm to have his office. Isn't that—"

"I'm leaving, John," she interrupted him, her voice firm.

"Huh? Where you going?" he asked.

"I'm leaving, John. For good. I'm glad you called so I could tell you. There's a note on the dresser in the bedroom."

"What do you mean?" John asked, bewildered. "What—? Stay right there. I'll be right home."

"It won't do you any good, John," Gloria's voice said determinedly. "I'll be gone when you get here."

"But you can't," he said. "We've got to talk this over. Now, you wait right there. Huh?"

"No, John," Gloria said. "When I saw that powder on your coat last night I knew it was no use. That wasn't a casual brushing of powder, but rubbed in—from Cloe's face. And the hearing was over at seven thirty. One of our neighbors was there and dropped in to tell me about it at eight thirty when he got home."

"But—," John stopped helplessly.

If you get rid of Cloe and have nothing more to do with her, you can tell me about it in a few months when you get straightened around," Gloria went on. "If you can't do that this is the end, John."

"But what'll you do, Gloria?" John said anxiously. "Where'll you go? This isn't the same world any more. You just can't!"

"I have a little money," she said. "I'll—I'll write you where I am so you can send money for—your children. I'll make out some way."

"Now you just wait right there, Gloria," John said firmly. "I'll catch a taxi."

He dropped the phone in its cradle and turned agonized eyes to Cloe.

"She's leaving me!" he said, unbelieving.

Cloe stared at the door, her eyes wide, her mouth opened in a rounded oh. Slowly her face relaxed. She smiled, pleased with herself.

CHAPTER FIFTEEN

THE HOUSE WAS EMPTY. John rushed from room to room, calling, "Dear! Where are you, Dear?" He had known the moment he entered the house that she was gone, but his mind refused to accept it.

Half sobbing, he explored clothes closets. Sisty's and Frankie's clothes were gone. So were some of Gloria's, though the dress he had so proudly bought her for Easter still hung on the rod, a little apart from the other remaining dresses as though Gloria had taken a last look at it before deciding not to take it.

That mental picture broke him down completely. Blinded by tears, he stumbled to the bed and sat on its edge, crying without restraint.

The doorbell rang. John leaped up, a light of sudden hope in his eyes. "She's come back!" he breathed. He left the bedroom and crossed the living room in long strides, flinging open the front door.

"How much longer you want me to wait?" the sour faced taxi driver asked.

"Oh," John said, his shoulders sagging. "You don't need to wait any more. I'll pay you now. Wait!" He hesitated. The urge to talk with someone overcame him. He followed the driver out to the cab, giving him Joe Pace's address. Joe wouldn't be home yet, but Martha would be a real comfort. If she was home.

The cab pulled up in front of the Pace's. John got out and paid the driver, then turned to go up the walk. As he reached the steps to the porch the front door opened.

"Gloria's left me," he blurted out as he caught sight of Martha in the doorway.

"You look terrible, John," Martha said. "Come on in. Joe'll be home from work in a few minutes."

John followed her into the living room with a feeling she hadn't understood what he had said. When she sat on the wide arm of an overstuffed across the small, too much furnished room and made no comment he became sure of it.

"Did you hear what I said?" he asked. "I said Gloria has left me and taken Sisty and Frank with her. I don't know where she is."

"Yes, I heard you," Martha said calmly. "That's the trouble with this new divorce setup. There'll probably be lots of divorces."

"But she can't get one without my consent," John said desperately. "I don't want one. I won't let her get one!"

"Why'd she leave you?" Martha said.

"It's just the way things happened," John said. "Some lipstick I couldn't explain, then some powder on my coat lapel."

"Oh," Martha said. "You were two-timing on her?"

"No," John said. He took a deep breath. "Look, Martha, things are different now than they were."

"You mean she should take it?" Martha asked with a show of slight hostility.

"No!" John shouted. Then more quietly. "I've been fighting to hold my job, make it more secure. To keep my home, and Gloria and the kids in it, safe and comfortable. It takes more than just ordinary effort now. Things aren't the same."

"I hear Joe," Martha interrupted. "You stay here. I'll explain to him."

There were heavy footsteps in the kitchen. Martha left the room.

From the kitchen came the sounds of their greeting. Then came hoarse whispers, a long and aggravating conversation carried on that way. John resisted the impulse to get up and go into the kitchen, and wondered why he did, deciding it was just the way Martha had told him to wait.

Finally heavy steps approached. Joe appeared in the doorway. A sympathetic grin flashed over his face and was gone.

"Martha tells me Gloria has left you, John," he said gravely. "Tell me about it."

"There's nothing to tell," John said, a mood of hopelessness settling over him suddenly. "I guess there was no way she could understand."

"I suppose women are all that way," Joe said. "They aren't broadminded."

"That has nothing to do with it," John said harshly. "I wasn't having an *affair*. I was just trying to hold my job. And finally succeeding at it. I was made manager of the publishing company today—only to find that my very reasons for getting that job had turned to sand under my feet."

"Go on," Joe said quietly.

"Remember what you told me about using the lie?" John said. "Well, it had to go a lot farther than even you guessed. I had to frame Alex Been or I would have been out on my ear. I had to have the help of Cloe, my secretary. There was no other way. Maybe she's in love with me—a little. I suppose most secretaries have to be a little in love with their boss or they look around for another job. That doesn't mean they're out to break up his home, or be his mistress.

"Framing Alex was a nerve racking experience. When Tombs called Cloe and me into his office we felt sure it meant the firing squad. Tombs was calm which made us even more nervous. You know the cat and the mouse act. But surprising enough he seemed pleased that Alex had jumped. He let us know that he had been worried about a weakness in Alex' makeup; he wasn't sure he would be able to stand up under the strain. Tombs told us that we would have to go before a party board and explain what happened. He intimated that we should tell them that Alex confessed to subversive activities and that he killed himself to avoid exposure."

"You can imagine how Cloe and I felt all this time. Then Tombs ushered us before this board or whatever you call it. To get caught would have meant worse than death, being sent to a slave labor camp. But Tombs took control and all we had to do was nod in agreement."

"Cloe held up beautifully during that trial. She had to. And so did I. We had gone too far to turn back. It was Alex or us. I wish to God it hadn't had to be, but Alex knew I was the logical man for the job he had but wasn't equipped to handle. I am sure he was working around to framing me.

"But after the hearing Cloe went to pieces. I had to take her home and quiet her nerves. She cried and cried. Sure, her head was on my shoulder. My arms were around her, comforting her. What else could I do? Push her away and say, 'No, no! My wife might object to a mere office girl being comforted by me. Keep yourself away from me!' Would you?

"All Gloria sees of it is the powder on my coat. She puts two and two together and gets a million. All of it against me. I suppose it's a form of rough justice."

"Gloria left a message?" Joe asked.

"I'm coming to that," John said. "When Mr. Tombs called me in he told me I was getting Alex's job as manager. Not only that, he was leaving the whole operation to me, getting out. So my worries were over. I made a beeline to the phone to tell Gloria the good news. She wouldn't listen. She just said she was leaving me. I got a taxi as quick as I could, but when I got home she was gone."

"Did she say she would ever come back to you?" Joe asked.

"She said maybe she would if I got rid of Cloe," John said bitterly.

"Cloe's too gifted to get rid of," Joe said absently, as though thinking aloud. "There'll be plenty of times when you'll need her genius and her loyalty. You have to keep her, and keep her fairly happy. At the same time you have to have Gloria and the kids back, or you won't be happy."

"You're talking in riddles," John said. "Gloria won't come back unless I get rid of Cloe, and I can't get rid of Cloe just by firing her, because she—well, she has too much on me. I'm stuck."

"Not necessarily," Joe said. "Remember how when you were little your mother made you do things you didn't want to, and after a while you got used to doing them and didn't mind? Like brushing your teeth?"

"What's that got to do with it?" John asked, mystified.

"As of today you're a big frog in the puddle," Joe said. "I happen to know. Here's what you must do. Get Tombs on the phone tomorrow and give him a smooth story about playing around with your secretary and your wife leaving you. Hint that you want a few strings pulled that will make her come back. He'll take it from there. Inside a week she'll be back. She won't like it, maybe, but after a while she'll get used to things, adjust herself to the inevitable fact that she can't have everything, and that she'll have to take the bad with the good. Maybe in time she'll come to realize that everything you do is because you love her, and that that reason can excuse a lot more than she had ever dreamed it could.

"And let Cloe know about it all. Tell her what you are doing about it, that you want your wife back and are going to get her back. She'll play things your way—just like Gloria will have to. The stakes for all of you are survival."

"Now go on home and get yourself some sleep," Joe said. "Tomorrow you do what I told you. I'll make a good communist out of you yet. You're doing lots of things you don't want to, to hold your home together. There's no reason why Gloria should live in the dream of the past and have things her own way even when they get to be unrealistic."

"That's right," John said wonderingly. "That's what it amounts to. I was making the sacrifices to keep her from making any. I'll go ahead with this. Thanks, Joe. You don't know how much this means. Thanks."

John stood up and shook hands with Joe. "Where's Martha? I want to thank her too."

"Oh she's probably out in back some where," Joe said carelessly. "I'll tell her. Drop around tomorrow evening and let me know how things look."

He had John's arm and was leading him to the door. "Take it easy, now, John," he admonished. He stood in the doorway until he saw John get into the bus at the corner. Then he closed the door and went into the kitchen.

"You heard everything, Gloria?" he said.

"Yes, Joe," Gloria Dow said humbly. "I know now that I shouldn't have left him. I'm going right home and tell him I'm sorry."

"You'll do nothing of the kind!" Joe said harshly. "If you do, do you know what will happen?"

"What?" Gloria asked.

"Cloe will become an out and out fighting she-cat," Joe said. "It's obvious she wants him. That's why she's done everything she has. You're going to get a room in a hotel and look for a job, and in a couple of days you're going to apply for a divorce. By that time Tombs will be at work. You won't get your divorce. They'll see you don't get a job. They'll force you to go back home. They may even have a talk with you and convince you. And when you do return home you must remember the tooth brushing story and be ungrateful, letting it slowly wear off."

"But why?" Gloria asked. "I don't understand!"

"I'll tell you after dinner," Joe said. "Get Sisty and Franky out of the back bedroom and don't tell them anything."

Martha looked up from the stove as Gloria left the kitchen and gave her husband a nervous smile.

"Sometimes I'm afraid of you, Joe," she said in a tone of voice that implied the opposite.

"You'd better be," he glowered darkly. Martha stared at him expressionlessly, then snapped her teeth at him defiantly. They were smiling when Gloria returned with Sisty and Franky.

An hour later dinner was over. Sisty and Franky were put to work doing the dishes while Gloria, Martha, and Joe went into the living room and turned on the phonograph to drown their voices.

"Now then," Gloria said. "You'd better do some real talking. The more I think the more I want to go back home tonight."

"I'm going to tell you something, Gloria," Joe said. "Something I should never tell anyone. When I get through you'll do exactly as I tell you—because you'll know you must. I know how to lick this thing. There's only one way to do it. That's to drive right up to the top of the heap.

"Putting it in words that make sense, what you drive to the top it can be likened to a car. When it stops driving you have to fix it. To fix it you have to have the tools to do it with. Then you can get it started again. Out in the middle of the desert if your car stops, sometimes all that stands between going on and staying there and dying is a simple little monkey wrench. You have to have the tools along with you. It you don't have a full kit at the start you have to pick them up here and there as you go, and you go only as far as your car and your tools will take you. Understand?"

"No," Gloria said. "I understand what you said, but I don't see what it has to do with the present."

"This," Joe said. "Cloe is a very valuable tool. I could have shown John how to get rid of her safely tomorrow. But he must keep her. She's a genius at a frame, and there will have to be plenty of frames to eliminate opposition on the way up the ladder. She's beautiful. I've seen her several times when I dropped in on John to go home with him. Right now she fancies she'd like to be married to John. I intend to coach him on how to steer her toward the idea of ambition. A few years from now she'll be indispensable as an agent and a schemer to clear the obstacles out of John's path. She'll be loyal, with the image of you, an unwilling wife, home only because John 'cold-bloodedly' pulled strings to force you to come back. That maneuver alone will make her content to let things ride in the direction of romance. What John does to you he could do to her if she tied up with him in marriage."

"I understand, now," Gloria said after a long silence. "But where is this going? You talk like you thought John is going to be more than the manager of the publishing company."

"Under communism you either go up or down," Joe said. "It's part of their system. Dialectical materialism, where there is nothing permanent, but only eternal conflict. In five years if John doesn't grow into a bigger job than manager of a two-bit company he'll be replaced by someone else who shows promise. He'll be out of favor, on the skids, and probably framed into a prison labor camp by some ambitious newcomer."

Gloria stared at the wallpaper design with round eyes, seeing the horrible uncertainty of the future as Joe had painted it.

"You'll follow my orders," Joe said quietly. "From now on. Won't you?"

"I'll follow your—orders," Gloria said. Suddenly she shuddered as though awakening from a horrible dream.

CHAPTER SIXTEEN

THE PHONE IN THE locked drawer buzzed discreetly.

"That'll be all right now, Cloe," John said.

"What are you going to do about Genevieve?" Cloe said.

"You don't like her," John said, fishing in his pocket for the key to the drawer. "I'll have her transferred under you," he concluded. Not missing the wolfish gleam that suddenly sprang into Cloe's eyes at the prospect of being boss over a girl she didn't like.

When the door closed behind her John opened the drawer and took out the private phone.

"This is Steffen Tombs, John," the heavy, throaty voice announced. "Do you have anything to report?"

"Everything under control, Mr. Tombs," John answered respectfully.

"How's your wife's attitude these days, John?"

"As well as can be expected," John said. "She's becoming—I think reconciled is the word."

"Ah well," Steffen Tombs said. "Few women grow up and realize that adult life isn't the same as childhood where they lived in an atmosphere of love and illusion, when she finally concludes that this is a man's world she'll be a good wife again. By the way, John, I'm having a small get-together at my house tonight. I'd like you and your wife to be there," It was a statement rather than an invitation. "A few people I'd like you to meet."

"Thank you, Sir. I'll be there," John said.

"An official car will call for you and your wife at eight o'clock. It will be formal." The click at the other end was a punctuation mark ending the call.

The car was a new limousine of the type manufactured only for those in the upper brackets of the new communist world state. There were two chauffeurs, in trim gunmetal blue uniforms over ramrod backs.

The heavy and often used forty-five automatic rode on the left hip of each of them. The faces under the narrow visors of the trim military hats were respectful.

They had arrived ten minutes early and rang the bell. John had answered.

"We aren't quite ready," he said, though it was obvious only Gloria could be not ready, since he was fully dressed.

One of the men held out a dressbox.

"We arrived early for a purpose, sir," he said. "Mrs. Tombs sent this dress made for Mrs. Dow, thinking perhaps she might be caught unprepared by the shortness of the notice."

"Well, thank you!" John said, surprised, taking the box. "Won't you come in?"

"We will wait in the car," the man replied politely. They turned and descended the porch steps.

John closed the door and went into the bedroom.

"Mrs. Tombs sent you a dress to wear, Gloria," he said. "Wasn't that nice of her?"

"I wonder what she's like," Gloria said, laying the box on the bed and opening it. "Oh!" It was a gasp of admiration.

She slipped into the strapless formal and posed before the mirror. "I didn't know they made anything like this any more," she said dreamily.

Impulsively she threw her arms around John and kissed him, then drew back quickly, her happy smile replaced by one of polite reserve.

"That's for having connections that rate me a dress like this one," she said. "Would you get my coat, please?"

John obediently brought her coat from the closet, a secret smile tugging at the corners of his mouth. "Here you are, moddom," he said, holding it for her to slip into.

"Thank you," Gloria said coolly, regaining her aloof manner. She went into the hall to the foot of the stairs. "Sisty, are you going to be all right?"

"Yes, mother," Sisty called down. "I won't be responsible for Frank staying in though."

"Frank," Gloria called. "Don't you dare go out tonight or your father will tan you good when we get home."

"Stop worrying, mother," Frank answered. "I'll be up 'til midnight on this school stuff."

"We're going now," Gloria called.

The limousine took them to one of the larger mansions built during the last two years to the east of the outer drive on the man-made shoreline of the lake made by the new communist city and state bosses right after R-Day.

The drawing room they were ushered into was a masterpiece of architecture and good taste.

Steffen Tombs, resplendent in full formal attire that gave his portly figure an air of majesty, stood beside a white haired lady like a benevolent giant beside a sixty-year-old Snow White.

"Good evening, John," he said, holding out a fat hand, his florid face wreathed in smiles of welcome. "And this is your wife,

Gloria? I've always wanted to meet you, young lady. You have my greatest admiration. This is my own wife, Mrs. Tombs. She may be old, almost as old as I am, but I wouldn't trade her for the most beautiful of the young ladies—which she was herself thirty years ago.

"I'm quite sure she was as beautiful when she was young as she is now," John said, smiling.

"What did I tell you, Anna?" Mr. Tombs said, still chuckling. "What did I tell you about John? I was right, wasn't I? Take him and his lovely wife in and introduce them to the guests." He pulled out an enormous linen handkerchief and mopped his brow, then turned to greet some others.

Within a few minutes John found Gloria maneuvered away from him by the ladies, and himself being shuffled from one small group of wary-eyed men to another.

Mechanically he was cataloging their faces and names, trying to remember them. Within an hour he was moving among them and driving their faces and names firmly home in his memory, casually asking each about his work, his family, and any little thing they cared to volunteer.

There was dancing at nine thirty. He danced with as many of the wives as he could, and felt sure each of them would remember him with pleasure.

When he danced with Gloria she was tense against him.

"What's the matter, Dear?" he whispered.

"It's that Mr. Jorn," she said. "He keeps looking at me. And he told me if I would drop up to his apartment some afternoon he would see that you get a better job."

John froze in midstep, going cold all over. Then slowly he resumed the dancing, steering Gloria gradually over to where Steffen Tombs sat regally against the wall, beaming over the room at his guests.

"Tell Mr. Jorn you wish to see him in your study, Mr. Tombs," he said quietly without interrupting his dance step.

A few minutes later he saw Mr. Tombs beckon a servant, then slowly, protestingly rise and waddle toward a side door. The servant searched the dance floor, then moved vainly through the dancers to a tall, swarthily handsome man. From the freshly catalogued information in his memory John knew that Jorn was one of the three city police commissioners, a very powerful man, both physically and in the Party.

From the corner of his eye he saw the man excuse himself from his dancing partner and follow after Mr. Tombs.

"Be back in a minute, Dear," he whispered after Jorn had left the room. He patted Gloria on the shoulder and went after Jorn.

"I'm sure I don't know, Mr. Jorn," Steffen Tombs was saying. "You'll have to ask Mr. Dow when he comes."

John pushed open the door and entered, closing it quickly, standing with his back to it.

Mr. Jorn straightened and turned to face him. On his face was the knowledge of why John had asked him here. A crooked smile slowly spread over his face.

"Really, Mr. Dow," he said mockingly. "Tonight we are having fun. I'm sure any business you wish to discuss with me can wait until tomorrow. Come and see me at my office. Have lunch with me. I insist."

John's smile matched Jorn's in its mixture of politeness and mockery. He shook his head.

"No, Jorn," he said. "I'm intelligent enough to know which of two forks in a road to take."

"Really, gentlemen," Steffen Tombs said, backing away from Jorn toward a settee. But John caught a glint in Mr. Tombs' eye that told him he was approving.

"I'm sure I don't know what you're driving at," Jorn said uneasily.

"Really?" John said coldly. Suddenly a flash of memory appeared in his mind's eye. The way a certain young lady had looked at Jorn earlier. It had puzzled him at the time. "But of course you don't. Actually it isn't I who should be here. It should be George Desmatte."

Jorn started in surprise.

Mr. Tombs was sitting down now. John saw him look across the room at drapes covering windows directly in back of Jorn, and nod barely enough to be perceptible. Those drapes parted. A white face appeared, and the blunt nose of a gun.

"Look here, Dow," Jorn said curtly. "Your insinuations are quite obvious. I don't like them. I think tomorrow morning I will start a thorough investigation of your party record."

"But you won't be alive tomorrow morning, Mr. Jorn," Steffen Tombs said casually. So casually that it took a second thought to understand the sense of his words.

John heard a deafening sound. At the same instant he saw the front of Mr. Jorn's head lift out and split open. One after another shots blasted out in the room.

In the silence that followed the white face at the drapes stared intently at John. Then it was gone.

"A stranger," Steffen Tombs hissed. "An assassin."

John nodded. He turned and flung the door open, rushing into the drawing room.

"Get the police!" he shouted. "A maniac just broke in and shot at us. He's running away. Get the police!"

"Are you hurt, John," Gloria cried, rushing to him.

Steffen Tombs appeared in the doorway, mopping his brow.

"I think he must have been attempting to kill *me!*" he said hoarsely. "But fortunately he missed both me and John. Only Mr. Jorn was killed, poor fellow." He mopped his face with his hand-kerchief and shook his head sadly, going to the nearest chair where he dropped wearily.

Gloria was staring at John, her eyes questioning.

"Look," John said, pointing imperceptibly.

Gloria followed his finger and was in time to see the expression on Mrs. Desmatte's face.

"But—" Gloria started to say.

She couldn't say any more. The men were gathering around John, congratulating him on his narrow escape in tones that could only mean they were congratulating him on Jorn's death.

Suddenly men in police uniforms were entering, dispersing themselves about the room.

"I am Captain Walters. I'm in charge here for the time being." He turned to the man nearest him and asked, "What happened?"

"All I know," the man, Fred Archer, said, "is that Mr. Tombs, Mr. Dow, and the dead man, Mr. Jorn, went into that room over there together and just as the door closed on them I heard the shooting start."

"How did they go in?" Captain Walters demanded. "Were they angry, serious, or what?"

"They were talking," Fred Archer said. Why? We're all friends."

"I would advise you to keep a civil tongue in your head, Captain Walters," Steffen Tombs said calmly. "The murderer is undoubtedly some disgruntled citizen who came here to shoot me. I didn't see his face. Mr. Dow didn't see his face. If Mr. Jorn saw it he isn't in a position to tell us. Examine your evidence and leave. We have a midnight dinner waiting for our guests. Or would you care to join us?" he added mockingly. "There's an empty plate now, you know."

"Thank you, Mr. Tombs," Captain Walters said, missing the mockery. "It will be a real pleasure. Go right ahead and I'll be with you shortly."

He went into the room where the shooting had taken place and started to give instructions to his men.

Steffen Tombs smiled at his guests and shrugged his fat shoulders, then rose with a heavy sigh and waddled toward the double doors to the dining room.

CHAPTER SEVENTEEN

"THREE SPADES," Martha said.

"You say you're sure some of those wives at that party had been up to Jorn's apartment?" Joe said to John.

"Three no trump," John said. "Of course I'm sure. I'd stake my life on it. I sensed the whole setup. Jorn as police commissioner could railroad any of those men to Siberia at any time. Some of those men whose wives had been up to Jorn's place must have known about it, but didn't dare do anything."

"Pass," Gloria said nervously.

"Four hearts," Joe said.

"Four spades," Martha said doubtfully.

"Double your four spades," John said. "When Gloria told me he had asked her to come up to his apartment I knew what I had to do."

"Pass," Gloria said.

"Redouble," Joe said. "So you went in there to kill him."

"I'll layout your cards for you, Dear," John said. "You're fingers are shaking too much. Not exactly to kill him, Joe. To tell him in front of Tombs to keep away, I guess. But when I got in there I realized it was no go. In the morning he would take care of me, and then he'd go after Gloria."

"Good thing that disgruntled taxpayer happened along," Joe said dryly.

"Wasn't it, though," Martha purred. "Play, John." Several more cards were played in silence.

"You know, John," Joe said. "Those men, or at least some of them, are pretty grateful to you about now. Some men try to climb by stepping on people. They usually fail. Some climb by lifting others up with them, or ahead of them. I knew an old mountain climber once. One day he said to me, 'You know, Joe—' He called me Joe. Friend of mine. He said, 'You know, Joe, it's always best to help the other fellow up ahead of you. Then if there's a loose foothold he'll do the stumbling.' I never forgot that."

"Well you're forgetting to play bridge," Martha said.

"Which reminds me," John said. "How would you like to work for the Moore Publishing Company, Joe?"

"Don't push me like that, John," Joe said. He studied the cards in the center of the table and selected one from his hand to lay on them. "No, John. I'd rather play cards with you than work for you."

"Let's finish this hand and have coffee," Gloria said. "There's so much talking we aren't doing any playing anyhow."

"That's the trouble with playing with women," Joe complained. John laughed while Martha and Gloria started talking, starring in Joe's direction at the same tune.

"How about it, Joe?" John asked when Gloria and Martha had gone into the kitchen. "I'm serious. Things are going to be very complicated for me from now on. I can feel it. I need you."

"It's no good," Joe said. "At least not yet. You over-estimate my worth. I'm an idle bystander."

"Stop that!" John said.

"Let's put it this way," Joe said. "Right now you're scared. If I move in and act as your crutch you'll always be scared. One of these days, yes. I'll go to work for you. But when that day comes you won't be in the publishing company."

"A Captain Walters to see you, Mr. Dow," the switchboard operator's voice said.

"Show him in," John said. "No, wait a minute! Ask him to wait just a moment."

Hastily he unlocked the bottom drawer and dialed Steffen Tombs' number on the secret phone.

"Captain Walters is here to see me," he said quickly. "I'll leave the receiver off and lock the drawer. Maybe you can overhear. If not, at least the phone can't ring."

After locking the drawer he told the girl to let the police captain come in.

"Good morning, Mr. Dow," Captain Walters said when he entered.

John smiled calmly, none of his inner tension showing outwardly.

"Have a seat, captain," he said. "I hope this is a friendly visit. I don't mind confessing I admired the way you handled things night before last. Not to speak ill of the dead, I can't understand why Jorn was over you. You have all the qualities of an executive that he lacked."

"Thank you, Mr. Dow," Captain Walters said. "Including the good sense not to play around with other men's wives, I hope."

"I wonder who will get Jorn's job?" John's tone was one of honest curiosity.

"That's hard to say," Walters said. "But what I came here for was more in the line of business than of pleasure. I want to ask you a few questions about that night. Had you ever met Jorn before?"

"Not until an hour before he was killed," John said.

"Your wife?" Walters asked.

"If my wife had ever been playing around with Jorn I would have killed him myself," John said, "regardless of the consequences."

"I see," Walters said sinisterly. "I would like you to explain why you asked Steffen Tombs to have Mr. Jorn step into the library, and why you followed after both of them had gone there."

John opened his mouth in surprise. His blank expression drifted into a lazy smile.

"I'm sure you are making a-suicidal error in judgment," he said calmly. "You are questioning the word of Mr. Tombs himself."

"I'm questioning no one," Walters said. "I know that while you and your wife were dancing you paused and spoke to Mr. Tombs. Immediately after, Mr. Tombs beckoned a servant who went to Mr. Jorn and asked him to go to the library. He did so. As soon as the door closed behind him you followed. I have all that from several independent sources."

"Oh, that," John said. "When I paused and spoke to Mr. Tombs I merely told him my shoes were hurting. By the way, how did your search for the murderer turn out? Were you able to track him?"

"Only as far as the pier," Walters answered. "He could have escaped by swimming or by boat. We sent out patrol boats, but they found nothing. Also, he could have been one of the employees and never left the property."

"I think I can see what you're hinting at, Walters," John said. "You're hinting that I asked or ordered Mr. Tombs to get Jorn into the library, and that I went in there to kill him, and did kill him. You're implying that there may have been an accomplice, a man who came in and shot Jorn at my request, then went out the window and made good his escape before we called you in.

"All that implies two possible things which can't be true. One—or if they are true your case is hopeless anyway. One, that I wield enough power to be able to order a man of Mr. Tomb's position around as I please. Two, that I planned the whole thing before I had even met Jorn, and everyone there except Jorn was a tool of mine." He grinned mockingly. "In such a case I would surely wield enough power in this city so that you would be writing yourself a ticket to Siberia if you tried to prove anything."

"This is the way I think," Walters said. "There are two possibilities. One, either you have no power at all, and were just a guest for the evening. Since I can't find a man who ran from that room I can order my men to say that there were no signs of one having done so. Then I can get a good case against you, and Mr. Tombs will let it go that way. Two, you have sufficient power so that even if you were guilty I could do nothing. In that case you can prove your power by making me commissioner as Jorn's successor."

"I haven't any power," John said. "But it's just possible I could see that you were made commissioner, if you're willing to be realistic about this."

"What do you mean?" Walters asked uneasily.

"There will be times when we can help each other, in various ways," John said knowingly. "It may be possible that I could have you killed if you ever turned against me, but I won't hold any threat over your head. Just remember if you become commissioner that my word to you in private is law."

"And if I don't become commissioner?"

"It might be because you aren't alive to accept the post," John said. "Meanwhile I would suggest you report the case as closed, due to lack of evidence sufficient to enable you to find the man who did the shooting."

"Yes sir," Walters said. "I'll wait another twenty-four hours before *writing it off.* Is that all right?"

When he had gone John unlocked the drawer and picked up the phone. "Did you hear it all right?" he asked.

"I couldn't hear a word," Mr. Tombs said testily. "What was said?"

"Could Captain Walters be made commissioner?" John asked.

"As a matter of fact I happen to know he's going to be told of his promotion this afternoon," Steffen Tombs said. "Why?"

"I thought as much," John said smoothly. "He was very affable.

I think he assumed I must be one of the inner circle because the purpose of his visit, as near as I could gather, was to hint that he would like to be invited to the next party at your house. He's already thinking in terms of being commissioner."

Steffen Tombs' rolling laughter came over the phone.

"Maybe he can at that," he said. "He seems a sensible fellow. And his estimate is quite correct. You are one of us. Oh yes, I knew there was something: do you think your Cloe has a level enough head to take your place?"

"Why," John hesitated, going cold inside, "I really hadn't thought about it."

"You'd better." Steffen Tombs said. "We're thinking of using you in a position where your abilities and judgment will be more useful to us. You will still oversee the publishing company from a distance. At this end of the phone, to be exact. I've merely hung on so I could keep an eye on your development."

John hung up, sweating. He sat very still, his fingers drumming on the surface of the desk, a frown on his face. Had Steffen Tombs been able to hear his conversation with Walters? He had to know.

He opened the bottom drawer on the other end of his desk and emptied its contents. The phone on his desk went into the drawer. There was a slight crack where the cord went in, but so much the better. If nothing could be heard over that phone, then nothing could have been heard over the other phone by Tombs.

Leaving the phone cradle in the drawer he asked the switchboard girl to get him Joe Pace's business number. In a minute Joe answered.

"This is John," John said. "I want you to do something for me. In a few seconds I'm going to say 'It's a nice day today.' I want to know if you can hear it or not. I'll say it in twenty seconds from when I say go. O.K.?"

"O.K. John," Joe said.

John watched the second hand on his wristwatch until it was straight up. "Go!" he said.

He laid the phone in the drawer and closed it. When the second hand had covered twenty seconds he said in a voice considerably louder than that he had used in conversation with Walters, "Four score and seven years ago."

"How was that, Joe?" he asked alter he opened the drawer. "Did you hear me say it?"

"No. Not anything but an indistinct mumble," Joe said. "What's it all about?"

"I just beat a full house with a pair of deuces," John said. "Thanks, and goodbye now."

He hung up smiling. Walters would get his promotion and believe it was his doing. He might never have any need to call on the new commissioner for any favor, but on the other hand the knowledge that he had a secret *in* with a powerful group, that was completely independent of any other he might have, would add to his self-assurance. This was something not even Steffen Tombs knew about. Maybe he wouldn't even tell Joe... No, not even Gloria.

After a while he buzzed Cloe. When she came in he went around the desk and took her face between his hands and kissed her. She pushed away.

"None of that," she said. "You worked hard enough making me get over being in love with you. Don't start me up again."

"That was just a congratulatory kiss," John said.

"What do you mean?" she asked.

"I'm firing you," John said. "Kicking you upstairs. Promoting you. In a couple of weeks I'll be taking over a new job. I'll still be your boss, but you'll be running this dump. They wanted to make it a man, but they gave me the say on it, since I will still be in charge, technically."

"Gloria!" John called, letting the front door slam and hanging up his coat in the bedroom closet before going to the kitchen.

"What are you so happy about?" Gloria said, looking up from the newspaper she was reading.

John strode over and took the paper out of her hands, then seized her shoulders and pulled her to her feet. She bent forward to kiss him. Suddenly she stopped, her face cramping queerly.

"Lipstick?" she said incredulously. "It's a long time since you came home with that."

"Oh, that," John said carelessly. "I just promoted Cloe to manager of the company. It'll save having to take her along with me to my new job."

"Wait a minute," Gloria said. "I'm all confused. I hear what you say but I don't understand it."

"Steffen Tombs is giving me a bigger job," John said. "Do I rate a kiss now?"

"When you wipe Cloe's lipstick off," Gloria said. While he was industriously doing so, "Did I understand you to say this is the end of Cloe working for you?"

"That's right," John said. "From now on I will just be the voice at the other end of an unlisted phone to her, just as Tombs was to me for so long." He sobered. "It will be much better that way, too. Her so-called hold over me has grown meaningless with time anyway. And now, with power to play with, she'll be just one of those tools that Joe was talking about the night we played bridge."

Noisy footsteps sounded on the back porch. There was a knock. The door opened. Joe Pace came in, followed by Martha.

"Did you hear the news, John?" He asked. "Maxim Vopinski has been assassinated."

"Huh?" John said, blinking. He turned and went to the radio switching it on.

"You won't hear it over the radio," Joe said. "I thought maybe you'd heard the news from Tombs."

"No," John said, turning the suddenly loud music down to a whisper. "How'd you hear it yourself?"

"The grapevine." Joe said. "Oh, the damn fools. Every one of them is known to the authorities. They were just left alive so that the government could keep tabs on all newcomers to their ranks. Now they'll be liquidated in the biggest purge since the week after R-Day. Maybe bigger."

"John just told me he's being promoted to a better job," Gloria said to Martha. Joe heard it while he was talking.

"What's the new job?" he asked.

"Tombs didn't tell me," John said. "I didn't have nerve enough to ask him. Anyway, I have a general policy of not asking questions of my superiors. They have a way of being irked by them."

"You put Cloe in charge of the publishing company and let her know that it was entirely your decision?" Joe asked quickly.

"How did you know?" John asked.

"I didn't," Joe said dryly. "I just knew that if you didn't you'd be in for plenty of grief in that direction sooner or later. I assumed you had enough sense to know it."

"I did," John said. "As a matter of fact, Tombs told me to place her in charge, but I didn't tell her that."

"Good boy," Joe said, relieved.

"You're staying for supper," Gloria said.

"No, no," Martha said. "I bought some nice steaks for our supper. We must be getting home. Joe just wanted to come over and find out if you had heard about Vopinski being assassinated."

"You might as well stay," John spoke up. "That roast is big enough for all of us and then some."

"Sure, let's stay," Joe said. He took John by the arm and pushed him gently toward the living room.

"Now then," Joe said gravely. "What was all this business today with the phone?"

"Just a little idea I had," John said carelessly.

"Let me tell you then," Joe said. "Since you intend to hold out on me. You had the phone off the hook in a drawer. You wanted to be sure that the private phone to Tombs wouldn't carry a voice in the room when the drawer was closed. Captain Walters came to question you. You got a bright idea and called Tombs and left the receiver off so he could overhear the conversation. But when you and Walters got into things you saw an opening for a good bluff. At first you were working it in the hope that Tombs would play along with you and get Walters made commissioner, but then Tombs told you he already going to be made that, and he also told you he hadn't been able to hear a word of what you said. So now Walters will believe it was your doing, and Tombs won't know that."

John was looking at him wonderingly. Joe saw the look and laughed softly.

"Never forget I'm on your side, John," he said. "We make a good team. You're a born opportunist, I'm a born planner. Between us we can—Let's see what your new job turns out to be. Maybe I'll go to work for you. Just maybe."

The two men looked into each other's eyes. At that moment they had reached a complete understanding of many things they—or at least John—had only half known before.

"Come on, we've got to get home. The Dows need some sleep tonight, even if you don't."

"O.K., Martha. G'night, John, Gloria."

And ten minutes later John Dow was stretching out in bed, already half-asleep. Eight hours. Yet up through layer upon layer of that incomprehensible reality known only as the mind, thought, consciousness, beyond the borders of the *World of If,* in that world we—by common agreement—call the world of reality, those eight hours were tolled by the pulse beats in the real John Dow's wrist. A period of a second or less during which a small galvanometer needle on the panel of an electronic machine leaped upward and back across the dial, and a counter behind the panel added another "hour" to the measure of "time" of John Dow's life in the dream world.

CHAPTER EIGHTEEN

JOE PACE SAT SMOKING A CIGARETTE, WATCHING THAT NEEDLE rhythmically jump back and forth, and also watching the "time" underneath it in a small rectangular slot as the numbers bounced into sight, to pause, then bounce again. Even as he watched, the year, 1953, changed to 1954, 1955, 1956.

Joe slowly ate a hamburger sandwich and sipped a cup of coffee while 1956 was replaced by 1957. 1958! The year of years! Perhaps not in known history, but in the background of things, in the undercurrents that control and direct history's unfoldment. He lit another cigarette and closed his eyes, letting memory rise to the surface of his thoughts. John had called him into his office...

"What have you gotten on that Equador oil deal, Joe?" John said.

"The Equadorian President is dead set against it," Joe replied. "He's been fed a lot of propaganda about the United States wanting to deplete Equador's natural resources. We might as well drop it."

"No," John said firmly. "All we have to do is get him to change his mind and we get ten million cash from a certain corporation. They don't care how we do it so long as they get what they want."

"That's a lot of money," Joe said.

"I got three million in advance for expenses," John said quietly. "I could foment a successful revolution down there with that kind of money, only—"

"Only it would result in a few natives killing each other," Joe said. "And you would consider yourself indirectly a murderer. I agree with you. But what other way is there?"

"There are other ways to use three million," John said. "What do you think of this idea? The Republicans will almost certainly get their man in the Presidency. He'll be one of three men. We could investigate those men, what investments they own, property, interest, and so on. Armed with that knowledge I could concentrate on getting close enough to them so that I could influence them to get tough with Equador."

"You—have—the—germ—of—an—idea," Joe said slowly, emphasizing each word. "The only weakness to it is that it doesn't have teeth to it, and can't have. Not directly. If you brought *direct* pressure to bear on anyone high in politics it would get you into trouble fast."

"That could be handled easily," John said. "A dummy setup to bring the pressure, then me to relieve it. There's all kinds of ways to use a combination like that. Maybe it could work into something. Not only from the financial standpoint, but from the political one."

"A thing like that could be a powerful tool," Joe said. "If you perfected it, it could rule both parties, and eventually put any man in office you wanted to, if—"

"If what?" John asked.

"If you were content to stay completely in the background," Joe said. "Not even the favors you ask in return for favors you've granted must seem to help you directly. For example, this thing on the fire now. Your desire must appear to be to help Equador by having the U. S. put pressure on their President for the good of international trade and the people of Equador. Which it will, definitely."

"Yes it will," John said. "It'll help Equador or I wouldn't have taken the job of putting it over."

"Then why don't you get it down to a system and develop it," Joe said. "In five or ten years you can make it big enough to work. Especially with this business consultant service you run here…"

1960, and Senator Whitlook's daughter lost thirty thousand dollars on the cuff in a gambling casino. John Dow through a friend high up in the city government of the city where it occurred had the place raided and the notes confiscated, returning them personally to the Senator's daughter, and loyally protecting her when her father heard in a roundabout way what had occurred. For friendship's sake with no thought of reward or recognition…

"But if you want to do me a favor, Henry, see what you can do about allocating funds for that development I'm so interested in. I vacationed down there last summer. Those people need it."

1961, and John Dow carried Gloria over the threshold of their new home on Lake Drive. There was the housewarming party…

"Look," John said in a low voice, glancing around to make sure no one could hear. "All three of you want the nomination. And all three of you are very good friends of mine. I want at least one of you to get it. But—well, there isn't much time, and two of you will have to withdraw or none of you will get it. You know that."

"You make the decision for us, John."

"O.K., but I want something out of it."

"Good old John. Always exacting his pound of flesh—to be paid to someone who doesn't even know him."

1964…"Well Joe, we've reached our goal. Both the Democrats and the Republicans are going to nominate the candidate I named to them. Whichever party gets the election one or the other of my men will be President!"

"And he'll follow orders, John, because neither of them believe they can get along without you. They can't. They need your decisions on World Policy."

1965…

Joe watched the years click in the small rectangle on the instrument panel, wondering what was going on in that imaginary world John was living in. He glanced at his wristwatch and was surprised to find it was after eight o'clock. It was beginning to get dark outside the windows.

"I've reached the point in time where I want to wake him," Dr. French said suddenly, stirring himself from the chair he had been half-asleep in.

"How are you going to do it?" Joe asked. "Don't forget he wants to remember everything when he's awake."

"I know," Dr. French said. "First I'll bring him part way out of it, to the point where he will tell me the highlights of what has happened. Then I'll bring him to full consciousness. It shouldn't take long, because there are only half a dozen things I want to ask him. Later, since he will remember everything, I can ask him more questions."

"Why not bring him all the way out first?" Joe asked.

"Something might happen to make him forget," Dr. French explained. "You see, he will awaken with the conviction that his dream has been real. For years and years in his dream he has been living in a world much different than this one. The conflict set up sometimes results in the subject refusing to accept reality again. And sometimes he rejects the dream life immediately no matter how we try to force him to keep remembering. So to play safe I'll have to ask my questions while he's still 'in' that other world."

"What will the questions be?" Joe persisted. "Personal? What he's been doing? What position he occupies? Will he have to answer them whether he wants to or not?"

Dr. Simon French smiled. "The answer to all your questions except the first one is yes," he said. "To that one, here is the list of questions."

He opened a notebook with full letter size pages. Questions were neatly typed, with space for the answers to be written in.

Joe read them hastily. Some of them could be dangerous questions applied to the real life situation. But the dream world?

"How closely will this dream world setup correspond to reality?" he asked.

"It's utterly different, I'm sure," Dr. French said. "You see, unless I'm very mistaken, the United States was taken over by the communists shortly after Mr. Dow entered the World of If."

"What!" Joe exclaimed. He blinked his eyes thoughtfully. "Well, then, it that's the case, ask him anything you want."

The doctor turned on the valve of the gas tank and laid the rubber tube so that the stream of gas played toward John Dow's nostrils. At the same time he slowly turned a knob on one of the panels.

His eyes were turned toward the large panel filled with small meters. Slowly the rhythm of their needles altered, sliding toward the center of the panel in their mass activity.

"John Dow!" the doctor said. "This is Simon French. Do you know me?"

The sleeping man's lips moved mutely, forming a silent yes.

"That's funny," Joe muttered. "Are you in his dream world as well as here?"

"He's on the threshold between the two," the doctor said. Then, "John Dow! You are commanded to speak! What is your occupation?"

"'I—I—'" The lips stuttered.

"Speak!" the doctor said sternly.

"I am manager of economic coordination for the western communist states," the answer came in a faraway whisper.

"That is a very powerful position," the doctor said, his tones full of admiration. "But also very surprising. You must have some very able assistants. Who, of all those around you, do you trust the most and rely on the most?"

"Hey!" Joe said softly. "That wasn't on your list!"

"Joe Pace," John said from far away.

"It was a question that just occurred to me on the spur of the moment," Dr. French said, looking up. "Do you know a man named Joe Pace?"

"Never heard of him," Joe said. "Must be someone he picked up within the dream world."

"The whole world is communist?" the doctor asked.

"The whole world is communist," John's voice came.

Joe watched Dr. French. The doctor was staring at John Dow's face, a strange look in his eyes. He opened his mouth as though to say something several times. Finally he picked up the notebook and began asking the questions written there, jotting down the answers as they came.

Finally he laid down the notebook and placed the stream of gas from the rubber tube so that it played directly at John's nostrils.

"You will open your eyes!" he ordered.

John's eyes opened, blinking at the light. They were doped looking.

"What do you see?" the doctor asked.

"I see you, Simon French," John said. His eyes turned to Joe. "And Jo—"

"John!" Joe said, rushing to the edge of the bed. "Speak to me. This is Craig Downing, your friend. Craig Downing. Do you recognize me?"

"Don't be so anxious, Mr. Downing," Dr. French said. "He'll be all right."

"Yes, I'm all right," John said, "Craig."

Joe relaxed. "Sure, John. You're all right."

"But—" Suddenly John's eyes widened. He stared around him, at the table of electronic instruments, at Dr. French, at the plates attached to his wrists and ankles. "So that's the way it happened," he said. "What time is it? Is it the same day?"

"Take it easy, John," Joe said. "Sure it's the same day."

Dr. French took off the helmet and plates, and took away the gas tube. John sat up and put his feet over the edge of the bed, working his face as the effects of the gas wore off.

"Do you remember everything that happened in that dream life?"

Joe asked anxiously.

"Remember it?" John echoed. "Listen—Craig. That was no dream!"

"If you're strong enough you can go now," Dr. French said. "The feeling of reality connected with that other existence will wear off by Monday. If it's all right with you I'd like to talk to you then. I'll call you on the phone for an appointment."

"Yes," Joe said. "Let's get out of here."

"I don't like it!" Joe said when they were out of the building. "I tell you there's something dangerous about that setup. He got you part way out and then asked you who your most trusted associate was. You told him Joe Pace. I have a hunch if he had known who I was we wouldn't have gotten out of there alive."

"Shut up, Joe," John said curtly. "I've got to have time to get my mind settled. I have the memories of two worlds to get used to. Right now I'm not too sure which one I'm in."

They reached John's car and got in. John looked it over thoughtfully. "Well," he said. "No car like this was ever made under the communists, so I guess I'm back in the capitalist civilization."

"Sure," Joe said. "I'm here."

"Ha!" John snorted. "You're in both places. You're one of what Dr. French called the *invariants.*"

"Let's get the paper at the next corner," Joe said. "I see a news stand there."

A minute later he was eagerly scanning the front page.

"It's in the headlines," he said. "Burk has been taken to the hospital psycho ward for observation."

"Who's Burk?" John asked. "Oh! He's the executor who controls the stock in Rexler. So that's the plan. A new executor will have to be appointed, and it will be possible to get him to sell the stock to us. Was it really Will Jones' idea, or yours?"

"Will's," Joe said. "Really. He's a sharp boy. It works nice and there's no after effects. They'll send Burk up to the State Hospital, and after a month or so someone will go up and see him and tell him the whole setup in private. He won't dare repeat it, because they'll put it down to a persecution complex. But it'll make him realize he wasn't insane, and a couple of weeks after he'll come out O.K., and probably keep his mouth shut."

John drove in silence, apparently unconcerned about anything except traffic.

"You say I was in that dream?" Joe finally broke the silence. At John's yes, "Was Dr. French in it somewhere?"

"I can't remember him in it," John replied. "The last part is rather hazy. I suppose that was because I was being lifted out of it. His voice, calling me out of that World of If would take hours of time the way it was there."

John turned off the arterial he was on into Joe's street. Three short blocks further he pulled to the curb. As Joe opened the door to get out, Martha and Gloria came out the front door.

"Come on in, John," Gloria called out. We're staying for dinner."

"I think I'd like to tell them what happened today," John said as he shut off the motor.

"No!" Joe whispered sharply. "You're still a little drugged. You don't seem to realize this whole thing smells of danger."

"I must be drugged," John said. "I can't see how it could be. But if you think so…"

Monday morning Joe was waiting for John with an expression that plainly told he thought he had the answer. Joe got in the car.

"I've got the answers," he said triumphantly, as John picked up speed again. "I asked myself how we were vulnerable."

"How are we vulnerable," John asked, seeming to be amused at the idea.

"Two ways," Joe said. "One, publicity backed with irrefutable evidence. Two, one or the other of us dying."

"Go on," John said calmly.

"I've been thinking of this idea of invariants," Joe said. "I'm an invariant in the World of If and the real world. There are others. What better way to find the secret, hidden invariant factors molding current civilization than by studying the World of If? Dr. French is an investigator. Most investigators search for facts. He puts men under hypnosis and has them dream. By comparing their dream lives he can arrive just as surely at the same facts."

"Of course," John said. "That's obvious from the accuracy of their annual business predictions."

"I'm talking about us," Joe said. "I mean he could, and probably has learned all about us *as we are.*"

"That's obvious too," John said. "I'm not particularly concerned about the Rexler Corporation knowing all that. What I'm interested in is what French knows about *what we will be.*"

CHAPTER NINETEEN

"DID YOU FIND OUT who the new executor is to be, Joe?" John asked over the phone.

"It's to be the bank itself," Joe answered. "The heirs are already down there demanding that the stock be sold at the ask price you've listed on the exchange. *Could be* it will go over, and we'll own Rexler by noon, since we now control the bank!"

"Then we can go over there and look through those files," John said. "I'm quite sure business trends are only one small part of their explorations of the coming year, and maybe they explore farther ahead than that!"

"Well," Joe said dryly, "if they do, maybe French knows already whether we will acquire ownership or not."

"I doubt it," John said. "It isn't detailed that way. Not so they can check it. At least that's my idea. They can only compare common knowledge. Things that will appear in the newspaper. Let me know the minute George Bennett calls you. I'm keeping things clear here for Dr. French's visit." He hung up. Getting up impatiently he paced around the office, frowning out the window.

Suddenly the phone rang. He took two swift strides and scooped it up. "Yes?" he said.

"Mr. Pace is on the phone again."

"John," Joe broke in. "It's through. We acquired the stock five minutes ago."

"Good!" John said. "That makes a whole lot of difference. Now I can make French tell me what he knows."

"Dr. French is on the phone," the switchboard girl said.

"Put him on," John said.

"Hello, Mr. Dow," Dr. French's voice erupted. "When will you have the time to spare to see me?"

"Where are you?" John asked.

"At my office."

"I can see you any time," John said. "Why don't you drop over now?"

"Thank you, I will," Dr. French replied. "I'll catch a taxi and be over there within fifteen minutes."

Ten minutes after he left the switchboard girl rang and said the doctor was in the outer office.

"Well, doctor," John said, getting up and advancing around his desk to meet him, "that was quite an experience I had Saturday. Do you know the strangest part of the whole thing?"

"I think I do," Dr. French said, shaking John's hand and smiling. "Others have invariably remarked the same thing that you want to say. That experience has settled into place beside your real life, so that you feel a sort of broadening of your horizons. You have lived two lives over a period of many years, stemming from two ways a Presidential election could have gone. It gives you a depth of perspective."

French paused and then said, "First of all, could I possibly meet Joe Pace? I'd like to put him under hypnosis too."

"He's out of town right now," John said vaguely. "I'll see him about it later. Why do you want to put him through that experiment?"

"More data," Dr. French said, grinning. "We scientists always want data, data, and more data."

"That's understandable," John said. "What's your next question?"

"That's all," Dr. French said.

"Surely you're curious about what happened to me during all those years!" John said, surprised.

"No," Dr. French said. "I know everything almost as well as you could remember it. I have the stories of over twenty people that lived through it, all agreeing on general detail. That's why I contacted you in the first place. I think I told you that."

"Why are you so interested in Joe Pace?" John asked. "It almost seems to me that was your sole object in the whole thing, to find the name of my closest business associate."

"Not at all," Dr. French said. "Remember, I asked you several questions under hypnosis."

"Oh, by the way," John said casually. "Craig Downing told me to tell you he would like to talk to you sometime about your work. He's very interested in it."

The phone rang. John frowned as he picked it up. "Yes?" he said.

"Dr. French is wanted on the phone," the switchboard girl said.

"For you, doctor," John said, holding out the phone.

Hello," Dr. French said while John listened absently. "Oh, hello Carl… What! Say that again! …Well, that certainly is unexpected, to say the least… Sure, Carl. I'll be back to the office in an hour or so. Bye."

"You sound like you've received bad news," John said, smiling slyly, and guessing what Dr. French had just learned.

"I have," Dr. French said. "I just learned that Rexler has a new owner. The majority of the stock was just sold a few minutes ago on the stock exchange. I wonder who could be so interested in us all of a sudden."

"Rexler is a money maker," John said. "Lots of people would like to own shares in it."

"But it's mighty peculiar, coming at this time," Dr. French said thoughtfully. "And, frankly, something that hadn't been expected. It worries me."

"Why?" John asked.

"The new owner can demand access to our secret files," Dr. French said. "That would be very bad for a lot of reasons. You see, they contain a lot at data on what is going to happen in the real world the next few months. Things that would be dynamite if they were generally known."

"You know, Dr. French," John said slowly, "you haven't told me something. I don't know what it is, but you've been nibbling at me on this with something definite in mind. Something connected with the near future and with me. What is it?"

"I don't know what would give you that idea," Dr. French said.

"Look at it this way," John said. "You have a lot at information on me and my activities in your files. This new owner might see them. I have a right to protect myself. I don't think you would use any information you might have in a dishonorable manner, but we can't know about the new owner."

"That's true," Dr. French admitted. "But let me say this. From what I know, I would like very much to get in touch with Joe Pace and let him spend a day under hypnosis before I say anything. Surely you can get in touch with him. He can fly here and come down tomorrow. Then, I promise you, tomorrow night I will not

111

only tell you everything you want to know, but turn over every scrap of data relating to you, so that the new owner will learn nothing about you. How about it, Mr. Dow?"

"It sounds attractive," John said. "Suppose you go back to your office and let me think about it. If I decide to do as you suggest I'll call you and let you know this afternoon."

Dr. French looked intently at John Dow for a moment.

"All right," he said quietly.

John watched him as he went out the door. He waited several minutes, then went after him to make sure he hadn't stopped at the switchboard.

"Dr. French leave?" he asked his secretary.

"He went right out," she answered.

"O.K." John said. "Tell Mr. Pace to come to my office."

He went back in and sat down, a brooding frown on his face. A few minutes later Joe came in without knocking.

"He knows Rexler has changed ownership," John said. "But he doesn't know we're the new owners."

"Good." Joe said, grinning delightedly.

"Also," John said, "he wants Joe Pace to spend a day in his lab.

In exchange he's willing to turn over everything relating to me tomorrow night, so that the new owner won't get it. A mighty attractive offer."

"But he doesn't know that you could go right down now and demand to see everything." Joe said. "Why don't you do that?"

"I don't know," John said. "I think it's mainly that I hate to confess to him that I lied about your name—on impulse. It was an impulse, you know. We had said nothing about that before we went in."

"But you know that he's going to find out who the new owner is before long," Joe said. "Then he'll know anyway. So why not now?"

"Not yet," John said. "And since we're the new owners, there's no pressure on us. We can wait. I'll call Dr. French up and tell him you informed me that you are ill, but you'll hurry back as soon as you're out of bed. That'll stall things. Maybe I can get access to those files anyway."

"I still can't see why you don't tell him you're the new owner?" Joe said.

"Hunches," John said. "A hunch made me introduce you as Craig Downing. A hunch tells me to wait."

"You know," Joe said softly, "this is the first time we've ever had a major difference. Every instinct in my body tells me Dr. French is very concerned about something, and that it has to do with us. Always before when I've insisted on something you've given in."

"I don't know why I don't this time, Joe," John said. "Let's let it ride until this afternoon, at least. O.K.?"

"O.K.," Joe said reluctantly.

"Oh, Joe," John said as Joe opened the door to leave. "I'm going out for a while."

John Dow parked his car in the same spot where he had parked it on Saturday. His steps were firm and sure as he walked the short distance to Rexler Research.

"Mr. Dow?" the young lady at the reception desk said. "I'm sorry, but Dr. French is busy right now, and expects to be for the rest of the day. An experiment is in progress."

"Tell him I must see him," John said. "It's important. Very important."

"I'll see what they say," the girl said doubtfully. She called upstairs and asked whoever it was that answered to tell the doctor Mr. Dow was there to see him on an important matter.

"You'll have to wait to see if he calls down," she smiled apologetically.

John Dow walked a few feet away from her desk, his eyes exploring the vacant hugeness of the room designed only to be a bank.

Behind the tellers a cage, recessed into the wall, was the massive door of the vault, containing all the data of ten or twelve years of research in two worlds.

So much that he didn't know. How many other Worlds of If were there besides the one predicated on a Presidential election going the other way than the one it did? And were those If-worlds the way the real world would have been? Or just a psychological growth. What of those people killed during R-Day? Not all of them had been killed on that day in the real world. Maybe none of them had. But they, and their insignificant lives, were not invariants. They weren't big enough, important enough in the world scheme, to have mattered either way.

Would they have died if the Presidential election had actually gone the other way? Nothing could ever be proven one way or another. The real past was unchangeable.

What was this mass mind that Dr. French had mentioned before? John had no doubt it existed. He was quite sure that his life under communism hadn't developed solely within his own mind. It had been too complicated. More to the point, many of the people in the World of If were people who had played parts in the real world utterly different. They were the same individuals, but their characters had developed differently, and genuinely. So many dozens of them that no amount of imaginative dreaming could possibly have invented them. They were the strongest argument for the reality of the *Worlds of If*.

The thought that they were real worlds struck John abruptly with full force. To be sure, they weren't real in the same sense as the material world. They were entirely mental, while the real world was cold hard atoms. But they existed somehow right now, in *something*.

In that *something* he was—must be—still going forward in time, living out his life just as he was here. But time there was different. In one day the way time went in the real world he had lived for a good many years.

But in the real world, under hypnotism, he could go back in time and relive his childhood, unaware of the future, which hid already unfolded.

The real world itself was also tied closely with a sort of mass mental complex, so that in its mental aspects, its social complexity, it was on a par with the Worlds of If, and perhaps operating from the same principles.

John went over to a couch and sat down. His thinking was leading him to concepts that were too vast to think about while standing.

He wondered if these different worlds had any effect on one another, or if they split sharply. Was some of current history under capitalism, democracy, influenced in some manner by the current history of the World of If where communism reigned supreme? And was that purely mental world of communism influenced to any degree by the world of reality?

The invariants! People, events that remained the same in the Worlds of If and the world of reality. And how many Worlds of If were there. Today, right now, he could go under hypnosis and have Dr. French impress on him that—that a communist revolution was finally taking place. And history would develop in a new If-world, with all its manifold ramifications.

There were even everyday practical applications. If he wanted to take a trip around the world he could go under hypnosis and take the trip. Then if anything undesirable happened he could cancel the trip when he awakened, and it wouldn't happen. But if he took the trip, would it develop exactly as it had in the dream world?

Or if he took it in the dream world and it turned out badly, could he keep from taking it in the real world when he woke up? That, essentially, was the crux of the whole matter!

"Dr. French wants you to come upstairs," the receptionist's voice interrupted John's thoughts. He turned. Her smile was like Gloria's in some indefinable way.

The same slender young man took him up on the elevator. On the way up John Dow thought back to that other trip on Saturday morning. It seemed an incredibly long time ago. In one way it was. It had happened before R-Day, and in the continuity of memory it had been many years before, as well as a mere three days.

Dr. French was waiting. John, stepped off the elevator, and heard its doors close while he shook hands with him. There was a certain tightness at the sides of the doctor's mouth when he smiled. John had known a man who did that when he was afraid. Why should Dr. French be afraid?

"What brings you over here this afternoon?" the doctor asked.

"I wanted to try something," John said. "I want to go under hypnosis and live out the next few days in detail as they will actually be. Could I do that?"

He was closely watching that telltale tightness to the doctor's lips. It increased.

"You probably could," Dr. French said, "but I wouldn't advise it."

"Why not?" John asked. "I realize it may not come out the way reality will. In fact, if it came out unpleasant I would use the experience to change it."

"It's not always possible to change things," Dr. French said. "I'd like to talk to you further before we decide anything. I have another subject under hypnosis right now who needs some attention. I'll show you to a room where you can wait. I won't be long."

He led him down the hall to a door next to the one he had gone through Saturday. It was a comfortably furnished room designed for people to wait in, with several chairs, a neat pile of magazines.

"It will probably be fifteen minutes," he said.

John looked around the room after the doctor had left. What had the man been afraid of? He had behaved like a man bluffing in a high stake poker game, or like someone concealing guilt, and afraid of discovery.

John went over and pulled up the venetian blind covering the window. Outside was a wide ledge. A fall from it wouldn't be fatal. The roof of the next building was only fifteen feet below. A one story restaurant building.

He returned to the door and opened it, sticking his head out into the hall. No one was in sight. Stealing softly along the hall, he pressed his ear to the door through which Dr. French had taken him.

He could hear no sound. Either the door was soundproof or nothing was being said. And every second meant danger of discovery and embarrassing questions.

He gave up and returned to his room, crossing to the window again. There was no time to waste. He crawled out onto the window ledge and edged along it, his back to the wall, until he was just beside the window.

The bulky form of the window air-conditioner projected outward over the ledge. John remembered the window from the inside now. It was double glass with dead air space in between the panes. There would be no possibility of overhearing anything except a loud shout from the room. But he wasn't as interested in what might be said inside as he was in seeing who the subject under hypnosis was.

Cautiously he twisted sideways, leaning until he could see inside. Dr. French was sitting in a chair beside the bed. The bed itself was empty.

John Dow frowned in perplexity. The table of instrument panels was visible. Pointers on dials were moving, showing that the instruments were in operation. The doctor, his back to the window, was making adjustments with the knobs at the bottom of one panel.

Suddenly John Dow noticed that all the cables from the instruments went to the floor and across it toward the other side of the room.

He looked at Dr. French's back, deciding that there was little danger of him turning suddenly and looking toward the window. He carefully leaned forward, his eyes following those cables across the floor. The cables ended in the base of a large device that hadn't been in the room Saturday.

On the platform of the base, rising to a height of five or six feet, and shaped somewhat similar to the chimney of a kerosene lamp was a cylindrical transparent container. Curved about its outer surface were wide bands of metal. The bands of metal, together with the shape of the cylindrical tube, were strongly suggestive of the insides of a radio, built on a giant scale.

Yet John's eyes saw nothing of this. They went at once to the figure standing upright within the large transparent tube.

It was Melva, the former switchboard girl. Under hypnosis!

CHAPTER TWENTY

AS HE WATCHED, an aliveness that seemed to surround her like an aura within the giant transparent tube, focusing into almost luminous brightness near the metal plates attached to her skin at various places in the same manner that similar plates had been attached to his own wrists and ankles two days before, she suddenly opened her eyes and saw him.

He saw her start in recognition, and drew back quickly, making his way along the ledge to the room he had left. He half fell through the window, picking himself up and going to the door.

Out in the hall he stopped. Should he burst into the doctor's laboratory? He couldn't know how much harm that might do to Melva. Her seeing him outside the window, and recognizing him, might already have done damage that couldn't be helped now.

He decided to wait. Neither the doctor nor Melva could leave that room without coming through the door. But the door remained impassively closed.

Ten minutes passed. Then the door opened. Dr. French came out.

"Tired of waiting?" he asked in such a friendly and unsuspecting way that it was obvious Melva hadn't told him about his looking through the window from the ledge.

"What were you doing with Melva in there?" John demanded. "What's that thing she was in?"

Dr. French stared at him, his eyes going wide. Then, slowly, his shoulders sagged, his face grew slack and tired.

"So you went along the ledge," he said dully. "It hadn't occurred to me that you might. There was no reason for you to."

"You aren't answering my questions," John said sharply.

Dr. French half opened the door and called back into the room. "Come into the next room when you are ready. I'll be there with Mr. Dow." He shut the door and led the way to the room John had left.

John stood near the door. Dr. French lit a cigarette with shaking fingers, took a deep drag, then dropped into a chair.

After a moment Melva came in. She smiled timidly at the two men and sat down, making herself as small as possible.

"Tell Mr. Dow what you learned, Melva," Dr. French said suddenly, keeping his eyes on the end of his cigarette and the lazy stream of blue smoke that curled upward from where it reposed between his fingers.

"I—I can't," Melva said, averting her eyes.

"Tell him!" Dr. French said, lifting his eyes for an instant, flashing authority in them, then dropping them again.

"But I just can't!" Melva said. She looked helplessly from Dr. French's averted eyes to John's intent stare.

"Tell me what you learned, Melva," John Dow said.

"Wait just a minute, Melva," Dr. French said. "Mr. Dow, I realize under the circumstances I'll probably get a flat no, but will you wait on asking questions until we can put Joe Pace under hypnosis to go through the same period I put Melva through just now?"

John hesitated, then shook his head. "I'm entitled to an explanation of this," he said.

"Let me say this before you make up your mind," Dr. French said.

"I didn't send Melva into the past to relive her life under a hypothetical change in history. I sent her into a probable future. The machine she was in is for that. It isn't as bizarre a contraption as it appears. It's just designed to help produce and maintain a deeper state of catalepsy, so that the subject can keep talking while living out the near future."

"So that's what it was!" John said. He turned his eyes to Melva.

"So you lived out the details of the coming few weeks? I'm very interested in that. I thought you were going to California? What happened?"

Melva turned her eyes helplessly to Dr. French. He nodded and returned his gaze to the tip of his cigarette.

"I went to Los Angeles," Melva said quietly. "I gave myself up. The next day I had a visitor. It was a lawyer, the one you had given orders to defend me. He told me—"

She paused, taking a deep breath.

"He told me," she went on, "that there would be some difficulty, but that he would follow your request even though he might not get his fee out of it, due to a possible tie-up of your estate through probate. You—you were dead."

"Dead!" John exploded.

"Murdered," Melva said quietly. She shrunk back in her char, her eyes wide and tearful.

John stared at her then suddenly relaxed, chuckling.

"I hadn't expected that," he said. "But of course it was just a hypothetical future. We can explore all the factors involved and I can avoid—getting murdered."

"That's just it," Dr. French said. "We can't explore all the factors, unless we can get Joe Pace here under hypnosis and get at those factors. Even then there's a strong possibility we can't. There are too many variables."

"Then we'll get Joe Pace here," John said.

"I sincerely hope you can," Dr. French said. "But I don't know whether you can or not. He's going to object. He may refuse to come."

"Why?" John asked. "Surely, he isn't the murderer!"

"He will be arrested for your murder," Dr. French said woodenly. "He'll get off. They won't convict him. The case won't ever be solved, but in my own mind I'm fairly certain he's the one who will be guilty."

"This is insane!" John said. "Imagine Dr. French, a quiet scientist who spends all his time in his laboratory. Doing what? Trying to solve a murder that hasn't been committed yet and probably—what do I mean probably! Definitely won't be committed! Nobody's going to kill me."

"You've been following the predictions, the business predictions put out by Rexler Research, for several years," he said quietly. "There was an ulterior motive in my putting you through the years from 1953 on, last Saturday. That purpose was to let you experience for yourself what I—we've been developing here in our laboratory."

John's eyes were wide.

"I see," he said. "So that when you told me I was to be murdered I wouldn't just shrug it off as an absurdity. But then, why don't you let me live out the next few days—"

"And be murdered in an If-world?" Dr. French said. "The human mind can't withstand that."

"I mean up to the point where I'm about to he killed," John said.

Dr. French shook his head. "We don't know the exact time or even the day. It's a variable. You will be dead by this Friday. That's all we know for sure."

"Simon told me enough of this Friday so that I couldn't go away without doing what I could to help," Melva said.

John looked from one to the other of them, nodding his head thoughtfully.

"And all the time I thought you were trying to find out all about me," he said. "That's why I had Melva arrested on what I thought would be groundless charges, to get her out of your reach until after Saturday." He looked past Dr. French to the window, a wondering incredulous light in his eyes. "This is so insane!" he exclaimed. "To be seriously discussing my coming murder!"

"I first found out about it almost a year ago," Dr. French said. "At first I wasn't too interested. But as the days went by—those in the future, I mean—I made up my mind to try to prevent your murder. I tried everything. Even if-futures in which I introduced hypothetical elements not predicted in flat-futures. In all possible futures you turned up murdered. Joe Pace was arrested, tried, and exonerated.

"Finally as a last resort I contacted you directly in the hopes that I could examine everything bearing on you. Whether Joe Pace killed you or not, only by solving the case that all possible futures show was never solved, and only by solving it before it took place, could I hope to save your life.

"In all the if-futures you are killed in dozens of different ways. Shot, poisoned, killed by a hit and run driver, thrown out the window of your office. The time of the murder varies from Tuesday morning to Friday afternoon of this week. All those details are variables. Your murder is an invariant. Unless we can find out who killed you. That, too, must be an invariant. It must be. We've got to find out *who* is going to kill you and try to prevent him."

"Why didn't you tell me all this that first day?" John demanded.

Dr. French shook his head. "You wouldn't have believed me. You would have thought me insane."

"That's probably true," John said. "Even now, with all the evidence I have from my own experience that your system of hypnosis contacts—if not a reality as genuine as this around us, at least the next thing to it, I have a hard time believing you enough to take this seriously." He stared at Dr. French speculatively.

"Where's the phone?" he asked abruptly. "I'll get Joe down here and we'll put him through the near future and see what he says. You say that in that thing Melva was in he will talk, so we can know what he's dreaming?"

"Yes," Dr. French said. "And we can learn what he's doing, or going to do, without him being able to keep still about it. Stay here. I'll get a phone and plug it in here."

"Well, Melva," John Dow said when Dr. French had gone, "this is more fantastic than the possibility that you actually would be wanted in some other city for something when I had the police arrest you."

"It certainly is," she said. Then they sat silently staring at each other.

Dr. French returned abruptly. The doctor plugged the phone into the baseboard phone outlet. John Dow calmly dialed the office and asked to be connected to Joe.

"Did he say when he would be back?" John asked. He hung up slowly, looking up at Dr. French.

"He's gone to the West Coast unexpectedly," he said. "He expects to be back tomorrow, but may have to stay longer. And he didn't say where he would be."

When he stopped, the only sound in the room was Melva's sharp intake of breath.

"Then it's too late," Dr. French interrupted the silence. "If he's to be the murderer he's already started his plan. He'll establish his alibi of being on the West Coast, and in some way return and kill you. Or maybe he hasn't really gone, and sometime after tonight he'll kill you. There's all sorts of ways he can work it." He studied John Dow speculatively. "Why don't you stay here?" he suggested. "We have living quarters in the building. You can stay here the rest of the week until after the danger is over. Does he know you came here?"

"No!" John exclaimed. "I just told him I was going out. For some reason I didn't tell him..." His voice drifted off. "I'll go home and have dinner, then come back this evening."

He took a folded blank check from his pocket and filled it out, then handed it to Melva.

"You'd better be on your way to Los Angeles," he said. "I'll be perfectly safe here. Joe, or no one else, can get at me here. This check is for the lawyer. I've made it out to you. When you get to Los Angeles give it to the lawyer." He smiled. "At least that part of the future won't come true."

"All right," Melva said, trying to smile. "But I'd rather stay with you until this is over."

"I'll be O.K.," John said confidently. "I'm warned. I know just about what to expect from Joe. I know him better than I know myself. And I'll be here where he can't get at me. I'll be back here tonight." He held out his hand, his smile one of dismissal.

Then she was gone.

"I'll be back about eight o'clock, doctor," John said. "I'll tell my wife I'm going to Washington or something. You'll be here?"

"I'll be here," Dr. French said.

"You know," John said, "the more I know you the more I like you. Did you know the controlling stock in Rexler had been sold?"

"No!" Dr. French said. "I thought Burk understood it wasn't to be sold under any circumstances!"

"Don't worry about it," John said. "I'm the one who bought it. You're going to have a bright future. I give you my word on that."

"Well, thank you," Dr. French said. "By the way, when you go down, don't say anything about this. I'll be here alone at eight o'clock, and the fewer people who know where you are, the less chance there is of Mr. Pace being able to find you."

"I know not to talk unnecessarily," John said laughing. "I'll be at the entrance at eight o'clock so you can be there and let me in."

He shook hands warmly with Dr. French, then left.

After he had gone, Dr. Simon French looked at the blanked expanse of the closed door. A full five minutes went by before he moved from where he stood.

Finally he sighed, as though awakening from a dream, and went to the door, opening it. Outside he went down the hall and opened the door to another loom and went in.

He crossed to another door and entered a small office. In one corner of the office was a desk littered with notes and records, some of them new, some from the vaults downstairs. Data on every detail of the near future that would affect mankind.

He looked down at those piles of information. Information he had vowed would never leave his hands to be read by someone not content to devote his life to pure research.

A bitter laugh erupted from his lips.

"Strange," his voice whispered in the silence of the room. "that I never thought to examine my own future and that of Rexler Research."

He bent down and opened the bottom drawer of his desk. When he straightened he was holding a gun in his hand, and on his lips was a sardonic smile.

There would be no risk. In every possible future the murder would remain unsolved.

John sat behind the desk in his office and relaxed. His fingers drummed the desktop for a moment and his brow furrowed into a frown of concentration. Finally the frown vanished and his mouth showed a satisfied smile.

He picked up his telephone and dialed a number.

Shortly: "Joe? Yes, I thought you'd catch on when I called from French's office. Yes, I'm sure of it now. I don't think we have to look any further. What makes me so sure?

"I never quite described Steffen Tombs to you, did I, Joe? Well, they're one and the same. Different names in two different worlds, but the same. What's that? Of course there's only one thing to do. We would have taken care of Tombs in due time— just as we'll take care of his counterpart. Dr. French.

"That's right, Joe. Take care of the matter. Nothing messy, you understand. Right. Call me later."

John Dow replaced the receiver and leaned back in his chair. That was that. And now he felt very tired and realized the strain of the past few days had been great. He must relax. And his family had received so little of his attention. He smiled when he thought of them.

There were no ifs or buts about Gloria and the children. Their love was an invariant.

He wondered what Gloria would have for dinner.

THE END

ABOUT ROG PHILLIPS

Rog Phillips...

...was born Roger Phillips Graham in Spokane, Washington in 1909. He started writing sci-fi stories during the 1940s for Ziff-Davis Publishing's two pulp giants, *Amazing Stories* and *Fantastic Adventures.* During this time he was one of the better writers in then-editor Ray Palmer's stable of steady contributors. Although he wrote many short stories, his real specialty was the short novel, of which he wrote dozens during his years at Ziff-Davis.

One of the high points in Phillips' career was the publication of his novelette, "Rat in the Skull" (contained in Armchair's "Science Fiction Gems, Vol. Two") which was nominated for a Hugo Award in 1959. Other memorable works were his novels "So Shall Ye Reap" and "The Involuntary Immortals," both originally published by Ziff Davis and later by Armchair. Phillips wrote under many assumed names, the most notable of which was Craig Browning. Phillips career was cut short by his early death in 1965.

If you've enjoyed this book, you will not want to miss these terrific titles…

ARMCHAIR SCI-FI & HORROR DOUBLE NOVELS, $12.95 each

D-41   **FULL CYCLE** by Clifford D. Simak
IT WAS THE DAY OF THE ROBOT by Frank Belknap Long

D-42   **THIS CROWDED EARTH** by Robert Bloch
REIGN OF THE TELEPUPPETS by Daniel Galouye

D-43   **THE CRISPIN AFFAIR** by Jack Sharkey
THE RED HELL OF JUPITER by Paul Ernst

D-44   **WE THE MACHINE** by Gerald Vance
PLANET OF DREAD by Dwight V. Swain

D-45   **THE STAR HUNTER** by Edmond Hamilton
THE ALIEN by Raymond F. Jones

D-46   **WORLD OF IF** by Rog Phillips
SLAVE RAIDERS FROM MERCURY by Don Wilcox

D-47   **THE ULTIMATE PERIL** by Robert Abernathy
PLANET OF SHAME by Bruce Elliot

D-48   **THE FLYING EYES** by J. Hunter Holly
SOME FABULOUS YONDER by Phillip Jose Farmer

D-49   **THE COSMIC BUNGLARS** by Geoff St. Reynard
THE BUTTONED SKY by Geoff St. Reynard

D-50   **TYRANTS OF TIME** by Milton Lesser
PARIAH PLANET by Murray Leinster

ARMCHAIR SCIENCE FICTION CLASSICS, $12.95 each

C-13   **SUNKEN WORLD**
by Stanton A. Coblentz

C-14   **THE LAST VIAL**
by Sam McClatchie, M. D.

C-15   **WE WHO SURVIVED (THE FIFTH ICE AGE)**
by Sterling Noel

ARMCHAIR MASTERS OF SCIENCE FICTION SERIES, $16.95 each

MS-5   **MASTERS OF SCIENCE FICTION, Vol. Five**
Winston K. Marks—Test Colony and other classics

MS-6   **MASTERS OF SCIENCE FICTION, Vol. Six**
Fritz Leiber—Deadly Moon and other classics

SENTENCED TO DEATH ON MERCURY!

In the most unbelievable manner possible, Lester Allison found himself hijacked to the planet Mercury. Once there he became a slave to a dying alien race, to be sold at auction to the highest bidder. However, the creature responsible for his kidnapping wasn't a yellow-skinned alien, but a scientist—a scientist from Earth itself, in league with the potentates of Mercury.

Allison might have resigned himself to his fate like the other humans who had come before him, but when a beautiful Earth woman came into danger, it set off a chain of events that threatened not only his life, but the lives of every living creature on the planet. A chain of events that culminated at Allison's scheduled execution: the Rite of the Floating Chop.

CAST OF CHARACTERS

LESTER ALLISON
All he wanted to do was have some fun at the local carnival. He didn't realize it meant a one-way ticket to Mercury.

JUNE O'NEIL
She was the first Earth female slave in Mercury's long history. And it caused a cultural uproar of unprecedented magnitude.

KILHIDE
He was probably as brilliant as any scientist back on Earth, but in the end he was just a vile traitor to his own race.

JO-JO-KAK
When you're 4,500 years old life can get a little boring, that is until a beautiful woman from Earth shows up.

SMITT
He'd been a slave on Mercury for a long time and he'd gotten used to it. Did he have any desire left for freedom?

TED TYNDALL
He might have been an okay guy back on Earth, but on Mercury you couldn't trust him when your back was turned.

SLAVE RAIDERS
FROM
MERCURY

By
DON WILCOX

ARMCHAIR FICTION
PO Box 4369, Medford, Oregon   97501-0168

*The original text of this novel was first
published by Ziff Davis Publishing*

Armchair Edition, Copyright 2012, by Gregory J.   Luce
All Rights Reserved

*For more information about Armchair Books and products, visit our
website at...*

www.armchairfiction.com

Or email us at...

armchairfiction@yahoo.com

CHAPTER ONE

"THIS way, ladies and gentlemen!" shouted the sideshow barker, pounding on a tom-tom. "Open to the public for the first time. The greatest mystery attraction ever offered for fifty cents. A rocket ship from the outside world!"

A few customers paid and passed through. Above the brightly painted canvas fence, the huge black chrysalis shaped hull gleamed in the midday sun. Lester Allison gazed. He dropped the wisp of foxtail grass from his teeth and edged toward the front of the crowd.

"Step right up, you handsome farmer boys," the barker sang out, with one eye on Allison, "It's brand new. There's no fake about it. It was found last week in a wheat field and this carnival bought it for your entertainment. Come one, come all, only fifty cents!"

Lester Allison yelled up at the speaker, "Who was in it when they found it?"

"Not a soul, my boy, not a soul."

"Then how'd it find its way to Earth?"

"Ah, there's the mystery! An empty ship from an outside world, and not a foot-track around it. Come in and get the whole story!"

Lester Allison looked around for someone to take in with him, but saw no one he knew. However, he gave a second look to the pretty girl who brushed past his shoulder.

The girl gave a quick anxious glance back through the crowd; apparently she was trying to get away from someone. She bolted through the canvas gateway without stopping to pay.

"Hold on, lady!" The barker made a pass at her.

"Here," said Lester Allison, slapping down a dollar. "For two."

"Thanks so much," the girl breathed a moment later. Lester Allison followed her through the open airlocks into the black ship.

"The luck's all mine," he said.

"Mine," said the girl, "if he doesn't follow me in, that is," she talked excitedly, "I'm running away—from home."

They pushed through the cluster of spectators within the ship.

"You oughtn't to wear such a bright yellow dress if you're trying to make a getaway. It caught my eye first thing—it and the yellow hat and your brown hair and—"

At a curious smile from the girl, Allison concluded he'd better not catalog any more of the items about her appearance that had attracted him. Nevertheless his gaze lingered on her pretty face.

"Pretty young to be running away, aren't you?"

Suddenly her dark eyes were intent on the door.

"Oh—" she began distressedly.

A slender young man came in and looked about furtively. The moment he spied the girl, he marched back to her.

"All right for you, June O'Neil," he said in a surly voice. "Your dad said come home. He meant it, too. He's sober and he's mad."

June O'Neil refused to speak. The young man tried to take her arm. She jerked away and scrunched down in her seat in the ship. He sat down beside her.

"Big-hearted of you," he said sarcastically, "to make me pay fifty cents to come in here and get you."

"You haven't got me," said the girl.

"Oh, *no?* Don't make me laugh…"

"Listen, Ted Tyndall," The girl's voice was low but every word was packed with fury, and the flash of her dark eyes gave Lester Allison a quickened heartbeat.

"I'm not coming home. That's final. I've had all of home and drunken fathers and quarrelsome boy friends that I can stand."

"*Zat* so?" Ted Tyndall mocked. Then his eyes took in Lester Allison, who stood, an easy six feet of country-bred manhood, at the other side of June's chair.

"Who's that?"

"I don't know," said June O'Neil quietly.

"I'm Lester Allison." The words were accompanied by a genial smile, which met with an expressionless stare from Ted Tyndall.

THE sideshow barker stepped inside the rocket ship and rapped for attention.

"Ladies and gentlemen…" (The group was mostly men; there chanced to be only one other lady besides June O'Neil.) "You are now in the main cabin of a mystery space ship whose secrets not only baffle science, they even baffle me. Mystery Number One: no controls are visible. Mystery Number Two: as I walk to the front of the cabin, the airlocks automatically close."

With a *swish* the doors folded, to become an imperceptible part of the black metal walls.

Ted Tyndall grumbled to the girl, "Now see what you've done. I'm stuck here for a lecture."

By this time most of the eighteen or twenty spectators were seated in the deep-cushioned chairs. Lester Allison started toward a seat as the carnival man continued.

"Mystery Number Three: the black metal of this ship is unlike anything found on this earth—"

Brmmm-brrr-wrrr-wham!

LESTER ALLISON awakened with the vague feeling that the universe had jumped a cog.

That dull aching roar—most of it seemed to be in his head. Some of it came through the wall that cramped his shoulder. He was too groggy to open his eyes. What a clamor of voices! That woman's unrelenting scream—again and again and again. Men shouting and wrangling and fighting. And, near at hand, the voice of that pretty girl, June O'Neil, her low spoken words fraught with terror. Lester Allison opened his eyes.

"He's alive, didn't I tell you?" the girl gasped.

Ted Tyndall's only response was, "Get me out of here! What the hell—"

"But he's hurt...he might be dying!" The girl's hands tugged at Allison's shoulders.

"Let him rot!" Ted Tyndall fairly screamed. "Get me back to the ground!"

Lester Allison took a deep breath and rolled onto his elbows and knees.

"I'm all right," he mumbled. "A little stunned. That sudden fall—"

His words were lost against the continual screaming. He staggered to his feet.

He saw June O'Neil's frightened, imploring face and heard her say, "No one knows why we took off. No one knows what to do."

Allison's attention turned to the distant sun blazing out of a black sky. It shot through the front cabin window and illuminated the frantic figures chasing through the aisles of the space ship. Some stood at the windows paralyzed with fear; some were fighting. Allison moved up the aisle toward the fight. Three or four enraged men had closed in on the carnival barker.

"You trapped us, you lousy—"

"I did not!"

"Get us back to Earth or we'll kill you!"

"What's the game, you crazy—"

"I tell you I didn't—" the barker protested.

"This knife means business…"

The sun flashed from the open pocketknife. The carnival man backed into a corner.

"Don't be a fool!" Allison snapped as he pushed through to the chief threatener. "Don't—"

HE caught the wrist that held the weapon, bore down with severe strength, and faced the threatener.

"Take it easy, friend."

"Take it easy! This fellow coaxed us in, didn't he? And locked the doors and—" The struggling man's grip relaxed as Allison's steel fingers tightened. The knife dropped.

"Let it lay," Allison snapped. "And don't be simple. That carnival guy's no space pilot. He's not *that* smart!"

Eyes turned toward the barker, whose jaw dropped with a comical effect. One of the threateners snorted, another chuckled, and the situation eased.

"Besides," Allison went on, "where are the controls? There aren't any. Say—how the heck does this thing operate, anyway?"

Naturally no one on board could answer that question. Lester Allison calmly picked up the pocketknife, folded it and slipped it into the owner's jacket.

"Hey—where do you think we're heading for?" another passenger spoke up.

Allison glanced out the window. "Either Mercury or Venus, near as I can judge. But probably Mercury, because we seem to be heading pretty close to the sun—and Mercury's the planet nearest the sun."

"Mercury..." the sideshow barker puffed. "And I only charged you fifty cents. Am I a dope!"

Ted Tyndall made his voice heard. "All right, smart fellow, if you know all the answers, turn us back."

Lester Allison's eyes roved along the walls hopefully. He wondered whether the, adjoining rooms might contain the answer. However, some of the men who had had time to explore shook their heads.

"We've searched high and low," said a one-armed man, "There's food and water and sanitary facilities, but nothing that looks like a control lever."

"Then we're in for a space jaunt," Allison muttered, "We may as well stop howling and make up our minds to it."

The other lady passenger, who had become hysterical, stopped crying for a moment, and then burst out afresh.

Ted Tyndall yowled, "You mean we can't get home tonight?"

"No, dear," the carnival barker mocked, mopping his forehead. "Better drop a note to mamma."

"Shut up, you damned—"

"Sit down!" Allison cracked the command, and Tyndall obeyed. "We've had enough roughhouse. Whatever we're in for, we may as well have order."

"You're elected to keep it," said the carnival barker.

Whether or not the barker meant it for a taunt, Lester Allison took it as a challenge. He looked from one to another of his fellow passengers.

An odd assortment, surely. A fat unshaved tramp, a one-armed man, a poorly dressed Negro, a bewildered old man who was deaf, several men who might have been machinists or farmers or white collar workers.

"You're elected," another of the men echoed.

In that moment Lester Allison forgot he was only twenty-three years old and that most of those years had gone into handling stubborn mules and running farm machinery. His eyes turned toward the woman who stood at the rear window, crying hysterically.

"Does anyone here know that woman?" he asked. No one did. He walked back to her. "Lady, we're going to put you in a room by yourself until you get quiet."

Immediately the terrified crying ceased. Quiet reigned. From that moment Lester Allison's authority was established. Whatever unknown destiny awaited the ship, for the present he was its master.

CHAPTER TWO
Inhabited Chasms

MERCURY grew like a crescent-shaped cloud bearing down upon the nose of the space ship. By this time the sun was far to the side. Lester Allison watched and wondered how soon the ship would cut its speed. A queer feeling, being tossed through the universe at the whims of—well, of *what?*

The men hovered close about Allison. No one talked. Everything had been talked out. Now there was nothing left but to wait and watch their common fate unfold.

Through Lester Allison's mind surged the memories of recent hours. The hysterical woman's shocking suicide…the bottle of deadly poison…the erratic note that proved she had been frightened crazy…

Allison had taken the bottle and hid it within his pocketbook for safekeeping. As soon as the dead body had been given a space burial, via the disposal chute, Allison had diverted the passengers' morbid thoughts as best he could.

Games had proved the best way. He had had the men make some bean shooters—bean shooting had been a favorite sport in his own boyhood—and he had organized a bean shooting tournament, good for several hours. But as the planet Mercury grew larger, the contestants' nerves became less steady, and the games had petered out.

When most of the passengers were asleep, June O'Neil came to Allison at the front window to help him keep watch. This hour would burn deep into his memory.

"You aren't a bit scared, are you?" he said.

"I haven't been since you took over. Whatever may come to us, there's nothing we can do now."

Then the girl laughed in a quiet confidential way. "Really, it's almost funny. All these men try to help me keep my courage up, and I think they're worse scared than I am."

Allison smiled at that, and his eyes looked at her long and intently. He had never before in his life been so impressed by a girl's spirit, nor so stirred by a girl's beauty.

To change the subject he said, "Is the boy friend still sulking? Don't worry, he'll come out of it."

June O'Neil blushed with resentment, "He's *not* my boy friend."

A short while later her words still echoed in Allison's mind as the girl stood silently beside him. Ted Tyndall was at the other side of her, and silent passengers were all around. The great unfathomable mass of Mercury grew closer, half lighted, half shadowed. They were headed toward the line that divided the misty white surface from the dark side of the planet.

"Stormy over there," said Allison, pointing.

"I could do with a storm," grunted the carnival barker. "Anything to break the monotony…"

"We're gonna crash…we're gonna crash!" Ted Tyndall gasped the words over and over.

The purring ship plummeted down, down through the clouds, through layers of blackness and brown twilight and gray fog. Down between banks of mountains, down—

"We're headed for that abyss," Allison muttered.

"*Which* abyss?" one of the others asked in an alarmed tone.

They watched in awe as the vast crevasses among the mountains gaped larger. The whole landscape was stitched with ragged gashes. Now they recalled their previous discussions about Mercury. How the planet always kept the same face to the sun. How hot it would be—and what the effects of the uneven heating might have.

"SEE any signs of civilization?" someone asked Allison.

The answer was obvious. On the surface, there wasn't any sign of life.

Was it at all possible that somewhere within those jagged depths there was a mind that contrived to direct their course so skillfully? Down into a funnel of pitch blackness they slowly coasted. Interminably down, like a car on an endless grade. When at last their eyes saw light again, it was artificial light…the dull red of flares reflected from red rock walls.

They stopped.

The airlocks opened. A puff of warm air blew in. Heavy atmosphere was tinged with odors that were at once mellow and pungent. Allison sniffed and took a deep breath. He felt puffy enough to float, the air was so buoyant and the gravity so light.

He led the way out, cautiously at first; then, at the sound of friendly human voices, he dropped all restraints. His passengers filed out after him, bounding and leaping and striding, curious at the sensation of new power in their feet and legs.

They were greeted by a volley of welcomes that figuratively brought them back to Earth. Welcomes shouted in good American slang—a puzzling thing, for they had conjured up all manner of perilous beasts and boiling cauldrons in their private nightmares.

But at the shouts of "What's happened back in America?" and "Give us all the news!" and "Who's president now?" and "Anybody here from Indiana?" all dangers seemed suddenly removed, or at least postponed.

The questions came from a dozen or more half-uniformed men, who passed out handshakes indiscriminately and made the robot ship's eighteen captives feel like prodigal sons. Then—

"A girl…" one of them uttered. All the uniformed men quieted, somewhat in awe, Allison thought, as if a fear or dread came into their thoughts.

"Who's in charge here?" Allison inquired.

An uncomfortable shrug of uniformed shoulders.

"In his laboratory. He'll drop around and take care of you after awhile," one of them finally answered.

"Who are you men, and what are you doing here?" Allison demanded.

The men glanced at each other and at their own distinctive garb; they seemed loath to answer. A curiously uniform group—all of them well-built men, youngish, perfect pictures of good health. The red lights gleamed upward across their muscular bodies. They were half-naked, like Egyptian gods.

The form-fitting garments about their loins and the mantelets on their shoulders were of fine mesh, woven from some unfamiliar red metal. Most of the brilliant mantelets were decorated with vertical white stripes—one over each shoulder or in some cases two.

"We're entitled to an explanation." Allison bit his words off carefully. "We've been taken against our wishes."

A man with double stripes over his shoulders answered, and there was a note of pathos in his voice.

"It is not our part to make explanations. We are…slaves."

"SLAVES—of *what?*"

"Of the Dazzalox."

"The dazzle—*what?*"

"The Dazzalox—the natives of this underground world. We were brought to Mercury by the robot ship, the same as you. You will soon be sold as slaves too—though the market is slumping just now, owing to the current deaths of two Dazzalox potentates.

"But no matter what happens to the market price," the man spoke as matter-of-factly as if he had been discussing the price of milk, "you'll soon be slaves too."

"The hell we will!" Allison's belligerent attitude only evoked smiles from the mantled men. They recalled that they too had bristled with resistance when they first came.

Allison's men began to mutter with anger, and their young leader voiced their sentiments.

"See here, we've come here by mistake. We need food and water, and a chance to rest before we start back."

At this all of the slaves laughed. Then the double-striped spokesman said:

"Don't mind us. We know just how you feel, but you don't realize what a trap you've fallen into. Take it easy and you'll be better off. Make yourselves comfortable on those circular benches and we'll see that you get some food and rest first thing. But as for starting back—forget it."

THE EXOTIC food might have been hothouse products: fruits and vegetables and nuts—rich blends of flavors and aromas and colors. Allison wasn't surprised that some of his men couldn't eat. The aged deaf man was definitely ill. Ted Tyndall had apparently lost all appetite.

But June O'Neil ate with relish. The sideshow barker and the man who had once threatened him with a knife feasted and joked together like old cronies on a picnic.

A deep-toned musical note resounded through a hundred distant caverns, and some of the slaves started away. Lester Allison finished his meal and started after one of them. A few light-footed bounds and he caught up.

"My name's Smitt." The man with the double stripes on each shoulder offered a friendly hand. "You want to look around, do you? I'm off duty now. On my way to the funeral—or rather funerals. Two of them. Big events on the Dazzalox social calendar. They love their funerals…or *farewells,* as they prefer to call them…sure, come along."

The deep-throated tone sounded again through the maze of red caverns. Allison glanced back at his party—they were stretched out on benches. Apparently they were in no danger. A few one-stripers were walking among them.

Smitt led the way over a red metal bridge that crossed a tiny gushing rivulet many feet below.

"We leave the Red Suburb here," Smitt said. "From this point on is the civilization of the Dazzalox—a dying race, and the proudest, haughtiest, most ostentatious sons-of-guns you ever saw. We slaves retreat to the Red Suburb in our time off, but most of the time we're at work here in the main city. Notice the change of colors?"

Allison saw that the red rock ended. Ahead were higher walls that stretched upward like fortresses of tightly packed columns—greens and blues and blacks. Apparently nature's tricks of heating and cooling accounted for these formations.

"A fascinating staircase there," Allison remarked.

"Thousands of years old, they say. My owner lives up there."

ALLISON'S eyes followed the magnificent sweep of the stairs toward the spacious shelf in the wall toward the roof of the cavern. It was too lofty for one to see into the home, but the rows of torches burning along the upper levels indicated a wealthy and pretentious built-in mansion.

"My owner's name is Naf," Smitt continued. "Rich and lazy. Sleeps so much that I have a lot of time—more than most of the slaves."

"Is Naf retired?"

"Rather. Everyone's retired here except us slaves. And even we are used more for displays and ceremonies than for handwork. Of course we gather and distribute the food. But the necessities of life were so well planned a few centuries ago that things almost take care of themselves—such as the gardens and underground orchards. Things live an interminably long time here, plants and people both."

They hiked along the corridors and riverside streets at a good pace. All of Allison's senses were on the alert, but he had yet to see his first Dazzalox.

He asked, "What do they do to pass their time?"

Smitt laughed. "Well, not very much. They polish up their old traditions and have funerals and bloodless wars and bragging parties and feasts. But they don't *do* anything— except eat and sleep. I've watched them for thirty years."

Allison gave a skeptical look, for Smitt didn't appear to be more than twenty-five.

"For thirty years," Smitt repeated, "and when I stop to realize that the older ones have gone on this way for centuries, I say to myself, 'No wonder they're ready to walk into their graves with their eyes wide open.' "

Bewilderment was piling upon Allison almost too fast. By this time he had viewed six magnificent staircases cut in deep-colored rocks and polished from ages of use. His eyes were dancing from the rows of luminous purplish white lamps that flanked the floor-ways. His ears rang with the untiring echoes of the funeral gong, drowned now and then by spouting waterfalls. Now he followed up a long narrow clay ramp, at last to look down upon a breathtaking sight.

"A stadium!" he gasped. "An underground stadium…"

"They call it the Grand March."

From above the tiers of seats they looked down upon the wide-paved parade ground that ran from end to end like an elongated gridiron. The whole structure filled a vast underground valley.

"My stars...there's room for two or three hundred thousand people!" Allison exclaimed.

"And only five thousand to fill it. A dying race. The native laborers died off a few centuries ago. The gardens needed so little care that the laborers became a superfluous class, who finally either died from misery or from trying to migrate under unfavorable conditions.

"Well, there's your five thousand," Smitt pointed down to the lower, sparsely filled tiers, "waiting for the first of the day's funerals."

Allison viewed the scattered audience incredulously.

"But those are people—humans."

"No, they're Dazzalox," said Smitt. "You'll notice a pronounced difference on closer inspection."

THE flame of excited curiosity in Allison leaped up. "They stand and walk and sit like ordinary people. A little more spring and hop to their step—but the gravity could account for that. Do they have human natures?"

"That depends upon what you mean. Lots of things pass for human nature," Smitt observed. "Most of it, I've noticed, has a lot to do with animal nature. These Dazzalox are as simple as children and as savage as beasts. Here come a couple of them now."

The two men slipped back into a convenient hiding nook, from which they could watch at their leisure without having to make any explanations for Allison's presence. The two Dazzalox—a male and a female—ascended the steps to take seats in the upper tier.

They were ornately dressed in highly colored mesh clothing. They were stockily bodied, but their bare legs were thin and sinewy, and their hard crusty bare feet were as ugly as an insect's.

"Kub-a-zaz-ola-jojo-kak—"

Now Allison saw his face. The male Dazzalox spoke in a metallic voice. It was an expressive face, but it looked as if it were made out of yellow chalk. The female's face was also of a single solid color, a slightly paler yellow. The female scolded like a bird.

"Is that a fair sample?" Allison asked. "What's wrong with their hands and feet?"

"Nothing. Adapted to living in rocks," said Smitt. "Did you notice their double eyebrows? Eyebrows below the eyes as well as above. I suppose their ancestors in the dim past enjoyed sunshine, but now most of their light comes from near the floors. *Lukle* gas torches. They've got *lukle* gas to burn, and plenty of other gases for other purposes."

"What are they saying?"

Smitt listened for a moment. "They're talking about the funeral that will follow this one. It's high time for old Jo-jo-kak to die, they say, because he's forty-five hundred years old."

"Forty-five hundred!"

"That's not as bad as it sounds, because we get a year here for every eighty-eight Earth days. By Earth time he's more than a thousand years old."

"But a thousand!" Allison searched his informant's face to make sure he wasn't being kidded. "Say, do they have old age pensions here?"

Smitt laughed, "If they did most everyone would be on the rolls. Long life and a low birth rate are the custom here. However, it isn't unknown for Dazzalox who are several hundred years old to still have children. Old Jo-jo-kak, for instance. Listen—"

The Dazzalox couple were still talking about old Jo-jo-kak, and Smitt interpreted their words.

"The language is simple. You'll get onto it in no time. Unless, of course, you decide to—er—go back right away," Smitt added with a wink.

"Sarcasm never ran a space ship," Allison retorted. "Maybe that's why you're still here."

SMITT laughed again, and Allison realized that in the past eventful hour a bond of friendship had sprung up between them.

"And speaking of space ships," said Lester Allison, "there's something that's burning me up. How the devil can this dying race of powdery-faced Dazzalox, who evidently don't have electric light, or automobiles, or radios—how the devil can they have robot space ships that slip out and gather up a load of Earth folks and chase back again like a homing pigeon?

"It's inconsistent," he continued. "There's a loose screw somewhere around here, and it's beginning to rattle in my ears worse than that funeral bell."

"Ah," Smitt sighed. "You're hot on the trail of the *brains* in this set-up. There's brains in these hills, all right. Sometime soon I'll give you a look behind the scenes, and you can draw your own conclusions."

Allison pondered his friend's words only to find that the mystery deepened.

The brains of this set-up?

Allison recalled an answer some slave had given him when he had just arrived: "The one in charge is in his *lab*."

Well, whoever he was—whether man or beast or robot or spirit—Allison resolved to see him.

The funeral gong silenced and the first of the farewell processions came into view.

CHAPTER THREE
The Symbol of Death

THE central figure of the funeral procession was an old male Dazzalox with long yellow hair who stood in the center of a moving platform waving his arms at the crowd.

"Where's the corpse?" Allison asked.

"That's it—the old man waving his arms. He'll be a corpse in a few minutes."

Allison was aghast. "But why?"

"Because this is his day to die."

"You mean he has to die, because it's his turn or something?"

"He *wants* to die. He's lived until he's tired of living. There's no sense waiting until you die a natural death here in Mercury. It just isn't being done. Voluntary deaths are getting more popular right along because—well, after all, it's the one way the Dazzalox have of escaping boredom.

"The old man set the date for this event a year or so ago. The same with Jo-jo-kak. It's the only pleasure these fellows have left on their social calendars."

"Pleasure?" Allison muttered. "Darned if I can see how death could be a pleasure."

"You aren't a thousand years old," Smitt retorted wisely, "But you can see for yourself that it *is* a pleasure for that old gent."

The procession was directly below them now. The crowd cheered in high chirping voices. Here and there the old man had the procession stop while he divested himself of a short speech, with many a vigorous shout and gesture.

"All memorized and practiced in private," said Smitt, "My owner, Naf, is working on his farewell now, though he hasn't set the date yet."

The color scheme of the procession, Allison noticed, was simple but striking. The old man with the yellow hair was dressed from head to foot in a flowing costume of bold black, with a black mask and black and white-striped anklets.

The moving platform was painted in black and white bars, and the human slaves who bore it wore mantelets with black and white stripes.

At last the procession came to a stop at the remote end of the Grand March, at a door in the rock wall also marked *with black and white vertical bars.*

"Those stripes must be the symbol of death," Allison remarked.

Smitt nodded. "The door leads into a long tunnel that is filled with death gas. Another bounty of nature. Death gas is plentiful and it provides a painless way to die. Any slave would be happy if he only believed he would eventually die by death gas, rather than by some Dazzalox violence—the Floating Chop, for instance."

The old man's last moment had come and he apparently gloried in it. He gave a magnificent bow arid, amid a flood of farewell cheers, leaped nimbly down from the platform and marched to the door. A slave opened it, the old man went in and the door closed...

"What happens to the body?" Allison whispered after silent minutes.

"Bountiful nature comes to the rescue again. The body remains in the tunnel untouched, but twice each year—that is, every forty-four days, Earth time—the boiling seas from the sun side overflow through all these caverns and sweep everything away. The people's homes, of course, are all high above the flood level, but the river beds and streets are washed clean."

ALLISON abruptly rose. "I'm going back to the Red Suburb," he announced.

"Come back in an hour or two," said Smitt, "if you want to see old Jo-jo-kak's farewell. In fact you might as well wait right here. There won't be anything going on until it's over. What's the hurry?"

"I just remembered something." Allison gave a wave and hurried off.

Smitt followed after him. "You'll get a kick out of old Jo-jo-kak. He's a bit eccentric... Allison, what the hell—"

Allison bounded down the long clay ramp with Smitt at his heels.

"That black and white door," Allison panted, and kept on running. "I just remembered there was a door marked like that back at the Red Suburb. My folks don't know the danger."

"Wait, let me explain!" But Smitt was losing ground. However, Allison missed the way and came to a stop in a dead end and then realized that his guide was still indispensable.

"That striped door is safe; that is, none of your gang will get in there by mistake. It's there for a purpose."

More explanation was sought in Allison's searching gaze. Smitt tried to wave the matter aside.

"Hell, quit worrying about things. You're well built and you'll be a cinch for the slave market. No striped door is gonna cross your path."

Allison stared. "What are you driving at?"

"Well, you may have noticed that all of us slaves fall into a uniform physical type. That's been a tradition since the first load of slaves came in—about forty years ago. The "boss" found out that the Dazzalox like well-built young American men, so that's what he gives them. People who don't fall into that classification are—er—spared the humiliation of becoming slaves."

"*How?*"

"By a painless process of elimination—the striped door. It's really a kindness, in comparison to—"

"*Kindness?*" Allison blurted out. He grabbed Smitt by the arms and stared at him hard. "They'd better not try any *kindness* on my group."

Smitt smiled calmly. "Relax. Don't misunderstand. I'm not hard-boiled. Down here the fates are different. I've learned to accept them. You'll have to, too."

"All right. What's the bad news?"

"Well, I glanced at your group. It was plain as day that there were five...uh..."unsuitable" ones out of your eighteen. By this time they have culled out—by way of the striped door."

"*Which five?*" Allison shouted.

"The deaf old man, the Negro...but only because he was sick...the one-armed man, the fat tramp, and...of course...the girl."

Down the cavernous lane they flew, Allison ahead, Smitt sailing after him in tow like a kite. When the red bridge came in sight, the gasping slave was left behind. Allison raced into the Red Suburb. A single glance at his group lying around on the benches, and he knew at once that some were missing.

"Where's June O'Neil?" he blurted to the first person he reached.

"Whose business is it?" Ted Tyndall retorted with a jealous smirk.

"*Where is she?*" Allison clutched the fellow by the shoulder.

"Damn it, what's the difference?" Tyndall snarled. "You're nothing to her. Lay off..."

TED TYNDALL sprawled to the ground without ever knowing what hit him. Other members of the party hurried up to Allison.

"She and some of the others went off with a fellow in a shiny white suit—a sort of big shot."

"*Which way?*" Allison fairly screamed.

"Up toward that striped door."

The men swarmed after Allison as he raced up the red rock path. He bounded against the striped metal panel. It opened inward. Blackness. Blackness and a strangely sweet smell like old flowers pressed in a book.

"Your flashlight," Allison barked at one of the men.

"It's dead."

"Then keep the door open for me—but don't breathe any of the air."

Allison took a breath, entered, groped along the jagged walls, lost himself in the blackness. In two minutes he was back, bearing a dead body. It was the one-armed man.

He caught his breath and rushed back in. Another man followed him. Two minutes...three... The other man returned empty-handed. Three and a half minutes—four—Allison stumbled out again, also empty-handed. He started to speak but fainted instead, and for a minute or two he was out.

"It's a death trap," the other man gasped. "We located three more bodies—the old man, the Negro, and fat Tubby. Didn't find the girl, did you, Allison?"

Allison shook his head. He breathed heavily, got up on his knees.

"I'm going back," he muttered.

"Give yourself a rest," said the man who had accompanied him. "Let someone else go."

The man's eyes turned to the sideshow barker, who quickly excused himself.

"I've got a weak heart," said the barker. "Let Tyndall go. He's got a crush on the girl."

Tyndall sneered. "The girl ain't in there."

"How do you know?" Allison growled, pulling himself to his feet dizzily.

"I saw the head man lead her on down that path," said Tyndall.

Allison bit his lips to keep from flying into a rage. He looked down at the corpse of the one-armed man.

"Leave the other bodies where they are," he said. "I'll be back later."

"And where are you going?" asked a slave with single stripes over his shoulders. Allison made no answer.

The one-striped slave snapped in an authoritative tone, "I have orders for thirteen new men. Get yourselves into these slave uniforms and memorize this list of rules. You are to be on the floor of the sales cavern in time to catch the funeral crowd. You've got less than two hours, and these rules are complicated, so get busy."

Allison grabbed the pile of slave uniforms and hurled them across the red rock floor.

"I'll take this up with the boss." he said. "Where do I find him?"

"At the end of this path," said the one-striper, "but it's your neck…"

CHAPTER FOUR
A Female Slave

"THE brains of this set-up," Allison muttered to himself as he sprinted. "A look behind the scenes—"

He stopped. Not twenty-five yards ahead of him the red rock path abruptly turned into an ornate entrance in the rock wall. Under red lights, the red stone carvings of the doorway glowed like a filigree of burning vines.

"The boss likes luxury," thought Allison.

A hum of motors came from within the place, smooth rhythmic sounds, music to one who appreciates fine machinery. A strangely discordant sound came from somewhere overhead. A ragged *tap-tap-tapping* on stone. Allison looked up.

His eyes beheld a solitary figure coming down a zigzag path. Where the trail came from Allison had no idea, but obviously it connected some other part of the maze of caverns to this red rock sanctuary of the big boss.

The solitary figure was a stone's throw above Allison, with several switchbacks to go before he got down to the red rock level on which Allison stood. Though he tapped along at a lively gait, apparently he was an old, old man—no, a Dazzalox.

His yellow face was wrinkled. His coppery hair hung long and uneven, his double eyebrows almost concealed his tiny eyes, although his head was bent downward. The tapping came from a bright copper-colored sword, which he used as a cane.

All this Allison caught in a glance.

"*That* can't be the head alien," he muttered. He ran on. He soon approached a doorway with a sign on it in English:

RING BEFORE ENTERING

Allison was in no mood to heed signs.

He had a single purpose: to make certain June O'Neil was alive and safe. He had thrown all caution to the wind. Now he dashed through the doorway and down a long glass-walled corridor. To his amazement this place was electrically lighted and had all the look of a gigantic subterranean power station.

"June!" he shouted. "June O'Neil!" His voice faded off into the hum of machines. He ran past room after room, and the passing sights fairly took his breath away. Everywhere were manifestations of power.

"June O'Neil!"

No answer, but the grinding of automatic engines came back, rolling out yards of shining metal goods. Ladles pouring molten red metal into ingots. Presses stamping out silvery ornaments. Charts of space routes flashing in neon. Automatic jewel cutters playing with precious stones under violet spotlights. Allison raced on. His voice rang weirdly.

He stopped to listen. Footsteps sounded dangerously behind him. He whirled to see a one-striper swing a club at his head. He went down.

His consciousness flashed back almost at once—before his captor got his hands and feet tied, in fact—but he was too helpless to struggle.

"Awake, eh? Hate to do this, brother," he heard the human slave mumble, "but orders are orders. Kilhide doesn't tolerate any rebellion."

Allison grunted sourly. "So that's his name."

"The boss'll have something to say to you. And then, if I was you, I'd get into a slave uniform like I was told."

The slave picked up Allison bodily and carried him back through the corridors to a brilliantly lighted room.

"Here's your rebel, Mr. Kilhide," said the one-striped slave. He eased Allison to the carpeted floor. Then at a flick of the finger from Kilhide in the farther end of the room, he went out.

ALLISON got his slightly blurred eyes into focus—and gasped. There before him sat the most imperious, the most uncommonly handsome individual he had ever seen. Dark, luxurious hair, swept back rebelliously over a sensitive brow. Chiseled, somewhat disdainful nostrils. A smooth, creamy brown complexion that was yet a little too smooth, a little too bland. And large brown eyes, intelligent, magnetic, which sparkled even in repose—but sparkled with malice.

If Kilhide heard Allison's little gasp of astonishment, however, he ignored it completely. It was only too evident that there was someone or something in the other end of the long room with which Kilhide was preoccupied. With the man's first words Allison understood.

"Now, Miss O'Neil, you realize how lucky you are that I brought you here instead of sending you with the others," said Kilhide's smooth oily voice.

Lester Allison gave a deep sigh. To know that June O'Neil was alive was cooling water to his thirsty soul. He could breathe again. The knots cut his wrists and ankles, his head hummed with pain where the club had struck him, but these things were trifles. June O'Neil was alive.

By squirming about Allison could see her at the farther end of the sumptuous parlor. She was looking at him; her dark eyes glistened and her firm breasts heaved. Allison could hear her strained breathing.

"Don't mind that wretch, my dear," said Kilhide, jerking a thumb toward Allison, "I get a problem child or two with every boatload. One snap of my fingers and they line up. More coffee? That's my own brand."

Allison had hated this man enough, sight unseen. But to find him a devilishly handsome American, gloating in riches gained from selling his fellow Americans into slavery—and now trying to twist this innocent girl around his little finger—well, it was enough to inflame Allison to thoughts of murder. But just now all he could do was listen. Kilhide apparently wasn't aware that his unctuous voice carried through the room.

"As I was saying, Miss O'Neil—June, if you don't mind—my fabulous wealth and my unlimited powers have come to me because I'm...let's say...smart. I know exactly how to play ball with these wealthy old Dazzalox potentates. From the day I cracked up with my trial rocket ship fifty years ago, I've played to their whims like nobody's business. Because I'm...smart."

"I see," said June O'Neil, trying not to let her eyes drift toward Allison.

"I give them everything they want. They give me everything *I* want. At first they were going to make a slave of me, but I convinced them they could have many more slaves if they would help me build a ship. I lost my first robot ship, but the second brought home the bacon."

"Why didn't you go back yourself?" the girl asked.

"To the Earth? Hell, what's Earth got that I haven't got! Nothing but more stupid people."

"Oh." June shuddered to think that any human being could be so saturated with disdain and egotism. She wanted to run, but she only sat, frozen, keeping one eye on Lester Allison.

"I suppose you think I can't keep up with Earth's scientific developments, living alone down here among these other 'lesser" Earthlings," Kilhide said.

June didn't answer. She was terrified, and obviously there was no way to break out of the situation.

"Well, you're wrong," said Kilhide. "I get new ideas from every boatload of slaves. There are always some newspapers in the men's pockets, and scientific discoveries are now regularly reported in the press. Whatever the Earth is building I eventually find out about—and duplicate. And do a better job of it, because my various red and black metals are superior to any steels or tungstens on Earth. Besides," the man stroked his little trick mustache, "I'm...smart."

"Mr. Kilhide," the girl rose and spoke boldly, "do me a favor."

"I'm doing you a favor, child. I'm going to marry you."

THE girl shrank back to her chair.

"What more could you ask?" said Kilhide with an arrogant smile. And he was that egotistical that he meant it.

"Send me back to Earth," said the girl weakly.

Kilhide snorted. "Earth! That's a helluva thing to ask! You told me you ran away from home. Well, you're away. Stay here. It's healthy. You can live for hundreds of years. The food gives you what you need to keep young. I've got everything you need," he made an elegant gesture toward the luxurious furnishings of the room. "To keep you happy. And I mean, happy."

He came close to June and tried to gather her fingers into his hands. She drew back. He laughed.

"You're afraid, child. You needn't be. Those rock-sleepers, the Dazzalox, won't know you're here, for they rarely come back to this end of the caverns, and the human slaves won't dare bother you."

Kilhide broke off his rhapsody to cast a glance at Allison, whom he had considered to be out of hearing.

He growled, "What are *you* gawking at?" He flung a mesh-covered sofa pillow at Allison's head, then strode down the room and painstakingly packed it against the other's face with a disdainful foot.

"I'm doing you a favor, June," Kilhide resumed in his confidential voice when he had walked back to her. "Of all the women the robot ship has brought here, not a one has been allowed to live more than a few minutes after arriving. In fact, the Dazzalox have never even seen an Earth woman."

A ragged *tap-tap-tap* sounded dimly from a corridor.

"Strange you didn't sell women for slaves," June O'Neil said a little sharply.

"Not at all," said Kilhide, too conceited to note the sarcasm. "Men have made perfect slaves. No use upsetting an established system. The Dazzalox like their traditions let alone. Moreover," the speaker again stroked his trick mustache, "since none of the women who came were both beautiful and intelligent, I've saved myself any annoyance by quickly disposing of them—*painlessly.*"

The girl winced. The *tap-tap-tapping* grew closer. Kilhide was too intent upon his purpose to notice it.

"You think me cruel, I suppose, but you're wrong, I'm just being practical…more coffee?"

"Please. It so strengthens one, you know," June almost hissed.

Kilhide started toward an adjoining room for more of his prided beverage, "By the time I return, I expect you to say that you are ready to marry me."

"The answer will still be no," said June O'Neil. "Most definitely."

Kilhide flushed, "May I politely remind you of the striped door we passed a short time ago?"

June fought the surge of anger within her.

"You may," she said shortly. "But first, the coffee...please?"

By this time Allison had shaken out from under the metallic pillow sufficiently to see the red flush that leaped to Kilhide's face. The haughty individual hesitated uncertainly in the doorway, then stomped into the adjoining room.

In the next instant June was at Allison's side, tugging at the tough cords that bit into his wrists. She wrenched her fingers, but the cords were stubborn and time was too short.

"Don't cross him," Allison whispered tensely. "He murders as easy as he lies... *Get away...*"

JUNE sprang away and appeared to be innocently examining a picture when the white-suited figure came back into the room. At the same moment a grizzled old Dazzalox with ragged, copper-colored hair hobbled in from the corridor.

"Jo-jo-kak!" Kilhide exclaimed in a disturbed voice.

Allison held his breath. Though he knew that the human slaves feared the savage Dazzalox as one might fear a cruel or stupid employer, it took the startled tone of Kilhide to convey the full value of the Dazzalox prestige.

"This is an unexpected pleasure!" Kilhide's enthusiasm rang falsely. He quickly changed his mood to one of gentle reprimand.

"You shouldn't be here. Today is your funeral...your farewell. Did you forget?"

"*Ak-ak-ak!...*" the old Dazzalox chuckled hoarsely. Then in broken English he announced that he had come to tell Kilhide farewell personally. He hadn't learned the language for nothing, he said.

Kilhide met him with a handshake and started to lead him back toward the corridor, but the wizened old Jo-jo-kak stood in his tracks and continued to shake hands—continued unconsciously until Kilhide pulled away. For Jo-jo-kak's beady little yellow eyes were now upon June O'Neil.

His eyes glittered and his double eyebrows blinked.

The rest of the world could roll into the boiling seas, but Jo-jo-kak's eyes would not unfasten from what they were seeing.

"Who be this?" he grunted.

"You'll have to hurry to get back for your farewell," said Kilhide nervously.

"Who be this?" Jo-jo-kak growled, shaking his copper locks.

"I—I'll have some slaves take you back to the Grand March," Kilhide evaded, "You're due now, and it's a long walk for you."

"WHO BE THIS?" The quaking old voice attained a genuine roar. The wrinkled old creature swaggered closer to the girl. He patted her brown hair and her full graceful arms with his unsteady sword.

"Female slave?" he yelped.

Kilhide reached for a bell and rang for assistance.

"So! Female slave," Jo-jo-kak crackled, "*Ak-ak-ak...*"

He dragged the sword down along the side of her dress, down to her shapely ankle. June walked back a step. He followed, and with his crude hand he caught her hair. She cried out. He jumped back with a ridiculous laugh.

"*Ak-ak-ak...* I want her!"

"Don't be silly," Kilhide snarled, "Please go on back."

"I buy her. How much?"

A sweat broke out on Kilhide's forehead.

"Buy" was a magic word between him and the Dazzalox. It was the magic that fixed things for him, and saved him from the Dazzalox's savage moods.

"You can't buy her, Jo-jo-kak. You're leaving. This is your day to die."

"No...I want her..."

With that the old Dazzalox potentate broke into a violent jabber that neither June O'Neil nor Lester Allison could understand, but from Kilhide's growing perspiration they knew that Jo-jo-kak held the high cards.

Some one-striped slaves arrived. The old Dazzalox turned to them and restated his case with renewed vigor, waving his copper-colored sword. Then he hobbled back to Kilhide and shouted in an accusing tone:

"Maybe *you* want her, so? Yes? She yours?"

"Yes," Kilhide hissed desperately.

"No!" cried June desperately. "Not in a million years..."

"*Ak-ak-ak!*" the old Dazzalox exulted. "She say she *not* yours. *Ak-ak-ak! I want her...*"

THE sting of the girl's open rejection blasted Kilhide's composure. He bit his words hatefully.

"Jo-jo-kak, she is your slave. No...I'm not selling her. I'm making you a gift. She is yours."

Jo-jo-kak went into a weird spasm of laughing and dancing and shouting. Then suddenly he stopped and turned to a slave.

"Go," he shouted. "Tell them there is no farewell. I do not die today."

CHAPTER FIVE
Underground Penthouse

THE slaves chased away with the strange command Jo-jo-kak had uttered, and the wizened old Dazzalox strutted out to the corridor, the proudest creature in the chasms of Mercury.

He accosted another slave and ordered him to go find his wife and bring her here at once. For June O'Neil had forcibly stated that Jo-jo-kak's wife (only Dazzalox and not slaves were permitted to marry) would have to accompany them, or she would refuse to go—a bit of swift thinking and stout bluffing on her part.

By this time Allison, who had tried in vain to break his bonds, gave way to a burst of temper. He shouted stinging words at the suave, handsome scientist, which under the conditions was all he was able to do. Kilhide was in no mood to take it. He responded with sharp kicks at Allison's prone body.

"Go ahead and kick me!" Allison snarled defiantly. "That ought to make you very happy. You're just a sewer rat—selling your fellow humans."

"My customers seem satisfied," Kilhide sneered.

"And that's all you care about. Giving those savage Dazzalox anything they want, just so you can have more power and wealth. You haven't an ounce of feeling for anybody but yourself."

"And why should I?" Kilhide snapped. "I'm a master scientist. To me, all the difference between average humans and these underground savages is less than the difference between two heads of cabbage. And I *hate* cabbage."

"Why, you damned, cynical—"

Another stout kick. "I'd kick your face to pulp if it wasn't for losing money on you. Get up, now!"

While Jo-jo-kak and June observed, Kilhide hoisted his prisoner into a chair, and as he did so he gauged the well-developed muscles of the young farmer's arms and shoulders.

"You damn fool, you could be a first class slave if you knew on which side your bread was buttered."

An excited one-stripe slave broke in upon the scene to report the pandemonium of the funeral crowd. Evidently five thousand Dazzalox at the Grand Parade had received the greatest shock of many a century.

A few minutes later, many smartly and colorfully dressed Dazzalox, men and women, crowded into the room, chattering and wailing at Jo-jo-kak, Allison couldn't make much out of the dreadful chaos, but he was sure they were upbraiding the old potentate because he had walked out on his funeral. Jo-jo-kak laughed at them, brandishing his sword and strutting around defiantly.

All the while, June O'Neil had been out of sight, having retired to an adjoining chamber to retouch her hair and make ready for the strange adventure. Now she entered the room.

At the sight of her, the group of blustering Dazzalox fell silent and edged back into a circle all around her. They gazed as if they were looking upon something unreal, something they couldn't quite believe.

But when Jo-jo-kak's wife finally arrived, she and her centuries-old husband led the female Earth creature out to the corridor to take her home with them. The Dazzalox were convinced that this thing of beauty was a fact. Some of them, indeed, could even begin to understand why old Jo-jo-kak had neglected his funeral.

CHATTER and cheering and the tapping of Jo-jo-kak's sword melted into the hum of machines, Kilhide called a one-striper.

"Have the mechanics service the robot ship for another trip," he ordered.

Then he turned to Allison, "Oh, yes...*you*. I was about to kick you in the face, I believe. Well, I haven't time now. But perhaps by this time you realize that the smart thing for you is to get into your slave clothes."

"What," said Allison deliberately, "would you do if you were in my shoes?"

Kilhide flushed, but there really was no answer he could make.

"Take him outside and cut his bonds," he snapped at the one-striper. "See that he and the others get ready for the market. Though heaven knows," he added as the slave dragged Allison out of hearing, "that the market is headed for a slump—the male market, anyway."

MANY hours after Allison, dressed in his red one-stripe outfit, had been stationed on the sales floor of the slave cavern, he looked up to find his old two-stripe friend, Smitt, grinning at him.

"So you haven't been sold yet," Smitt observed.

"None of us have been sold," said Allison. "Scores of potentates have examined us from head to foot, and made us prance and climb rocks and repeat Dazzalox words, but they didn't buy. Kilhide marked us up, marked us down, and down some more; but still no sales."

"That girl," said Smitt with a sweeping gesture, as if that were enough to account for everything. "You never saw such a stir. These sleepy old Dazzalox are all in a dither. Most of them haven't seen her yet, but they know she must be something terrific to make old Jo-jo-kak miss his funeral.

"Now they can hardly wait for the Challenge Parade that Jo-jo-kak has promised. Did I ever tell you about the Challenge Parades they have here?"

"You told me they put on big shows to impress each other with their wealth."

"That's what it amounts to," said Smitt. "Although to them, it has a lot more meaning, because it has carried down from the centuries when they had wars, and each potentate would parade his army and challenge the world. Now they don't have armies, so they parade their families and slaves and jewels and their famous weapons. Such an orgy of display you never saw…"

"Tell me something…" said Allison in a voice of quiet confidence.

But just then their conversation was interrupted by the attendant in charge of sales, who dismissed the one-stripers from the salesroom, for the business day was over. Allison jogged back to his temporary quarters at the Red Suburb and Smitt, being off duty, accompanied him.

Allison, being hot and dusty, stripped and got into the natural shower bath that gushed out of the rock wall.

"Tell me," he resumed, while Smitt prepared some food for him, "is Jo-jo-kak interested in this Earth girl simply as an ornament for his display, or… Hell, man, you know what I mean."

Smitt shrugged his shoulders sympathetically. "I wouldn't want to say."

Allison frowned worriedly. "Of course, she's beautiful," he said. "There's no denying that. And if these Dazzalox have an eye for beauty—"

"The point is," said Smitt, "that no Dazzalox ever saw an Earth girl before. She's a novelty. Any Dazzalox who can have her for his Challenge Parade has gained a big edge on all his fellows. That's what Jo-jo-kak is after. Still…"

"You should have seen the look in his eye when he saw her," said Allison. "I don't trust him. She was clever enough to call for his wife before she would go with him. If it hadn't been for that…"

SMITT shrugged. "They're Dazzalox. We're humans. We slaves have never had any attraction for the Dazzalox women."

"Dazzalox women aren't attractive," said Allison.

"Through our eyes, no, of course not."

"It would be a pretty pickle if the Dazzalox potentates saw through our eyes." Allison dried himself on a towel of matting and got into his one-stripe uniform.

Smitt munched at a ripe fruit thoughtfully. He began to see what Allison was driving at.

"Say, this thing might turn into some kind of avalanche. Already the potentates have found out from us slaves that there are *more* of these Earth women where this one came from. And when they take a notion they want something…"

Allison caught on instantly. "They know that Kilhide, with all his scientific magic, will get it for them somehow."

"Exactly."

"Kilhide is having the robot ship serviced," said Allison dryly.

"The hell! Damned louse!"

"I thought you approved of Kilhide and all his thievery and 'gentle' murders and—"

"Kilhide's a devil," Smitt muttered under his breath, glancing about to make sure no other slaves were within hearing. One never knew what fellow slaves might be talebearers.

"We lick his boots because he's got us. It's futile to fight—so we don't care whether we live or die. But if he starts shipping women here for slaves—"

"There'd be something worth fighting about," snapped Allison. "Which way to Jo-jo-kak's? I've got to see June O'Neil."

LESTER ALLISON skipped up the long circling staircase as nimbly as a squirrel. The red flame of his torch fluttered over his bare arm. It was a torch of porous stone. It was Smitt who had shown him how such torches could be made by soaking a strip of gray stone in liquid fuel and touching it to a blaze.

Another round of steps and he found himself on the uppermost level beneath the cavern roof. Before him a semi-circle of dim flares outlined the railing that enclosed the open shelf of rock: the combination balcony and front porch of Jo-jo-kak's built-in mansion.

A momentary impression of carved arches and ornamental furniture, then Allison's eyes lighted upon the figure of the girl standing before a natural mirror of polished black rock.

"June," he called softly.

The girl turned and her face brightened.

"Lester…"

She ran to him and he caught her hands. Then, rather in awe, he stepped back to gaze at her.

"You're—you're beautiful!"

Allison couldn't remember ever having said those words to a girl before. Certainly no words could have been any more appropriate, even if he did explode them quite unintentionally. June O'Neil was dressed in all the splendor of an Oriental queen.

"It's part of my costume for the Challenge Parade," she said. "There'll be a headdress too, and some ornamental hangings from each wrist. All the Dazzalox in this neighborhood have been working on it for hours, but just now they are all away, making more plans."

"Then you're...alone?"

THE girl nodded. "It's wonderful of you to come, Lester. I've been so worried about you."

"Nothing to worry about," Allison laughed, involuntarily rubbing the bruises on his face that had come from Kilhide's boot.

At once they fell to talking of all that had happened. The head of the long, circling stairs seemed an ideal place to sit. They were close together, and their very closeness made them realize that they were two adventurers in a land of hidden perils—adventurers who couldn't lose hope as long as they were looking in each other's eyes.

"It's good to be with you," said Allison. All the longing and desire to be alone with this girl that had kept his heart pounding in the interminable hours on the space ship, and the torch-lit hours since, flooded over him. His arm held her tightly.

"Are you afraid here?" he asked.

"Not as much as when Kilhide talked to me. I shudder for fear of Jo-jo-kak's finding me alone; but his wife takes care of me, and I feel safe with her. She's much younger— only three hundred Mercury years. I think she must have been badly upset because he didn't go ahead with his farewell, though she pretends everything is just fine."

"Has anyone been to see you, June?"

"Who would there be—but you?"

"I thought perhaps Ted Tyndall—"

"He still despises me for bringing him here. He'll blame me to his dying day."

Allison was silent for awhile. Together they watched the lights of the streets below, the Dazzalox coming and going, the ribbons of water chasing through the ravines.

"Wouldn't it be beautiful up here," said June, "if we could only forget all the fears and troubles that are closing in on us?"

"It's easy to forget everything else when I can look at you," said Allison, conscious that his face was very close to hers.

"This place is like I've always imagined a lush penthouse would be," she half-whispered. "Only here the sky is a rock roof right above our heads. Could you pin some little lights up, Lester, for stars?"

Lester Allison wasn't sure why he chose that moment to kiss her. He only knew that his lips came close to hers and all at once he was lost to everything except June O'Neil. Then swiftly the dangers surged back into his mind, and their lips parted reluctantly.

"That's just to remind you," he said softly, "that I'm with you in whatever happens."

The girl looked into his eyes intently and nodded without smiling.

"If my plan works," said Allison, "I may get you back to Earth soon. Kilhide is preparing his spaceship for another trip." June looked at him questioningly. He added, "I'll keep you posted."

"You'd better go now," she implored. "They'll be coming back soon. The way Jo-jo-kak has been blustering around with his sword, I wouldn't put anything past him, I hope I don't have to be near him in the Challenge Parade." She laughed lightly.

"Is it something you dread? I never know what to expect of these Dazzalox."

"I'll be all right," said the girl bravely. "It's probably foolish for me to worry."

Her mind flashed back to Kilhide—Kilhide, giving her to this erratic old potentate; Kilhide, waiting to see her humiliated as an ornament in a Dazzalox display; Kilhide, who held all the power over every human being in these chasms.

"I'll be with you," Lester Allison repeated as he said goodnight.

CHAPTER SIX
The Living Ornament

THE holiday brought the full five thousand natives to the gayly decorated Grand March stadium. They came early, in a more than ordinary festive spirit. Challenge Parades of past centuries had often been hundreds of times as long in the preparation, but none had ever evoked so much excitement or suspense as this one.

"Girl! Girl!" was the cry everywhere.

From the hour that the famous Jo-jo-kak had walked out on his funeral, that magic English word had taken the Dazzalox civilization by storm. It was on every Dazzalox's lips this hour. Whatever else old Jo-jo-kak might have in his parade, the important thing was that he would exhibit the most novel—and according to rumor, the most beautiful—living ornament ever seen.

Lester Allison watched from a front seat. He was with Smitt, who had chosen seats within hearing distance of Naf, his owner. While the excited talk and cheering gathered momentum, Smitt quietly described to Allison the highlights of a few previous Challenge Parades that had made indelible impressions.

Allison was most impressed to learn that slaves were sometimes killed at these affairs.

"Not for any reason, you understand," said Smitt, "except that the Dazzalox become intoxicated with the spirit of the spectacular. I've seen them place two slaves on the top of a float and make them maul each other with battle axes, just in order to keep the audience applauding."

A huge door unfolded from one wall and a single magnificent float came into view. It actually floated in; for the Grand March was built over a river, and for this occasion the floor through the center of the stadium had been removed, section by section. The waters rippled brightly with the colored lights of a thousand flares.

"That artificial river bed is as old as their civilization," Smitt remarked. "You wouldn't guess it, but there is a funnel-shaped depression right out there in the center, that is used for some of their ceremonies—the Ancient Rite of the Floating Chop, for example."

"Tell me later," said. Allison. He was intent upon the approaching float. It was a huge floating pyramid, bearing many a handsomely arrayed Dazzalox. But where was June O'Neil?

Uniformed slaves towed the pyramid slowly, like a canal boat, from one end of the Grand March to the other. Brilliant lights flooded the tower of steps, which were resplendent with knives, swords, jewels, battle-axes—all arranged in patterns that would have made an artist gasp for breath. The action of the figures was dazzling. Gaudy Dazzalox, both male and female, kept up a continuous procession of running up and down the sides of the pyramid.

The only quiet figure was the wizened old Jo-jo-kak himself, who sat on the top of the pyramid. And his time was coming.

But among all the startlingly grotesque creatures, Allison still failed to find a single human being.

The crowds also grew impatient for what they knew must be coming—the mysterious living ornament that had been promised.

"Girl! Girl! *Kap-ja-zaz-o-Jo-jo-kak-uf-ta-ju—girl!*"

The cries were an intoxicant to Jo-jo-kak. At last he leaped to his feet at the top of the pyramid and brandished his sword. The other Dazzalox sat down on the lower tiers and turned so they could watch him.

EVEN with five thousand creatures clamoring for the surprise, the old potentate held them off long enough to make a speech. The pyramid floated the length of the Grand March and back again, with Jo-jo-kak shouting at the top of his withered voice, and with the crowds bawling at him so loudly that no one could hear a word he said.

At last he stepped down on the second step from the top level. With his unsteady sword he struck at the top step. A lid opened.

The five thousand silenced. It was suddenly so quiet that Allison could hear the excited old potentate puffing.

The girl rose up out of the top of the pyramid. She stepped down to the second level. The lid closed. She ascended to the pinnacle, stood there motionless, her arms outspread.

The silence was perfect. Even Jo-jo-kak's breathing must have stopped in that moment.

The ornamental draperies that hung from the girl's wrists trembled slightly, and with every tremble Lester Allison's heart fluttered. To him, her radiant beauty was overpowering. To the Dazzalox... He could only wonder.

Jo-jo-kak swung his glittering sword in a broad gesture of triumph and shouted in a loud croaking voice:

"*Girl!*"

"*Girl! Girl! Girl!*" the crowds echoed, and wave after wave of cheering followed while the pyramid passed between the sides of the stadium.

Then someone started a new cry and the crowds picked it up. Old Jo-jo-kak pranced around the fourth level below his living ornament, listening to first this section of the crowd and then that, then tossing his head back and laughing and slapping his sword against his side.

"What are they shouting?" Allison demanded of Smitt.

"They say there are too many ornaments. They want to see the girl."

Just then Jo-jo-kak pranced up three steps and flashed his sword through the air toward the girl's head. Her ornamental headdress shattered and fell. Her brown hair cascaded down over her shoulders. The crowd roared.

Jo-jo-kak jogged down to the fourth step and hobbled around the pyramid a few times and then went up again. Another shaky stroke with his sword. The flowing ornaments from the girl's left wrist slipped down onto the steps.

"What are they yelling now?" Allison asked excitedly.

"More!" Smitt answered.

Allison gasped. "He wouldn't dare—"

"He'd dare anything."

June O'Neil's left wrist was bleeding.

Jo-jo-kak again did a limping grotesque dance around the fourth level. Then up the steps again. More clumsy, treacherous sword work. The girl winced.

"The damned fool!" Allison muttered loudly. "The filthy old—"

Smitt clamped a hand over his mouth. "Quiet! There's nothing you can do about it."

"Nothing," Allison spluttered. "Oh, if I only had a gun…"

"If *any* of us had a gun," Smitt mocked bitterly under his breath, *"If…"*

Involuntarily Allison's hand plunged into the pocket of his slave uniform. Only useless things: scraps of gray porous rock from a torch, a pocketbook, and his handkerchief wrapped tightly around something—what was it? Oh, yes, the old bean shooter he had used to win over all the others on the boat.

PERHAPS—but what was that bulge in his pocketbook? Why, it was tiny bottle of deadly poison, poison that had once effected a quick suicide. Poison… Porous stone… A bean shooter…

The girl's bleeding left hand fell to her side. She lifted it up again. Both arms were bare now. She held them out as best she could.

Up the steps came the wrinkled old creature with his ugly crackling laugh. His yellow eyes glittered as he danced around the girl, prodding her body with the point of his sword. Avidly the other Dazzalox cried for more.

Again the sword jabbed perilously at June O'Neil's garments. The blue ornamental band that covered the girl's breasts severed. For a moment the side below her extended right arm was whitely naked; then a long dark line of blood appeared.

Jo-jo-kak hobbled back down to the fourth step and tossed back his ragged coppery head of hair and laughed like a demon. The crowd went wild with cheering.

Then something mysterious happened. Jo-jo-kak straightened up with a jerk. His skinny arms shot out, his gnarled fingers extended. His sword clattered down the steps and swished into the water. The breathless crowd heard the clatter and the splash.

Jo-jo-kak grabbed his mouth. A trickle of blood dripped over his lower lip. He spat and choked and with both hands fought at his mouth, all the while reeling about on the fourth step like a man who has been stabbed.

His wrinkled yellow face grew dark. His arms drooped. His eyes tightened. He fell.

He slid only a few steps, for his crusty yellow hands and feet caught him. He hung on the side of the pyramid, head and face downward, and his ragged coppery hair showered down toward the water. He was dead.

ALLISON and his fellow one-stripers lay about on the floor of the slave sales cavern. The men complained of the endless hours of waiting.

"Hell, if we've got to be slaves," one of them grumbled, "I wish someone would buy us. I'd rather work for a Dazzalox than have to answer to that swine Kilhide all the time."

"Me, too," said another. "But who wants men-slaves now? All the potentates are putting in their orders for women slaves. I hear several of the old boys have put off their death dates."

"And some of their women are up in arms about their breaking traditions," said a third. "But if the potentates want Earth women, they'll get them. That's Kilhide for you. Ain't that so, Allison?"

Allison didn't answer.

"He hasn't said a word for hours," someone grunted.

"More like weeks. Brooding about the girl, probably. It's a good thing he got away long enough to fix up her scratches, though. Even if he did get lashed for it."

A Dazzalox potentate then came past, stopped to inquire for Kilhide, and went on. The conversation resumed.

"Funny about that thousand-year old codger falling dead right when he did... But if he hadn't, he might easily have killed the girl, the way he was going."

"He didn't just fall dead, however," said another man carelessly, "according to something I heard."

LESTER ALLISON looked up sharply. "What did you hear?"

"I heard that he was killed somehow…by some slave…though Tyndall wouldn't tell who it was or how he did it."

"Tyndall?"

"He's the one who saw it happen…at least, he claims he did."

"Where is Tyndall?" Allison asked apprehensively.

"That big shot Kilhide and some potentates took him over for a conference. It won't take them long to find out what he knows."

The group waited for Allison to say something more, but he didn't. His manner was puzzling.

Someone finally asked, "Whatever happened to that rebellion you started when you first got here, Allison? Thought you were going to get us a ride back to Earth."

"Come close and listen to me," Allison said coldly. Then his voice lowered to a whispered undertone. "The robot ship will soon take off. I've found out when it goes and who goes with it. A few trusted slaves. They're being sent to America to gather up a load—all girls. When they take off, Kilhide will be at his lab, working the automatic controls."

One of the men asked, "But how will these slaves get people to come aboard? After all, the people on Earth—particularly in our country—will be mobilized, wary of the return of this kidnapping space ship, and when it does reappear…well…"

Allison's face twisted, "Kilhide has an answer for that, too. No matter how many trips this damned shuttling space vessel makes, it'll be landed each time at night, disguised, camouflaged, on the outskirts of a town or the edge of a woods. I don't even want to think about how Kilhide's slaves will kidnap folks."

There was a swelling chorus of angry mutters.

"Can't we get to Kilhide?" one of the group bit out through clenched teeth.

"Not a chance," said Allison. "He's got more protection than a dictator. *But*...by careful timing, there might be a chance for one or two—possibly three—of us to slip aboard during the crucial five or ten seconds just before the take-off."

"Let the girl go, for one," said the sideshow barker.

The other men voiced their agreement. She should have first chance.

"I suggest we draw straws for second, third and fourth chances," said Allison, "and we'll follow through as long as our luck lasts."

The straws were prepared. But just as the draw was to begin, the sound of footsteps outside made Allison hold up a warning hand.

"*Pssst!*" he whispered. "Make out like we're playing some game."

A moment later Ted Tyndall walked in, and behind him came three Dazzalox carrying ornamented battle-axes, followed by Kilhide. It was Kilhide who spoke.

"Allison, the Dazzalox want you for the murder of Jo-jo-kak."

Allison's eyes met Kilhide's and read the evil delight that lurked there in the handsome scientist's saturnine, gloating face. Kilhide, however, could not meet the other's accusing stare. His own eyes lowered and came to rest on the straws the slave men held in their hands.

"What is going on here?" Kilhide demanded, full of suspicion. "Not drawing lots for some little trick, are you?"

"You don't think," Allison fairly purred, "that any of us are that clever—do you, Kilhide? If you have made us slaves, at least you cannot deny us the right to play an occasional game."

Kilhide flushed darkly, made as if to say something, and then retired from the room in momentary confusion, gesturing to the three Dazzalox to take Allison along. Allison rose leisurely, glanced back at the men who had been about to draw straws, and surveyed Ted Tyndall with amused, contemptuous eyes. Tyndall's face turned away.

"Let my good friend Tyndall have my straw," Allison said as he left in the center of the three Dazzalox. "Perhaps— perhaps he likes to play games, too. Perhaps there will even come a time when he will be 'it'."

AT a snails pace the robot ship moved along the cavern runway, its gleaming black metal nose pointed toward the unlighted tunnel that would let it escape, somewhere miles beyond these buried chasms, into the void.

The rocket motors thundered.

Several men in slave uniforms waited, concealed in a deep shadowy crevice. The drawing of straws had gone through according to Allison's original plan. Ted Tyndall, in fact, had taken Allison's place with an almost sweating eagerness.

Silently the men counted off the seconds. Another one-striper came running to them a moment later from the other end of the crevice and whispered his news breathlessly.

"Allison couldn't get her to come!" he gasped. "She's determined to stay."

"Hell…" the carnival barker muttered. "We should have guessed that she wouldn't go unless Allison did. Wish I'd given Allison *my* chance. If there was only time—"

"Not a chance," said the news bearer: "They've just convicted him of murder. He's sunk."

The ship rolled to a momentary stop to take on Kilhide's trusted slaves. It was time to act. Since the girl hadn't come, the barker's turn was automatically raised to first. Ted Tyndall's chance moved up from fifth to fourth.

"Why can't I have her place?" Tyndall begged. "After all—"

"You're *fourth*," the barker snapped. "Heads up— All ready? Remember what Allison said. We jump out of here at our own risk. Either we make it or we don't. Ready, number two?"

Number two stood directly behind the barker, number three next, Ted Tyndall and the rest followed in line.

The ship eased to a stop. On the opposite side of it Kilhide's minion would enter. There was a click; the airlocks on this side automatically pushed open.

The carnival barker dashed out.

Number two failed to get started, for Ted Tyndall gave him a violent push and crowded out ahead of him.

Then above the sound of the idling rocket motors an automatic gun rattled. The barker and Ted Tyndall fell. The other men fled back through the crevice as hard as they could go. The robot ship roared away exactly on schedule.

CHAPTER SEVEN
War of the Sexes

LESTER ALLISON lay on his stomach a fortnight later, his chin resting in his hands, his eyes watching the Dazzalox traffic come and go.

The heavy metal bars of his prison door afforded a comprehensive view of Dazzalox life, and in the many hours he had been here—an estimated twenty-five days, Earth time—he had gained much insight on the rising conflicts within this subterranean race.

A sharp, bitter conflict between the sexes.

At first, when he had been hailed into the absurd courts of native justice, he had been mildly surprised at the pronounced difference of opinion between the males and the females regarding his degree of guilt. To his astonishment, even old Jo-jo-kak's widow had made a stout appeal in his behalf.

"This slave not kill," the unbereaved spouse had declared in her prided English words. "Jo-jo-kak, his time to die. He try to escape death. He die."

The other women had carried their superstitions even farther. It was the official duty of the Dazzalox women to uphold and defend the great traditions. When they discovered that their males were yielding to a strange urge to break traditions, they were sure that Jo-jo-kak's death should be interpreted as a warning. Nothing less.

To Allison's grim amusement, many of the old men had cancelled their death dates, as if life had suddenly taken on a new interest; and this, the women complained, was upsetting to their careful plans for the distribution of food and properties. But back of it all, Allison knew, was a deep-rooted female distrust of the ill-suppressed desires of their males for "girls."

If this Allison slave was guilty of a murder, the women whispered among themselves, then he should still be dealt with leniently; for he had put a timely end to the most undignified and ungracious exhibition of any Challenge Parade in their memory.

But although the Dazzalox women considered that the murder had been well timed, if murder it was, the male Dazzalox were exceedingly angered that the act had occurred just when it did. They had been crying, "More!" to old Jo-jo-kak, and he had been complying.

Indeed, the Challenge Parade had been on the point of making memorable history when Jo-jo-kak's death brought the excitement to an end. The murderer deserved death. No, he deserved the worst kind of death.

Between Ted Tyndall's eyewitness account and the telltale bottle of poison which Allison had dropped and broken in his haste, there had been no difficulty proving guilt. The only question that Kilhide had left open to the potentates was: what was the most appropriate sentence?

Allison closed his eyes as these thoughts flooded through his mind for the thousandth time. The perspiration trickled over his half-naked body. He knew that before the manner of his death had been decided upon, other things had happened to make his case a spectacular issue.

The most important thing was that the robot ship had returned on schedule seven days ago after its week's trip to Earth to dump twenty-five nice-looking girls—stolen from a factory in the eastern United States—into Kilhide's lap.

"There are now over a hundred male slaves; there are twenty-six female slaves in our society," Naf, Smitt's owner, had reminded his fellow potentates, speaking in their native tongue during the last session of Allison's hearings.

"Unless we deal firmly with the murderer of Jo-jo-kak, we may expect more trouble from the male slaves."

The potentates had applauded vigorously.

"If the females are to be our slaves, we must have complete freedom in our management of them." Naf's words had led to enthusiastic cheering. A severe execution seemed in order.

ANOTHER potentate had hit upon another need for such an execution, saying, in effect, "If these female slaves are treated to the bravest and most daring of our Dazzalox performances, in which we put to shame the poor fighting skills of their males, they will be convinced that male slaves are insignificant compared to us. The most daring and spectacular way for us to execute this murderer is by the Ancient Rite of the Floating Chop."

So, in spite of demands for leniency from the female upholders of tradition, Allison had been condemned to die by the Floating Chop.

And what had happened to the anger of the women aroused by these masculine strategies? At that very moment Allison could look out into the streets and see groups of female Dazzalox talking in ominously low tones. The conflict was gathering fury. It had been gathering all the past weeks. There were subtle signs here and there that the lid would soon blow off.

Allison felt a poignant wish that he could live to see what form the conflict would take, and whether the women would dare to do violence. But he doubted whether he would live to find out, for he was to die by the Floating Chop.

When? He wondered.

Perhaps not until this orgy of buying and selling the new females had subsided. Not until the arrogant old potentates had had their turns at staging ostentatious Challenge Parades to impress these lovely females slaves with their grandeur and power. Not until the speculation on the slave market had passed its first frenzied wave.

Perhaps not until the boiling seas had swept periodically through these streets and river beds, to wash away the filth and grime and half a Mercury year's accumulation of bodies from the death tunnels. The blue dust from the stone streets was constantly in the air, so thick and fast came the traffic of hard, crusty yellow feet, and so long had it been since the sea had swept through.

"How's the boy, Les?"

Lester Allison looked up into the grinning face of Smitt. A flicker of disappointment came into his own visage.

"You couldn't get her?"

"Not yet, Romeo. But I'll try again soon. It's devilishly risky, you know. As long as she's with Jo-jo-kak's wife, she's safe. But with these potentates practically fighting over girl slaves…"

"I know," Allison muttered. "I see plenty of it from this angle, with the slave mart right across the street from me. Those poor girls are scared to death. They fell into a pretty mess of hell when they came here. Did June send any message?"

"Her love, and this." Smitt passed a package of food through the bars. Allison took the package with eager be-grimed fingers. Smitt grinned broadly and knowingly.

He mumbled, "I've begun to figure out your side of things finally. That is…" He shuffled his feet like a bashful boy with something embarrassing that had to be said.

"What are you driving at?"

"Well, at first I thought you were a fool to try to fight against Kilhide's racket. It was too much like batting your brains against a stone wall. But since that load of females arrived, I've sort of picked up the feeling that life is worth fighting for."

"You mean—"

"Her name's Mary," said Smitt, as if that explained everything. He added, chuckling, "I know of three other fellows who've got it as bad as I have. They've been dead to themselves for years down here, but the minute some girls came along and began to look at them as "heroes," darned if the fellows aren't pawing the earth for a chance to put the hammerlock on Kilhide and take a shot for the void.

"If you were just on the other side of these bars, Les, that rebellion you've been propagating— Listen…what's that?"

"Another load of girls," Allison muttered. "Two trips in two weeks."

THE subterranean canyon filled with the percussion of the robot ship.

Before the sounds stopped and the echoes died, hundreds of Dazzalox bounded down their steps and through the streets toward the Red Suburb.

Soon another twenty-five attractive working girls were lined up in the slave market across the dusty plaza from Allison's prison, and instantly the bewildered creatures were surrounded by a chaos of buying and selling and trading—a chaos of shrill bird-like voices screaming and quarreling in an inhuman tongue. Potentates hurried to the market with many of the first crop of girls—and with groups of two-stripers to make exchanges.

Smitt was still sitting outside Allison's bars when Kilhide breezed past, then turned back to say, "I'm looking for June O'Neil. Have you seen her?"

Allison's fighting temperature jumped. His words clogged. Smitt answered with a blank stare. So far as Smitt knew, she was with Jo-jo-kak's widow.

"Find her for me, Smitt," Kilhide snapped. "With prices skyrocketing, she ought to be back in circulation."

Smitt saluted and he and Kilhide went their separate ways. Allison glanced dully at the package of food.

Half an hour later Smitt returned to the barred opening, and worry showed on his face.

"She's gone, Les. What do you suppose—"

"What did Jo-jo-kak's widow say?"

"*She's* gone, too."

"Where?"

"I couldn't find out."

"Didn't any of the Dazzalox women see her go?"

"Les, you'll think I'm blind and deaf and cockeyed. But by George, I couldn't find *any* Dazzalox women—not alone!"

Allison's eyes shot across to the crowd of Dazzalox men. Apparently most of the male population had turned out to swarm about the slave mart. He glanced up and down the main thoroughfares, toward the rock-walled vestibules and shadowy side streets where a few hours earlier groups of women had been conferring in hushed tones.

"Something's up, Smitt," Allison said with a snap of his fingers. "I'll swear I haven't seen a female Dazzalox since these new girls came in."

The package of food caught Allison's eye. He shuffled its contents and there he found the answer—a penciled note from June.

Dear Lester,

This is to tell you that the Dazzalox women are going to migrate. Jo-jo-kak's widow has confided this to me. You can guess how desperate they are about their broken traditions when I tell you that they debated whether they should run away or commit wholesale murder upon all the males. They seem to feel that the sooner their race comes to an end, the better. It is the only answer, they say, to their outraged traditions.

"They're the damnedest lot..." Smitt hissed. "I never could understand them and their traditions."

ALLISON read on.

They talked of escaping these caverns through some ascending passages. I don't know whether they can.

"They run the risk of death from the sea," Smitt muttered. "And if they find their way to the top, they'll be scorched to cinders, from what Kilhide says."

Allison read feverishly now. *For appearances' sake I must go with Jo-jo-kak's widow. But I can't give up believing that you may yet escape, Lester. You must. I shall try to break away from the women before they leave the caverns, and wait for you. But if you do not come— I will tell myself to the last that somehow you must have escaped them and flown back to Earth. I shall always love you. June.*

Lester Allison leaped to his feet and shook the bars.
"Get me out of here, Smitt! I've got to get out..."
Smitt's hand shot through the bars and flattened over Allison's mouth.
"Quiet! You'll have Kilhide on your neck..."
"But *June*—"
"I'll go after her," Smitt said, and for once he wasn't grinning. "If Naf comes looking for me, tell him—nothing."

ALLISON stalked the prison cave hungrily. All the food June had sent him that day had been devoured, and the closely eaten rinds of the fruits had washed away with the gushing rivulet that pounded incessantly down a jagged wall of his cave and chased through a barred opening to deeper ravines beyond.

He was scarcely conscious of his hunger. He was keenly conscious, however, that it had been hours and hours since Smitt set out to bring June back. And during those hours— what a terrific hullabaloo! The Dazzalox men had discovered what had happened, and they had forthwith exploded into an enraged brand of pursuers.

A thousand or so pairs of female yellow feet had thudded through the dusty caverns, leaving only the echoes of angry shouting and clouds of purple dust in their wake. What had followed when the males finally overtook their rebellious runaways several miles up the canyons, Allison could only imagine.

But evidently the males had administered some sort of persuasive argument, either by force or threats, for the women had at last begun to dribble back.

"That ends that," thought Allison, as he watched group after group straggle homeward. "Or is it only the beginning?"

The more closely he observed, the more he wondered. The thing he particularly noticed was that the groups of females who trudged past within his hearing were not speaking to the males who followed them. The husbands might growl and shout threats and dictate demands, but the women only huddled closer together and said nothing. Were they refusing to squander their energies on a verbal quarrel, Allison wondered.

"Violence ahead," he muttered to himself.

Whenever the women passed near the large violet flare, he thought he could see a certain glint of desperation in their yellow eyes. And suddenly he discerned in that blazing desperation a glint of hope for himself...

IF only these mad Dazzalox women would unleash their fury soon enough, he might escape the Floating Chop.

And if Smitt was right about some of the slaves; *if* they were ripe to risk Kilhide's guns; and if they could storm the upper secret chambers of Kilhide's lab, where the controls to the robot ship were thought to be hidden—

If... But these were runaway dreams, with less chance to succeed than the runaway Dazzalox women. Allison's dizzy thoughts boiled down to one single thing: If Smitt didn't come back soon with the news that June O'Neil was safe, he'd go crazy.

JUNE came to him hours later, tired and dirty but still beautiful. Allison kissed her passionately through the bars of his prison, and she smiled while he brushed the rock dust from her cheek and her shoulder.

"Thanks—thanks more than I can tell," said Allison to Smitt, who stood by, grinning. Then Smitt was off on business of his own, and Allison and the girl were sitting side by side with only the black vertical bars between them.

Food and drink passed through the bars. June made believe they were dining in luxury; and as her dark eyes flashed smiles at him and her hair fell against his shoulder, the luxury became genuine for Allison.

"You must go get some rest," she said, after he had listened to her story of the women's ill-fated venture. "I'll be safe for a time, surely. The Dazzalox will probably turn in for one of their three-day sleeps after all this turmoil."

The girl's smile quickly vanished. "No, there are other plans," she spoke with tense restraint. "Desperate plans. I—I can't—I mustn't talk of them."

She was pale, and Allison felt the blood leave his own face. "Tell me."

June shook her head. "All the way back I heard them talking. The men boasted, and the women whispered," she hesitated. "I didn't hear all the details. I didn't want to. I couldn't," she choked. "Then men were talking about—"

"A circus in the big arena?"

The girl nodded. Allison felt the cold surge through his spine. So at last the Floating Chop was at hand...

"They're going to have this orgy of cruelty at once," said June. "It's their savage way of forgetting the slap the women have just given them. As soon as they had turned the migration back, they began to clamor for a celebration—and the first thing they thought of was Jo-jo-kak and you."

"And the Dazzalox women?" Allison asked. "What do they have up their sleeves?"

"Wholesale murder," June answered.

"How soon?"

June gave him a quick frightened look. "Almost too soon," she said. "Perhaps as soon as they can pick up enough knives—as soon as the signal comes. Then they'll all strike at once."

"Don't tremble so," said Allison softly. "There's still a chance for us. I've got a scheme..."

A shrill brassy gong sounded from somewhere down the torch-lit street. It clanged out three inharmonious notes in rapid succession. Then it came again, and again. Ominous triple clangs.

AT once Dazzalox men and women hurried down the distant stairways. Dazzalox potentates led their elaborately adorned female slaves down the streets. Two-stripers and Mercurian natives paraded together in hastily arranged formations—toward the Grand March.

Friendly slaves slipped past Allison's prison to give him a sign of farewell or a word of tasteless hope. Hope that snatched at straws.

"Your strategy?" June asked for the third time. She too, was snatching for straws in these last minutes. She knew that no condemned creature had ever lived through the Floating Chop.

A slender Dazzalox in a gaudy green athletic suit bounded past, swinging a gleaming black ax. A crowd chased after him, cheering him. Some of them stopped to hoot at Allison for a moment. They raced on toward the stadium.

"Your strategy?" June repeated in a tight voice. Her lips trembled.

"I'm going to fight for time," Allison answered. "If the women are on the verge of a slaughter that nothing can stop—well, I may take advantage of it. They probably plan to spring their knives as soon as the men are intent upon my execution ceremony."

"Yes." June was staring off into the gloomy distance.

"Then if I can only stave off death until the women strike," there was a distant hope in Allison's eyes, "then my death party will be forgotten—at least, there's a speck of a chance. If I can, I'll bolt for the narrow stairway at the lower end of the stadium. You know…to the left of the striped door."

"Stairway," the girl echoed dazedly.

"So that's my strategy…to hold on to dear life till the women give their signal and hell breaks loose."

A group of armed Dazzalox officers rounded a corner and came toward the prison.

"If I only knew what signal the women will wait for," came Allison's final whisper. And then he kissed the girl. The officers opened the barred door and led him away.

"Signal!" June moaned and she sank to the floor in a paroxysm of sobbing and despair. She had not had the heart to tell him that the signal the Dazzalox women had agreed upon was the deathblow at the Ancient Rite of the Floating Chop.

CHAPTER EIGHT
The Floating Chop

THE chains on Lester Allison's wrists led him back and forth before the stadium crowd. He was royally hooted. All the Dazzalox words for "killer" and "criminal" and "monster" were hurled at him. He had learned the Dazzalox tongue only to be mocked by it.

The four uniformed Dazzalox who marched him around kept the two long chains stretched tight so that they themselves were never close to him. They were not only playing safe, keeping out of his reach; they were shunning him.

"Let them delay all they want with their damned preliminaries," Allison thought to himself. He clung to his one false hope tenaciously.

Such a sinking feeling assailed him as he had never known before. As if death were already leading him by the hand. As if he had already departed from everyone in the world.

Even the one-stripers and two-stripers he glimpsed here and there among the assemblage of glittering Dazzalox were completely apart from him now. Their bondage was nothing compared to his. But their fates would come in time—and what would they be? Allison wondered. The chain whipped and jerked at his left wrist, a signal to turn back.

His blood chilled each time they led him past the pool in the center of the arena. A circular section of the flooring had been removed from over the hidden river. That circular pool was to be the scene of his execution.

Allison's eyes followed the three floating discs, each ten or twelve feet across and apparently made of tightly compressed faggots from some subterranean timber or root, that circulated within the pool. They were like three huge doughnuts in a kettle of grease, except that the grease was green water and the doughnuts were like round meat-cutters' tables, hacked and scarred from ceremonies immemorial. The chains led Allison on.

Glancing upward, he saw that there were a number of female slaves here and there in the crowd. Some of them were in gold and blue slave costumes, others still wore their American clothes; but all were richly adorned with bold Dazzalox jewelry and medals and trinkets. They sat near wealthy potentates. Probably they were too baffled, Allison thought, to know what was going on.

And yet it was their innocent presence that was figuratively to bring the universe crashing down upon the Dazzalox race. At this very moment, how silently the Dazzalox women sat at the sides of their unsuspecting males, like charges of electric death awaiting the flip of a switch.

Back toward the pool the chains pulled Allison.

Now his eyes widened in horror as he counted off three Dazzalox, lithe and well muscled. Each of them wielded a black metal double-edged ax, and all three were now enthusiastically engaged in warming up.

They pranced around the open arena in their athletic uniforms, glittering with polished medallions. Attendants tossed fruits in the air for them, which they deftly sliced with their flying axes. Up in one piece, down in eight—and the crowds hailed the feat with lusty cheers.

At last Allison was released into the circular pen—a fence of vertical iron bars that enclosed the pool. His wrists were free again; his mantle was removed. He wore only his slave trunks. Bars clanged after him.

So this was the arena for his execution! Without hesitation, Allison plunged into the pool.

A dozen easy strokes took him across and he climbed up on the narrow walk that bordered the pool. The walk, like the ten-foot discs in the water, was chipped and hacked, Allison sat with his back against the bars of the fence and let his feet rest in the cool water. His arms involuntarily jerked and trembled.

"Stall for time," he kept saying to himself in a voiceless whisper, "Just keep stalling for time."

ONE of the floating discs brushed past his feet. He kicked at it, then leaped onto it. It was as buoyant as cork. He crossed to the other two discs—the flow of the river through the pool kept them in constant circulation—and jumped back to the narrow walk.

Now, amid a loud ovation, the three muscular choppers entered the pen and the gate was fastened behind them. They stood together ceremoniously, with their long-handled axes uplifted, while an official on the outside made a presentation speech.

The crowd listened breathlessly. Between the announcer's sentences Allison could hear the bubbling of the river as it seeped along under the stadium floor, into the eddying pool, and out again through its under-floor passage. Perhaps—

No, the very words of the announcer extinguished a sporadic hope that flashed through Allison's mind—the hope of an under floor escape. In substance the announcer said:

"...and he has been condemned to die by the Floating Chop. There is no escape from the Floating Chop. The surrounding fence is made of strong bars with spears at the top. Beneath the water there are walls of metal bars and of stone that narrow to a point. The culprit must either meet his death by the ax—or drown.

"The choppers have a sporting chance to kill him. If they succeed before drowning overtakes him, they shall win the

Ancient Award of the Floating Chop. A salute to their success!"

The choppers, standing in a line across the pool from Allison, swung their axes in circles and called out some unintelligible response in unison. They came to attention again while the announcer finished.

"Remember that the rules cannot be violated," he said, in effect. "The culprit's members must be severed in a precise order: first, the two feet, then the two hands, finally the head. You are now ready… Begin!"

The subterranean canyons rocked with yelping cheers of the male Dazzalox.

Eagerly the three choppers tightened their grips on their axes. One dressed in green started around the circular walk in one direction; An orange ax-man took the other. A yellow one stood where he was. Allison dived for the center of the pool.

He came up to see a yellow-clad form floating toward him on a disc. He caught his breath and looked for an open corner. There wasn't any such thing. Not as long as the two choppers were running around on the narrow circular walk.

Allison swam for a disc and climbed up onto it. The advantage of Mercury's slightly lighter gravity kept surprising him as he accustomed himself to the water. But other less pleasant surprises soon flooded in upon him too swiftly for him to collect his thoughts—surprises in the form of leaping choppers and spinning axes.

He sprang backward from the disc barely in time to escape the black streak that whizzed past his feet. He plunged for the center of the pool and stayed there, treading water, studying the vicious yellow eyes, trying to gauge where the next attack would come from.

The yellow chopper floated near him on a disc. The ax-man's double eyebrows were squinted menacingly toward the water; his wicked blade was poised. He was trying to sight Allison's submerged feet. He floated past without doing any damage, and the crowd clamored for action.

THE green chopper was dancing about on the next disc, swinging the flat of his ax against the waves to slap water into Allison's face in order both to enrage and confuse him.

Suddenly the orange man plunged from the side, ax and all. He swam underwater, but the waves showed where he was coming. Allison surface dived and cut well under him.

Another dive sounded, and Allison looked up from a depth of several feet to see a chopper coming straight down toward him. With a swift twist Allison plunged deeper. He realized by now that the advantage of vision was with whoever was underneath, for all the light came from above the pool.

But suddenly it dawned on him, as he scraped against a narrowing wall, that the cone itself was a treacherous trap. The deeper he went, the easier it would be for three ax-men to close in on him. He switched back, barely passing a third diver as he shot upward. A hard hand clutched at his ankle. He kicked out of it and bobbed up to the surface like a jumping fish. An instant later he was up on the ragged walk, panting furiously.

Three ugly Dazzalox heads came up. Three axes caught on the edge of the walk and the choppers pulled themselves up with practiced skill.

There was a moment's hesitation while the green ax-man gibbered a word of instruction. Then two of them came racing around the perimeter, one from each direction. The third leaped out to a floating disc and waited.

Allison dived again. There was nothing else to do.

He made as if to dive deeply; then with distended eyes searching the green waves for forms above him, he switched back to retrace his course. It was an old trick he had used when he was a boy playing tag at the lake. Five seconds after the three choppers dived for him, he was upon the surface again.

But he was well aware that all the tricks he could muster would not last long against their teamwork...

To the utter amazement of the roaring, bellowing crowds, Allison's wily tactics lasted for most of the next half hour. By that time he was approaching complete exhaustion, both physically and mentally. Had it not been for the rules, his hands and head would never have survived the ceaseless attacks. As it was, nine times the ax blades had bit into his legs.

Three of the cuts stung him constantly. The sharp pains soaked upward through his legs, and blood and strength seeped away from him. But there was nothing to be done about that. The crowd yelped for action and the three choppers closed in on him again.

Allison dived deeply. For the first time he allowed himself to go down—down—down.

The walls of the cone narrowed around him. If the choppers should follow... But an upward glance told him they were still floundering several feet above, trying to locate him. If the fates would only give him the one break he craved!

He groped at the bottom of the cone. His search was futile. He had hoped his hands might fall upon an ax lost in some previous tournament, fallen to the bottom of the cone, forgotten. Again he explored.

No such luck. All his groping hands found in the point of the cone was slime. Slime and bits of bone.

Slime! He cupped his two hands into it, then up he floated—up to the surface with bursting lungs.

HE caught sight of the three ax-men back in their positions. He heard the crowd wail for action. Action! In another moment they would get it, if the gods of luck would give him half a break. Treading water at the edge of the pool, *he smeared his slimy hands over the walk.*

The orange chopper bounded toward him with a devilish gleam in his yellow eyes. Three swift bounds—and a grand slip! Flying arms and legs, orange body, black ax—all went careening into the fence. The chopper made a swift scramble to recover his ax. Allison was too quick for him.

A tense gasp echoed through the stadium, a long gasp that melted into worried mumbles.

The yellow and green choppers who had started around the ring to their fellow's rescue stopped short, for the orange form plunged into the pool. In his place stood the slave they were to execute—a well-muscled human being *with an ax in his hands.*

They jabbered savagely for a moment. Outside the cage the announcer roared something at the frenzied crowd.

Allison understood. The rules were automatically off. The choppers were to strike anywhere—and strike to kill! No more playing around. This culprit was a dangerous creature.

Another ax was passed through the bars to the orange executioner. Three attendants outside the pen came toward Allison and debated trying to reach in and take the ax away from him, but decided against it when he flashed the weapon deftly toward the bars.

"Stall for time," Allison thought, but the words had a sickly taste in his mouth. How *much* time—or had the women forgotten their resolve? Pain shot through his feet. He felt weak from loss of blood. He wanted to lie down and faint away.

Now two of the ax-men began to close in on him from each direction as before. However, this time they did it more cautiously, more desperately. A disc floated toward Allison's edge. The yellow chopper was on it. There was no more stalling. It was kill or be killed. One false move would be the end.

Which way to strike? That was the question that beat through his mind. His right-handedness determined he would throw his stroke in the direction that would give his right arm full play. Automatically he plunged to his left to meet the approaching green chopper.

But fate waited in his path—the slime.

Three steps he bolted, then his footing gave way. He shot outward over the water. But as his foot gave a final kick against the edge of the walk, he flung his ax back with all his strength, squarely at the green body. The force of a madman went into that blow and followed through as the ax shot out of his hands.

His plunge carried him deep into the cooling waters. His hands were free now. He plodded on in a downward direction. He didn't want to come up again. His strength was almost completely gone. He felt that drowning would be so very easy, so simple. He clung to the slanting wall and waited.

No one came after him. Things began to go black. His hands loosened...

Even before Allison's face cut through the surface of the water to gasp air, he was conscious of the terrific screaming that filled the stadium. His lungs inhaled air, bleary sight returned to his eyes, blood-chilling cries of terror crowded upon his ears. What a weird, terrifying pandemonium...

The tiers of the stadium were a shambles of mass murder. Knives flashed again and again upon the writhing bodies of male Dazzalox. Blood gushed and streamed down the steps.

Males and females grappled in death struggles and tumbled down, tier after tier, to roll onto the open pavement of the Grand March.

So the hour had struck at last—the fatal hour that might spell the doom of a race in the ghastly clash of sex against sex!

CHAPTER NINE
Destiny

WHAT signal had set the shambles off? Allison's eyes swept the bloody scene and returned at last to the pen of his own intended execution.

Across the pool from him the gate was open. The orange and yellow Dazzalox choppers were outside, now running as if to the rescue of a friend, now halting as if overwhelmed by the scene of terror. They glanced back, and Allison's eyes followed their glance. Their green-suited teammate lay motionless on the walk beside the pool.

The ax, which had sunk deep in his heart, still hung there with its handle pointing almost straight up. Blood flowed in a crooked stream along the water-tracked walk to an ancient ax mark at the pool's edge, and from there the eddying waters carried it away.

Allison dragged himself up out of the water, rolled against the fence and lay there, bleeding, quivering, wondering at the fact that he was still alive. The two departing choppers looked back at him, but their hearts had evidently gone out of their jobs. It was throngs of angry women advancing upon them that absorbed their attention now. The last that Allison saw of them they were backing away and defending themselves wildly with their axes.

Two slaughtered potentates rolled down the stone tiers and thumped into the bars of the cage. One of them was Naf, Smitt's master. His wrinkled old face was a contorted mass of yellow chalk. He had weathered a thousand Earth years only to die from a black knife in his side.

The dead and dying bodies rolled down, and those Dazzalox still alive scrambled across the tiers—to kill or to be killed.

Allison was relieved to see that his fellow humans of both sexes were clambering to the upper reaches of the sloping sides and finding exits. His eyes sought for June. He remembered telling her he would try to escape by the narrow stairs above the striped door at the farther end.

And someone was there! Someone waving at him—a girlish figure with brown hair and a blue and gold costume.

"June..." he sighed, half aloud, "June...June..." The very name gave him strength. Allison tottered dizzily to the door of the cage, waving at her.

He paused. Several hundred Dazzalox males and females were battling to death on the open pavement before him. Armed women were charging about in small groups. Getting through that mad milieu wouldn't be easy. He looked about for a weapon. The only thing he saw was the ax buried in the green chopper's bloody chest. He turned from the sight and plodded through the battleground unarmed.

"Lester...you were wonderful!" The girl bathed his face with her kisses and tears. "Don't mind me. I'm so happy, I just have to cry."

But the next moment June dried her tears and became instantly practical. She hastily tore strips from her garments to bandage his bleeding feet and legs. A crevice protected them from the spectacle of the bloody war, and they tried not to hear the thudding of feet and the wailing and cursing of males.

"The women must have got off to a good start," Allison remarked, lying back on the rock floor and closing his eyes.

"You should have seen the first attack. It went off like clockwork."

ALLISON asked innocently, "What started them off?"

"The signal you gave them."

"The signal I gave them?"

"They had agreed that the death blow would be the signal to attack. You finally furnished it when you threw your ax at one of the choppers. They couldn't have waited much longer, anyway. In fact, you provided them with the ideal moment. It was such a stunner to the Dazzalox males, to see you cut down one of their heroes, it was almost equal to an anesthetic."

"I'll bet," Allison said grimly. "But what next, after they finish with their men? Do they start in on us humans?"

"There's only one human they've sworn to get."

"Not Kilhide?" Allison came bolt upright.

"Yes. They blame him for encouraging the men in this mania for female Earth slaves."

"We can't let them get Kilhide!" Allison snapped. As the final bandage was tied he came to his feet. "Kilhide's the only one that can get us back to Earth!"

Hand in hand they ran down the clay ramp as fast as Allison's painful legs could travel. They dodged groups of fighters in the streets; they closed their ears to death screams from bodies that had been hurled into ravines.

They glimpsed the fall of an aged potentate from the top of a stairway; heard a moment later the scream from the terrorized American girl who had just fought free of his grasp; saw the stricken Dazzalox crash to death over a torch light. Wincing, they turned their eyes away as the flames puffed up from his yellow hair and eyebrows. They hurried on.

"Where's Kilhide?" they shouted together at a two-striped slave who came running from the other direction.

"Layin' for the trouble makers. Watch out…he killed a couple of them at the suburb," the slave retorted without stopping.

They slackened their pace as they neared the red metal bridge. A severe voice barked at them from the shadows.

"This way, you two."

They turned to see the gleaming pistol move out into the light. Back of it the sleek white-clad form of Kilhide appeared.

"So you escaped your fate, Allison," said the evilly handsome scientist with a twitching smile. "You'll not escape this one. You happen to be superfluous to my purposes, and this hour was made to order for ridding myself of superfluous people. Your friend Smitt will also qualify. Now, Allison, step away from the girl…"

"No!" cried June O'Neil. "Please…you can't…not unless you kill us both…"

"Don't be throwing yourself at the feet of a corpse, Miss O'Neil. It only annoys me." Kilhide twisted his little trick mustache into a cynical scowl. "Besides, it's bad taste for one of your rank. You're soon to be queen of these caverns…when the Dazzalox have had their fun, and I…"

Lester Allison and June O'Neil were no longer listening. Their eyes were intent upon the six figures who were cautiously stealing toward the scientist from behind his back. Now Kilhide's words broke off as he saw shadows creep along the perpendicular wall.

THE man with the gun whirled. He faced a group of Dazzalox women with knives and axes in their bloodstained yellow hands. The group bore down upon him. His pistol blazed, and three of them fell. The others swamped him with their blades. His arms clamped over his chest and his gun fell. In another instant he would have died with a knife in his throat, had Allison not interfered.

But between the efforts of Allison and June, not to mention Jo-jo-kak's widow, who chanced to be one of the attackers, the assault was brought to a sudden halt.

"*Ja-ik-lif! Ka-lib-or-taf-ki-damik...*" Jo-jo-kak's widow cried, pulling the other women back from the fallen slave master. "It is enough! We leave him to die..."

THE spacious corridors of Kilhide's laboratory were seething with American men and women, who talked in low excited undertones. Though most of them wore the uniforms of Dazzalox slaves, their faces glowed with hope and enthusiasm. They were on the verge of freedom. They talked of a swift return to Earth.

Whenever their conversation slackened, Allison, sitting near the door, could hear the roar of the rivers outside. The periodic floods of Mercury were scouring the rock dust and filth from the streets. Powerful torrents were sweeping the dead and dying bodies away through unknown subterranean channels, bearing them to the boiling seas on other sides of the planet.

Allison watched through the glass doorway. The winds, generated by the floods, kept the red torches flickering and the shadows of the Red Suburb quivered. Occasionally—but rarely—a rush of water would slap over a flame and extinguish it.

"June asked me to tell you that Kilhide is beginning to stir," said a voice at Allison's shoulder.

"Tell her I'll come soon," Allison answered.

"Smitt and the others haven't returned?"

"Not yet."

Allison's eyes turned again to the red scene, coming to rest, as always, upon the crumpled striped door beside the gaping death cave. Earlier he had seen the three Dazzalox women smash that door with axes and then themselves fall victims to the escaping death gas. Now the last of those three women was caught by a wave and borne away, and only the battered fallen door was left as a monument to their mad determination.

Poor insane Dazzalox women, Allison thought. Not satisfied until they had turned the last stone upon their own extinction. They had released the invisible death that would rise to slay every male who escaped the high rocks.

Four hooded figures came bounding along the path.

"The door…" Allison called. "Unseal it…"

Someone obeyed, and Smitt and his three companions entered; the door was sealed again. The four men removed their oxygen masks.

"Well?" Allison asked, facing Smitt.

Smitt shook his head slowly. "Complete slaughter," he said. "Every striped door is down, I don't think there's a living soul left out there, human or Dazzalox. We found a few of both up on the shelves, but they were gone," He added, turning away, "We didn't find—Mary."

ALLISON put a hand on his shoulder. "Your Mary is here," he said. "She came in just after you left—and none too soon. I think she'll be all right."

IN an inner chamber Allison glared into the eyes of Kilhide. The dying scientist had been given every medical attention. He knew he could not live many hours longer, but he fought death as bitterly as he had fought his fellow men.

"You've got to live," Allison said to him fiercely. "You've got to live long enough to send these people back to Earth."

Kilhide muttered profanity. "So that's why you wouldn't let them kill me."

"There couldn't be any other reason," snapped Allison. "You've got to come through."

"You can't threaten me, Allison," the sick man answered sardonically.

"For God's sake, man, show us how to operate the robot ship before it's too late."

The dying man answered with a sarcastic, taunting laugh.

"You've got to do it, Kilhide! You've got to send us back."

"You can go to hell and fry," Kilhide sneered, and then he closed his eyes.

June and Allison and the others who were at his side during the next two hours were convinced that he never once returned to normal consciousness. All his feverish raving was simply the welling up of repressions and hatreds and loves, dreams and ambitions and scientific secrets that were imprisoned within his warped, complex mind.

Two hours they heard of the most eloquent raving that ever passed a scientist's lips, a dying genius, declaring himself to be the mastermind of the world!

Allison listened in awe; Smitt snatched at every word of information; June, with her practical turn of mind, seized pencil and paper and captured the flow of words in shorthand.

For the fever-stricken slave master was at last the glorified figure he had always dreamed of being. He was host to the world's leading scientists. They were evidently circled around him, and his maniacal eyes glittered upon them as he talked. His delusion was complete.

He commanded them to carry him through his laboratories from top to bottom while he lectured upon their wonders. All through his ravings, he acted as though his delusions were being carried out to the letter. He extracted promises that they would never reveal his magnificent secrets to the rabble from Earth, nor to the world tourists who might come to this place.

He began with the robot ship's controls, followed through the power plant, started through the shops—and then, in a burst of rage over imagined enemies from Earth, he collapsed. A minute later, the amazingly brilliant, incredible evil Kilhide passed on to the eternity for which his whole life had been a fitting preparation.

WITH the aid of gas masks, Allison, Smitt and three other men had rebuilt the doors across the death caves. They had needed something to do, they said, while they counted off the days of waiting for the robot ship's final return trip for its last load. Only ten persons remained. Today was the day.

June and Allison strolled along the clean streets, surveying the strangely quiet world. All signs of the war were gone. The air was fresh. The waterfalls and rivulets gushed with lively music that seemed more melodious, now that there were no harsh Dazzalox voices.

Strangely, in the many days that had passed since the fighting and the invisible death took their toll, not a single living Dazzalox had been found. In a sense, Allison thought, the women had won a complete victory.

But tears often came to June's eyes as she thought of Jo-jo-kak's widow and the curious friendship that had grown up between them.

"I'm sorry we couldn't have saved her life," said Allison.

"But she wouldn't have been happy living on, after her civilization was gone," June replied. "It is just as well."

Allison smiled at her curiously. Somehow she had reconciled her feelings to the insane violence the women had committed.

"But I understand how they felt," said June, reading his thoughts. "It wouldn't be much fun to live after you've lost all faith in your own civilization."

There was something deep and serious in her dark eyes that Allison appreciated.

"You have some pretty big thoughts for such a young girl," he said. "Were you thinking things like this when you ran away from home? Perhaps you had lost faith in your own civilization, too."

"And if I had," she answered, "what would you suggest?"

"Come," said Allison, taking her hand. "I'll answer that one when we reach the top of this stairs."

They climbed the winding steps to the balcony where, not so many weeks ago, they had first kissed. They looked across to other torch-lighted mansions of the silent, uninhabited city. They saw Smitt and Mary strolling along the street below them.

Elsewhere, they knew, three other couples who had lingered to take the last boat back to Earth were also enjoying the quiet romantic atmosphere of this lost world.

"You were going to suggest..." said June.

"That if we don't feel the call of our old civilization too strongly," said Allison, "we might all stay here and build a new civilization of our own."

"Make our homes here?" June crept closer into Allison's arms and there was a bewitching eagerness in her dark eyes— an eagerness for new adventures concerned with life, not death.

Allison kissed her. For a time no word was spoken.

"We five men have been studying the machines," Allison said presently. "Kilhide has left us the foundation for marvelous developments. In time we'll come to appreciate him more—after we've forgotten what kind of person he was."

The girl in Allison's arms shuddered slightly.

"But Kilhide's science isn't civilization," Allison went on. "At least, it isn't everything. There have to be people that want to live together. Honest, genuine people...like you and Smitt and Mary..."

"I can name the other seven by heart," said June, smiling up at him as if to help him with his pretty speech.

"I saw to it that only these five couples would be left for the last load," Allison said. "Right now the other four men are asking their sweethearts, just as I'm asking you, whether they would be willing to marry and stay right here."

"The other four girls will say yes," June answered with a faint twinkle in her eyes. "I know, because they've talked and dreamed and planned every hour while their men were out rebuilding the doors."

"Then," said Allison softly, drawing the girl tighter in his arms, "why not make it unanimous?"

THE END

If you've enjoyed this book, you will not want to miss these terrific titles...

ARMCHAIR SCI-FI, FANTASY, & HORROR DOUBLE NOVELS, $12.95 *each*

D-1   **THE GALAXY RAIDERS** by William P. McGivern
         SPACE STATION #1 by Frank Belknap Long

D-2   **THE PROGRAMMED PEOPLE** by Jack Sharkey
         SLAVES OF THE CRYSTAL BRAIN by William Carter Sawtelle

D-3   **YOU'RE ALL ALONE** by Fritz Leiber
         THE LIQUID MAN by Bernard C. Gilford

D-4   **CITADEL OF THE STAR LORDS** by Edmund Hamilton
         VOYAGE TO ETERNITY by Milton Lesser

D-5   **IRON MEN OF VENUS** by Don Wilcox
         THE MAN WITH ABSOLUTE MOTION by Noel Loomis

D-6   **WHO SOWS THE WIND...** by Rog Phillips
         THE PUZZLE PLANET by Robert A. W. Lowndes

D-7   **PLANET OF DREAD** by Murray Leinster
         TWICE UPON A TIME by Charles L. Fontenay

D-8   **THE TERROR OUT OF SPACE** by Dwight V. Swain
         QUEST OF THE GOLDEN APE by Ivar Jorgensen and Adam Chase

D-9   **SECRET OF MARRACOTT DEEP** by Henry Slesar
         PAWN OF THE BLACK FLEET by Mark Clifton.

D-10 **BEYOND THE RINGS OF SATURN** by Robert Moore Williams
         A MAN OBSESSED by Alan E. Nourse

ARMCHAIR SCIENCE FICTION CLASSICS, $12.95 each

C-1   **THE GREEN MAN**
         by Harold M. Sherman

C-2   **A TRACE OF MEMORY**
         By Keith Laumer

C-3   **INTO PLUTONIAN DEPTHS**
         by Stanton A. Coblentz

ARMCHAIR MASTERS OF SCIENCE FICTION SERIES, $16.95 each

M-1   **MASTERS OF SCIENCE FICTION, Vol. One**
         Bryce Walton—"Dark of the Moon" and other tales

M-2   **MASTERS OF SCIENCE FICTION, Vol. Two**
         Jerome Bixby: "One Way Street" and other tales

If you've enjoyed this book, you will not want to miss these terrific titles...

ARMCHAIR SCI-FI & HORROR DOUBLE NOVELS, $12.95 each

D-11   **PERIL OF THE STARMEN** by Kris Neville
THE STRANGE INVASION by Murray Leinster

D-12   **THE STAR LORD** by Boyd Ellanby
CAPTIVES OF THE FLAME by Samuel R. Delaney

D-13   **MEN OF THE MORNING STAR** by Edmund Hamilton
PLANET FOR PLUNDER by Hal Clement and Sam Merwin, Jr.

D-14   **ICE CITY OF THE GORGON** by Chester S. Geier and Richard Shaver
WHEN THE WORLD TOTTERED by Lester Del Rey

D-15   **WORLDS WITHOUT END** by Clifford D. Simak
THE LAVENDER VINE OF DEATH by Don Wilcox

D-16   **SHADOW ON THE MOON** by Joe Gibson
ARMAGEDDON EARTH by Geoff St. Reynard

D-17   **THE GIRL WHO LOVED DEATH** by Paul W. Fairman
SLAVE PLANET by Laurence M. Janifer

D-18   **SECOND CHANCE** by J. F. Bone
MISSION TO A DISTANT STAR by Frank Belknap Long

D-19   **THE SYNDIC** by C. M. Kornbluth
FLIGHT TO FOREVER by Poul Anderson

D-20   **SOMEWHERE I'LL FIND YOU** by Milton Lesser
THE TIME ARMADA by Fox B. Holden

ARMCHAIR SCIENCE FICTION CLASSICS, $12.95 each

C-4   **CORPUS EARTHLING**
by Louis Charbonneau

C-5   **THE TIME DISSOLVER**
by Jerry Sohl

C-6   **WEST OF THE SUN**
by Edgar Pangborn

ARMCHAIR SCIENCE FICTION & HORROR GEMS SERIES, $12.95 each

G-1   **SCIENCE FICTION GEMS, Vol. One**
Isaac Asimov and others

G-2   **HORROR GEMS, Vol. One**
Carl Jacobi and others

If you've enjoyed this book, you will not want to miss these terrific titles…

ARMCHAIR SCI-FI, FANTASY, & HORROR DOUBLE NOVELS, $12.95 each

D-21 **EMPIRE OF EVIL** by Robert Arnette
THE SIGN OF THE TIGER by Alan E. Nourse & J. A. Meyer

D-22 **OPERATION SQUARE PEG** by Frank Belknap Long
ENCHANTRESS OF VENUS by Leigh Brackett

D-23 **THE LIFE WATCH** by Lester Del Rey
CREATURES OF THE ABYSS by Murray Leinster

D-24 **LEGION OF LAZARUS** by Edmond Hamilton
STAR HUNTER by Andre Norton

D-25 **EMPIRE OF WOMEN** by John Fletcher
ONE OF OUR CITIES IS MISSING by Irving Cox

D-26 **THE WRONG SIDE OF PARADISE** by Raymond F. Jones
THE INVOLUNTARY IMMORTALS by Rog Phillips

D-27 **EARTH QUARTER** by Damon Knight
ENVOY TO NEW WORLDS by Keith Laumer

D-28 **SLAVES TO THE METAL HORDE** by Milton Lesser
HUNTERS OUT OF TIME by Joseph E. Kelleam

D-29 **RX JUPITER SAVE US** by Ward Moore
BEWARE THE USURPERS by Geoff St. Reynard

D-30 **SECRET OF THE SERPENT** by Don Wilcox
CRUSADE ACROSS THE VOID by Dwight V. Swain

ARMCHAIR SCIENCE FICTION CLASSICS, $12.95 each

C-7 **THE SHAVER MYSTERY, pt. 1**
by Richard S. Shaver

C-8 **THE SHAVER MYSTERY, pt. 2**
by Richard S. Shaver

C-9 **MURDER IN SPACE** by David V. Reed
by David V. Reed

ARMCHAIR MASTERS OF SCIENCE FICTION SERIES, $16.95 each

M-3 **MASTERS OF SCIENCE FICTION, Vol. Three**
Robert Sheckley, "The Perfect Woman" and other tales

M-4 **MASTERS OF SCIENCE FICTION, Vol. Four**
Mack Reynolds, "Stowaway" and other tales

If you've enjoyed this book, you will not want to miss these terrific titles…

ARMCHAIR SCI-FI & HORROR DOUBLE NOVELS, $12.95 each

ARMCHAIR SCIENCE FICTION CLASSICS, $12.95 each

ARMCHAIR SCIENCE FICTION & HORROR GEMS SERIES, $12.95 each

www.ingramcontent.com/pod-product-compliance
Lightning Source LLC
Chambersburg PA
CBHW030312180626
46810CB00003B/1034